Heidi Edmundson was born by the sea and grew up surrounded by the legends of Northern Ireland's spectacular Causeway Coast. Her parents and grandparents ran guesthouses in Portrush and she spent summer holidays working in the White House Department Store and the change box of Barry's Amusement Arcade.

As a child, she was fascinated by myths and fairy tales of all kinds. She was an avid reader of mystery stories and wanted to be Nancy Drew. Her love of crime fiction continued into adolescence when, one summer, she discovered a box full of Agatha Christie books with the original Fontana covers.

After attending Coleraine High School, she went to university in Dundee to study medicine and has worked as a doctor since 1994, predominantly for the NHS.

She currently lives in North London where she has been a consultant in Emergency Medicine for over ten years. She is a passionate advocate for staff wellbeing and building positive workplace cultures.

When the COVID pandemic began to take hold in Britain in March 2020 she experienced first-hand the importance of having a daily creative practice to manage stress and anxiety. She originally planned to write a short story but surprised herself by discovering that she had a lot more to say, and she enjoyed creating a crime to solve as much as reading about one. It was the next best thing to being Nancy Drew.

DARKNESS
IN THE
CITY OF LIGHT

Heidi Edmundson

Constellations Press

First published in 2024
by Constellations Press

Typeset by Constellations Press

Printed and bound in the UK by Biddles, Kings Lynn

A CIP record for this book is available from the British Library

ISBN 978-1-917000-02-4
eISBN 978-1-917000-12-3

*This book is dedicated to my father
who bought me all the books I wanted as a child.*

Introduction

One evening last summer, a strange red star appeared in the sky. A red star has always been associated with death and destruction in the City of Light. In the past, it was thought to predict war, calamity or plague.

No red star had been seen for centuries. We are all very modern in the City now. We don't suffer from things like plague anymore. But we are also a superstitious people. Perhaps it comes from living by the sea and from having so many ancestors who were sailors.

There was already something strange in the City that summer. The atmosphere had been building oppressively, like the heat. It was an oddness that I couldn't quite put my finger on, and nor could I shake the feeling off.

It was not long after the red star had been sighted that the first of the mermaids was found murdered on the beach.

Chapter 1

Nowhere on earth is like the City in the Sea. Nor are any people like her people.

from *A History of the City in the Sea, Part 2 – The City of Light*
Professor Justin Lambe

My name is Vulpe Tempest and this is my story. It's not just my story, it's the story of several others, too, but as I'm the one who survived, I'm the only one left to tell it. And that should give you some idea of the kind of story we are dealing with here.

It might also give you the faintest flicker of an idea about me: a tantalising little clue about the type of person I am. Or maybe not. Maybe I will surprise you. I certainly surprised myself. Often the person that we think we are is not necessarily the person that we actually turn out to be.

It is also the story of the City in the Sea. Well, it is *a* story of the City, for something that the City is not short of is stories. There are as many stories about the City in the Sea as there are stars in the sky.

The City in the Sea used to be known as the Dark City but now it is called the City of Light. It is important to draw a distinction between now and then. For then was a very long time ago and now is right now. And it all started with the arrival of glass: glass transformed the City.

'Glass,' as my old history teacher would say, 'brought with it both light and lightness. Glass lit us up and glass lifted us up. It elevated us. It brought a brightness and an airiness to the City.

Glass opened us up like a burst of song from a bird at dawn. It was glass that made us glorious.'

So, we went from being the Dark City to the City of Light. We believed that we had been transfigured. We had had our caterpillar days, our fat larvae days, our hidden-away-in-darkness days and we had burst free of our cocoon days and now we were dancing our best, butterfly days. That's what we were all taught when we went to school.

Well, let me tell you, that darkness still exists. It has hidden itself right at the very heart of the City. And all around the edges too, waiting to swallow us whole like a fog from the sea. Oh yes, the darkness is still there; it is all around us. The boundaries aren't as sharp and crisp as you might think. The darkness is bleeding into the light, mixing with it like blood on sand; like mermaid blood mixed with sand and sea and spilled champagne.

And let me tell you something else: a world of glass is a world of reflections and distortions, as well as a world of light. Glass breaks, it cracks, and it shatters. And when it does, it leaves a sharp edge that can slice and cut and fillet: an edge that can kill a man, or woman, or mermaid.

So, the next time you toast your success, don't clink that glass too hard, for it will transform itself into a weapon in the time it takes you to say 'Cheers'. And when the party's over, be careful what you do with your empty bottles. In the time it takes to kiss people on the cheek and wave them on their way, I've seen someone killed with a champagne bottle. In fact, I was very nearly killed with one myself.

At the time of this story, I was, as people say, between careers. I was working in the office of a private detective, my uncle,

Timeon Tempest. Uncle Timeon had inherited the business from his father, my grandfather, who had inherited it from his. Like many people in the City, the Tempests were originally sailors but Great-Grandfather Tempest had decided that he preferred a life on dry land and opened the agency. Interestingly, my father, Uncle Timeon's older brother, had decided that *he* wanted a life at sea and had become a merchant.

Uncle Timeon kindly employed me as a favour to my father. The City is very forward-thinking like that; it encourages young women in the workplace. In the beginning, helping out involved posting things and making coffee. It sometimes involved making up excuses for Uncle Timeon. Pretending that he was out when he was in. Or that he was in, but indisposed, when he was out. But as time wore on, he allowed me to get involved in other things. including some of his more straightforward cases.

Not long before the sighting of the red star, Uncle Timeon had gone away on a holiday. It was at that point in the summer when the heat becomes unbearable and anyone who is able to, leaves for somewhere more pleasant.

Uncle Timeon did not usually follow this practice, but last year he claimed that he needed a few restorative weeks in the clear air of the mountains. This was obviously a lie; we all knew he had gone to spend time with a certain lady friend of his. For a private investigator, Uncle Timeon was very easy to investigate.

The plan was that I would keep the agency going over the summer. There was some deception involved, though Uncle Timeon preferred to call it 'sleight of hand'.

'Don't turn work down,' he said. 'Just pretend that I am out for the day and then post me the details. We can string them along until I get back.'

Of course, he didn't use the term 'string them along'.

'Anyway, nothing ever happens in August,' he added. 'The City is dead. Anyone who is anybody has gone away. And as for those that are left behind, it is too hot to get up to no good.'

As somebody who was nobody, I was finding the heat stifling. I got up to open the window: a pointless exercise, as it just let in even more of the heat.

'And,' said Uncle Timeon, before he left, 'you can take on a couple of things, if you like. Just the simple ones, mind, nothing complicated.'

In retrospect, this was a stupid thing for anyone to say, let alone a private detective. For the truth is that we don't really know whether something is simple or complicated until we reach the end. And by then it is too late.

I had not grown up wanting to be a private detective. All through my childhood I had wanted to be an artist. I am named after the famous artist Vulpe du Temps. Maybe being named after an artist made me believe that I could be one. But what we believe we should be is not necessarily what we are. The City has a famous art academy which is also very forward-thinking and admits young ladies from all sorts of backgrounds, even young ladies like me. Unfortunately, when I applied, they did not think that I was, quote: 'quite ready yet'; I needed more 'life experience'; aka I was not good enough.

So, I took my sketch books and paints and drawings and threw them off the Bridge of Truth and Knowledge at midnight. That was just over a year ago now, and I have had plenty of life experience since then. But has it helped my painting?

I wouldn't know. I haven't lifted a paintbrush since I threw my old ones away.

Chapter 2

Sometimes a minute's silence is worth a decade's conversation.

from *A Broken Heart and Larynx* Nate Innings

It was mid-afternoon, my least favourite time of day. The heat was unbearable and the light was harsh.

I had just settled down with an iced coffee and a Florentine from the café across from the office. I needed a little pick-me-up to keep me going through to the evening. But before I had a chance to get picked up, there was a knock at the door. I hastily hid my purchases in the desk drawer. Uncle Timeon had impressed upon me the need to look professional at all times.

The woman who entered was a couple of years younger than me, perhaps. She seemed shy; at least, she came into the room shyly, which isn't necessarily the same thing. But, in her case, I think it was. Her hair was cut short and shingled at the back. It was very fair, almost silver. It had a shine to it like the shore when the tide is out. As she came in, I felt a pleasant coolness as a sea breeze broke through the heat. It brought freshness, along with the smell of the water.

She appeared nervous, but people who come here always are. That was the first thing Uncle Timeon told me when I started.

'You will have to be extremely soothing,' he had said. 'Everyone who comes here needs to be soothed.'

At first, I thought that he was exaggerating. I often felt that Uncle Timeon spoke as if he was acting a part. He sounded the way a detective does in a book (the only experience of detectives that I had really had). But in this instance, he was right.

'It's because they think they want the truth,' he had replied when I asked him why. 'But most of them don't. Most people come here hoping that we will find that the lie they have believed was the truth all along. We are in a rare position, in that most people want us to prove them wrong. That's why they are nervous when they arrive; they are nervous that they might be right.'

'Does no-one want the truth, then?'

'I suppose some people, who have been believing the lies for a very long time, might. To believe a lie is a complicated and exhausting thing. You invariably have to believe more and more lies and half-truths to sustain it, until you no longer know what's real or imaginary. And the truth rarely brings happiness. Grieving what is lost is often the price that has to be paid for freedom from the lies.'

'Very cheerful,' I had said. 'Are there no happy endings? What about when we find stuff – people or things?'

'Well,' said Uncle Timeon. 'When we find money, people are grateful, but money rarely brings the happiness we think it will. And when we find people, well, often the found don't want to be found and that can cause all sorts of upsets. I suppose if it is pets – dogs or cats, say – then people are happy. Well, maybe not cats. Cats have no loyalty. But dogs, yes. There are happy endings if dogs are involved. As long as the dog is alive, that is.'

I introduced myself to the young woman, who told me that her name was Lina.

'So,' I said, 'what is the problem?' I spoke in a gentle voice: a soothing voice, as Uncle Timeon would call it.

'It's my friend,' she replied.

She looked out of the window towards the shore and twisted her little bag in her hands. It was one of the new, fun bags, which came in all sorts of shapes. Hers was formed like a seahorse and covered in glass beads.

I didn't say anything.

That is what Uncle Timeon had taught me to do. 'Silence,' he had said, 'acts like an oyster knife. It's like a thin blade that slips into a tightness and then pop, they open right up.'

He was right about this too. It was a technique that I had used very effectively on several occasions. In my personal life, that is, not at work. I almost never got to interview the client on their first visit. Uncle Timeon insisted on doing that himself.

After a few minutes, Lina said, 'She's vanished. Gone missing.'

'When?' I asked, keeping my voice soothing, trying to sound like a friend, not an interrogator.

'A while ago,' she said, evasively.

Evasiveness is always a clue that someone is holding something back. Sometimes, with a little patience you can get it out of them. Other times, you have to accept that they will only reveal what it is when they are ready.

'Tell me what happened,' I said, soothing as balm on a wound.

'We had a big fight.' This came out in rush.

'What about?' I said, leaning forwards slightly.

'Oh, this and that,' said Lina, looking away.

I said nothing and we sat, listening to the sounds in the street below. Someone was whistling a tune that I couldn't quite place; someone laughed. I looked at the bookcase opposite and read the titles on the spines of the books: *An Introduction to Detecting*, *The History of the City in the Sea: Books 1, 2 and 3*, and *An Atlas and an Encyclopaedia of Rare Illnesses*. I moved my gaze upwards and studied the plant that we never watered but that never quite died, and the strange drawing of the red fish that hung in a dusty frame beside the clock on the wall. But Lina didn't continue. Even silence wasn't opening this oyster.

'What is your friend's name?' I asked, changing tack.

'Ruby,' replied Lina. 'Ruby Alleck.' She spelled it out.

I wrote it down in my notebook.

'And what does she look like?' I asked. 'Do you have any photographs?'

Even though most people do not own a camera, there are always people standing around taking your photo for a fee. Those they do not sell, they use to advertise their work, so pretty girls dressed up for fun and adventure are always in demand. I imagined that Lina and her friend would have been the type to have been snapped. Dogs and babies were also very popular.

A man had recently sold a camera to Uncle Timeon. He told us that one day the photograph would replace the portrait. However, having an artist's eye is also necessary to taking a good picture. He offered to give me a lesson or two at a good price. I declined, as I obviously do not have an artist's eye, good or otherwise, and the camera remained in its box in a cupboard.

'I do,' said Lina, interrupting my thoughts. 'Somewhere at home, but I may have lost it.'

She seemed anxious. 'Is it important?'

'It will help,' I said. 'Can you describe her in the meantime?'

'Oh, she is beautiful,' said Lina. 'Really beautiful. She is tall and slim with long, red hair and big, green eyes. Everyone says how beautiful she is.'

Most of us have experienced the pain of having a beautiful friend: someone whose looks have the power to eclipse our own; whose mere presence sucks all the light from the room and directs it on themselves; who can 'put us out' like a candle, extinguish us. The beautiful ones tell us their beauty is as much a burden as a blessing. But I have never been fully convinced.

You did not need to be an investigator to deduce that this could have been the 'this' or the 'that' that Ruby and Lina had argued about. It also explained Lina's evasiveness. There was probably a man involved somewhere. There was often a man involved, in my opinion. Again, this came from my personal rather than professional experience.

Looking at Lina, I suspected that she also had her fair share of admirers. She had a fragility about her that I was sure many men would find irresistible. A silvery, elusive quality. She was like moonlight reflecting off water.

'So, do you have her address?' I asked. 'Last known address, I mean.'

I assumed that Lina did not have a current address or she would not be paying me money to find Ruby, who would, in that instance, not technically be lost, just not speaking to Lina. But, then again, you can never tell.

Lina shook her head.

'She had a room across the canal, near the Bridge of Truth and Knowledge,' she said, 'but I don't know the official address.'

'Could you find it?'

Lina looked doubtful. 'I only went a few times. I don't know if I could remember the way.'

To be honest, the City is renowned for being hard to navigate. It is full of dead ends and canals with no bridges.

'Anyway,' said Lina, 'she doesn't live there now.'

I was about to say that that didn't matter, that someone might know something, when another thought occurred to me.

'How do you know?' I asked. 'If you don't know where it is and you haven't seen her, how do you know she isn't living there?'

Lina went red. 'I just know.'

I made a mental note to revisit this later.

'How do you know Ruby?'

'We've known each other forever. We met at school.'

'Do you know her parents? Might they know where she is?'

'They're dead,' said Lina quickly, looking away.

'What about a job?' I asked. 'Does Ruby have a job?'

'She was working at the DT Watch Factory.'

'Did she ever introduce you to any friends from work?'

Lina shook her head.

I asked Lina a couple more questions and then told her how much we usually charged, how we calculated expenses, that sort of thing. She seemed happy with that and did not try to argue, which was unusual. I handed her a contract and got her to sign it before she could change her mind. I was now supposed to write the details down and send them to Uncle Timeon's address in the mountains... which was, in fact, a post office in a nearby village.

It was only afterwards, when I was writing the letter, that it struck me as odd that Lina had not enquired after Timeon Tempest himself, or indeed his son. The agency was called Timeon Tempest and Son, Investigators. The sign had not been changed to reflect the fact that Uncle Timeon was neither of the original investigators, nor that he had no heir.

I often wondered whether he was sad that he had no son to follow him. Or no son that we know of, my mother would say frequently, as she pursed her lips. She was very disapproving of Uncle Timeon's lifestyle choices.

But if Uncle Timeon did feel sad, he never showed it. He occasionally discussed changing the sign to Latin as he was a great admirer of the Romans.

'I always think things in Latin have a certain gravitas,' he would say, smiling at his little pun.

I liked the idea that Lina had assumed that I was a real detective. Perhaps that is why I decided to do what I did next. I didn't send the letter. I decided I would take on the case myself.

Although Uncle Timeon had told me that I could look into a few simple cases, I knew he didn't mean a missing person case. But, then again, how hard could it be? It wasn't like it was a kidnapping with a ransom. Or someone important whose absence would be noticed.

It was just two friends who had fallen out over a man. I would find Ruby and persuade her to meet with Lina over coffee and cake or a glass of wine. Or even one of the new fashionable cocktails that were becoming all the rage. Girlfriends shouldn't fall out over a man. They should stick together. All the women's magazines: that is what they said.

And I should know this better than anyone.

For a moment, I thought about my ex-lover. And I felt the old, familiar pain. Not in my heart but in my stomach. My heart didn't feel broken, but my stomach twisted and clenched. I felt a sharpness like thousands of pinpricks and, for a moment, it was hard to breathe. Despite the bright glare of the sun, it seemed dark in the office. I felt desolate and empty.

As for plenty more fish in the sea, I rarely felt one pulling at my line or even caught a glimpse of one passing by. And on the rare occasions when I did, they invariably turned out to be red herrings.

By the time I had written my report, I decided that it was too late to start investigating. The sensible thing would have been to go home. I was supposed to be going out later. But I was reluctant to get ready in this heat and even more reluctant to go out. I decided to sit around the office, killing time.

I reached into the big drawer under the desk where I had hidden my iced coffee and Florentine. The ice had melted, and the coffee was tepid. It was impossible to tell whether it was a cold drink that had warmed up or a hot drink that had cooled down. The Florentine was a sticky mess. I drank and ate them just the same. Uncle Timeon always had the morning paper delivered, so I read it for something to do.

That is how I learned that a mermaid had been killed. Her mutilated body had been found on the beach at dawn, just beyond all the cafés and ice cream parlours: cheerful, happy places with pink and blue candy-stripe parasols and a carousel for children.

She had periwinkle-blue hair and had a little bag covered with glass beads. It was shaped like a starfish, and that pitiful little detail made me want to cry.

Mermaids have been associated with the City in the Sea since the beginning of time: since before it was the City in the Sea, in fact. Back then, long before humans lived here, it was just a rag-tag collection of mud islands in a swampy lagoon. The mermaids would come ashore and bask in the sun.

When humans arrived, the mermaids continued to visit. They used magic and potions and glamour to take on human form so that they could walk unrecognised amongst the people. According to one legend, mermaids whispered in the ears of the early settlers, telling them where to find fresh water and the best places to fish; according to another, the first mermaids came from the spirits of dead sailors. This montage of memories and visions is what gives the City its elusive and haunting quality; what makes it simultaneously distinctive and familiar.

It was with the arrival of glass that the mermaids started coming in ever-increasing numbers. The City of Light sparkled and shimmered, drawing mermaids to it like a flame draws moths. They came in great swarms and shoals and stopped disguising themselves. They came from far away, swimming and splashing through the sea, singing, dancing, and laughing as they approached.

But there was another side to the mermaids, a darker side. They ate the fish in the lagoon and claimed the beaches as their own. People began to feel that they were becoming a nuisance, that there were too many of them and they were far too powerful. All sorts of rumours circulated. Some people began to whisper that the mermaids wanted to reclaim the City for themselves. The land had once belonged to them, after all, and it was the humans that had stolen and built on it.

Some said that mermaids did not have blood in their veins but freezing seawater. They had something hard and glittering inside them and their souls were like salt. Moreover, they had different ideas about love. Mermaids loved in a cold-blooded kind of way. They might sweep you up with the passion of a storm – all waves and winds and high tides – but that quickly subsided, leaving you adrift. In the end, a mermaid will always abandon a human lover to return to the sea.

So, the City Fathers ordered the mermaids to leave. Patrols with dogs, feral cats, and city foxes were set up to guard the beaches. The mermaid pools were filled with sharp stones and broken glass. Great nets were strung up across the lagoon to stop the mermaids entering. However, many of the nets were knitted by old ladies who were sympathetic to the mermaids. They infused the yarn with a potion which rendered the nets useless.

In any case, the mermaids had been visiting the City since the beginning of time and they weren't going to stop. They didn't need to 'own' the City to feel that it was theirs. They came in smaller numbers and reverted to disguise, hiding themselves in plain sight, but they still came. They could only spend a certain time ashore, but it was more than enough time for them. Some stories say that they managed to buy property in the City. Even today, a few of the little wooden fishermen's houses down by the beach are rumoured to be mermaid-owned, as are some of the jewel-coloured bathing huts.

It's common knowledge that you can tell when you are in the presence of a mermaid because you can't help but think of the sea. And their reflections look different; they flicker like sunlight on water. Some old houses have a 'mermaid bridge': a wooden plank or, occasionally, a sheet of glass laid over a pond. Visitors to the house have to walk over the plank so the host can check their reflection, and see whether it is safe to admit them.

According to the paper, whoever had killed the mermaid had tried to cut off her tail. It had been a frenzied attack and she had sustained multiple cuts and slashes. The more I read of the article, the more I wished I hadn't. They had sliced off her gills and laid them on top of her eyes. I wish I didn't know that. Once you know a thing, you can never unknow it.

Why on earth would anyone want to kill a mermaid? Mermaids matter to us. Mermaids are like a distorted reflection of ourselves. They are a slippery, silvered version of who we might be.

The paper had a grainy photograph. I could not stop my imagination making up more vivid images. They worked their way deep inside me as though they were splinters of broken glass.

Chapter 3

The stitches in an embroidery are like clues. Individually, they might appear insignificant, but together they create a solution.

from *A Woman's Guide to Needlework* CK Lusk

Eventually, I could delay no longer and I headed for home.

The office is situated in one of the oldest parts of the City. Several properties in the street had once been owned by the famous du Temps family. The building opposite once sold art supplies and had a small gallery space. It was the first place that Vulpe du Temps, my namesake, had exhibited her work. It is now a barber's shop called du Trims, and had recently acquired a display of larger-than-life barbers' implements: scissors, a razor and a shaving brush. They are made of glass and are attached to the front of the building and rotated by an elaborate mechanism that resembles the insides of a clock. I find them sinister. I always avoid walking on that side of the street, much to the amusement of Uncle Timeon.

Just beyond the library, the Vulpe du Temps Library to be precise, the street seems to come to a dead end, but it is actually a dog's leg. As I entered it, I had the strangest sensation that I was being watched. I checked the street behind me. But there were just the usual people doing their usual things. It was not busy, but it was not empty either. I shivered a little, recalling the news of the dead mermaid. I was obviously becoming overly fanciful, but I hurried along the little alleyway just the same.

The alleyway opens into a pretty square, where I rent a room in one of the houses. Legend has it that the central garden belonged to Madame Martinet, a mysterious figure whose spirit lives on in the City. In the past, people used to leave gifts of fruit and sweets in places that were sacred to her. Sometimes, if I bought a bag of cherries, I would put a couple for her on one of the benches.

My landlady, Cassiopeia, works as a seamstress in one of the fashion houses in the City and often takes in extra sewing to make a little more money. She is an old friend of Uncle Timeon. He had found me the lodgings shortly after I started to work for him. I wanted to feel independent. Many young women live away from home now in the City. It is a very modern thing to do.

Naturally, my mother disapproved. She imagined that I led a much more exciting life than I actually did. Only in my wildest dreams did I have the income and the opportunities to lead the kind of life that my mother believed that I was leading. She constantly worried that I would not get enough hot dinners and so tried to make me come home as often as possible to eat with her.

I ate with Cassiopeia most nights. And if Cassiopeia were to go away, I would be happy with bread and cheese and even happier with cake. Eating with Cassiopeia was not part of the agreement, but she said that she always ended up cooking more than she needed. This was not really true; it was because she liked the company. So, every evening we went through the ritual of her telling me that it would only go to waste. And I replied that it would be a shame to waste good food, a sin even, and I would come down and join her.

Cassiopeia liked to talk about Uncle Timeon. Sometimes, she could not stop herself from smiling when I said his name. She smiled in such a way as to suggest that there was a story there. It was never told but was implicit, always present, ticking away in the background like the clocks in her dining room. She also liked to discuss the cases with me. I imagined that I was not supposed to do that. But what Uncle Timeon didn't know wouldn't hurt him. Anyway, I got the impression that, once upon a time, he had discussed cases with her too. Cassiopeia has a very sharp mind. Sometimes, I wondered if it was Uncle Timeon that she liked, or the person she became when she was with him.

Cassiopeia had lost her husband. She told me when I first moved in. I said that I was sorry.

'I'm not,' she replied, adding, 'He is lost to the sea.' He had not met a watery end, but had jumped onto one of the many ships that thronged the port and sailed away and left her. I can never work out if she had been friends with Uncle Timeon before or after she was married.

I never told my mother any of this. I did not feel that it would make her any less worried about the hot-dinner situation. In fact, I imagined that it would make her angrier. Maybe even angry enough for her to have forced me to go home.

Cassiopeia collects clocks and weather houses, and several were chiming the hour as I went in. Something was different. It took me a few moments to realise that they had been joined, on time, by the cuckoo. The cuckoo was never on time; he always ran five minutes late.

Cassiopeia called to me to join her for a drink. She knew that I was going out so wouldn't want to eat. Cocktails had become all the rage recently and Cassiopeia had embraced this trend. She was mixing gin with a bitter orange liqueur of which she was particularly fond.

She is not a tall woman, but she has a fierce quality about her, mixed up with something exotic. She reminds me of the pictures that I have seen of the warrior women who came on horseback from the east. On that day, she had her straight, black hair piled on her head like a priestess. She was not originally from the City of Light but had come here as a young woman. She was from a mining town somewhere in the north. 'A place where it is always raining, and the landscape is wild,' is how she always describes it.

She had been doing her embroidery. She is very fond of embroidery and is always making pictures which she designs herself. They generally contain an old saying, such as *What is a shipwreck but a journey with an unexpected destination?*

She always embroiders her signature at the bottom.

'It's because embroidery is as much of an art as painting is,' she told me.

She too had wanted to be an artist. She always seemed sad when I said that I was finished with painting, and was always trying to persuade me to start again.

I commented on the cuckoo and his time-keeping.

'That new clock-maker was able to fix him,' she replied, as she handed me my drink.

We sat, lost in our own thoughts, enjoying the first sips and listening to the sound the ice cubes made as we swirled our glasses. It had become a little ritual which we both liked to savour.

'How was your day?' she asked, as the ice cubes began to melt.

I did not want to tell her about Lina. I had a hunch that she would disapprove of my intention to look for Ruby and try to dissuade me. To avoid the subject, I showed her the newspaper. 'Why would anyone want to kill a mermaid?' I asked. 'They are just so beautiful.'

'That is the thing about beauty,' replied Cassiopeia. 'Some people want to destroy it because it enrages them.'

We sat in silence again, each in our own worlds, considering this. Then Cassiopeia mixed us another drink. 'It is the start of the weekend, after all,' she said, lightening the mood.

I was still thinking about the dead mermaid an hour later as I sat in my room, killing the last little bits of time before I had to leave.

I regarded my appearance in the mirror. The heat had made my short black hair stick out at all angles. It made me look like an angry bird trapped in a tight space, pecking, scratching and flapping its wings.

I scowled back at myself. Who scowled first, I wondered, me or my reflection?

Cassiopeia called up to remind me of the time. Who could lose track of the time in a house full of clocks? I thought. The air was thick with their ticking and chiming. For reasons that I did not understand, Cassiopeia was heavily invested in my attending the party.

'You look lovely,' she cried, as I came downstairs.

'Wait,' she added, and ran off to return with a pair of earrings shaped like dragonflies. They were made of silver and enamelled in different shades of green and blue.

I slipped them into my ears.

'Enjoy yourself,' she said, giving my arm a little squeeze as I went out into the evening.

Chapter 4

'That's why they have music at parties,' said Caitlin. 'To drown out the sound of people crying. There is always at least one person crying.'

from *The Curious and the Restless* Daisy Daily

The street was busy with people coming home and people going out. The invisible line that demarcates the hours of the day from the hours of the evening had been crossed. It felt like the day had exhaled, loosened her clothing, and kicked off her shoes. She had acquired a loucheness: a seductiveness, suggesting limitless possibilities and opportunities to misbehave. Then I remembered where I was going, and the angry bird inside my head began to flap its wings.

I caught sight of my reflection, watching me from the surrounding glass and water. Reflections from the water re-reflected in the glass and reflections in the glass re-reflected in the water: all shimmering and shaking and floating around in the gentlest of evening breezes. Reflections of houses, trees and the sky all mixed up together, tangled with each other: broken up, fragmented, and distorted like bits of a puzzle not yet solved, like pieces of a jigsaw jumbled together, with only the faintest clue as to what the final picture would be.

I entered New Park by the east entrance, the Longitude Gate. There is a Latitude Gate on the north side and several other smaller entrances. It is far from being new. It was constructed in the boom years after glass had arrived in the City. It had been designed in the 'new style': that is, neatly regulated and laid out with wide paths and well-marked flowerbeds. The trees are all in orderly positions, each with its own plaque bearing its name in Latin (much to Uncle Timeon's approval), a description and a little about its history.

However, New Park is not without its wildness. The story goes that whilst it was being laid out, the gardeners would work hard every day and pack away their tools in the evening. When they returned the next morning, they found that their work had been destroyed. Plants had been dug up and strewn around, paths that had been laid were now obscured. Bags of earth and rubbish had been opened, and their contents tossed about. At first, the city foxes and wild dogs were blamed, and guards were employed. But the destruction continued with not even a glimpse of the perpetrator.

Eventually, someone suggested that it was the work of Madame Martinet. The City Fathers speculated that she was angry about the park, that she felt that she was being overlooked or disrespected. One of them had the idea to wall off an area and call it the Martinet Garden. They allowed it to grow wild. In the centre, they built a fountain decorated with fruit and flowers, the things that people had traditionally left as gifts for her. The destruction stopped and they were able to complete New Park.

I passed the Martinet Garden on my right and followed the directions on the invitation. The park was busy, groups of people gathering to enjoy the evening. Friends greeted each other as they threw rugs down on the grass and set out loaves of bread, cheese and bottles of wine and beer.

Astrid had picked a pretty corner for the party, but I would have expected nothing less. It was the prettiest corner in a park full of pretty corners. There were wicker chairs painted in shades of aubergine, turquoise and saffron and strewn with silk cushions, which gave them an air of opulence. Tiny glass jars of many different colours, each with a candle inside, hung from the branches of the nearby trees. Alongside them, there were hundreds of glass bubbles of the type called mesmerises that the people from the islands, on the edge of the lagoon, use to decorate their houses. Streamers of silver and pink caught the light in the gentle evening breeze. She'd better hope that that is safe, I thought. Imagine if one of those jars broke and a candle fell setting fire to a streamer.

Two long tables with white linen tablecloths had been placed in a L-shape. One had savoury things: mini sandwiches and little pies. The other was weighed down with cakes and pastries of every description, including strawberry tarts, and meringues in different colours. In the centre, a huge three-tiered cake was covered in pink icing and little silver balls, the birthday candles on the top waiting to be lit. At the other end, under a willow tree – or *Salix Babylonica*, to give it its Latin name – stood a barman with a crimson bow tie, making cocktails in a shaker of smoky pink glass.

It was as if they had brought the inside outside. Or as if, with a combination of the sheer force of her personality and her money, Astrid had turned the outside into the inside. There was something magical about it. In the bandstand, the band was warming up, an anarchy of sound before it organised itself into music. There would be dancing later. That's how it had all started, with dancing. But, then again, doesn't everything?

I spotted Astrid easily. Tonight, her resemblance to a goddess was even more pronounced than usual. She was the fairest of them all, to use the language of a fairy tale, the language that we were fed as little girls. We were stuffed full of it like foie gras geese. No-one prepared us for what we should do if we grew up not to be the fairest of them all.

Astrid had an effervescence about her, like the bubbles in a glass of champagne. I suffered a fleeting stab of irritation at her happiness. When she saw me, she waved enthusiastically but approached with a slight hesitancy, affording me a little pleasure. I had a sudden impulse to walk away, but I stood my ground. I did not take even one step to meet her. Let her come to me, I thought.

She gave me a hopeful smile. Hopefulness rarely ends in disappointment for the Astrids of this world.

I returned a little glassy smile, a smile that could shatter: a smile that could drain blood. When I said hello, my voice was stiff and high like a huge swell of water being forced through a very tight space.

I went rigid as she hugged me. I did not close my eyes. I had been fooled like that once before. She smelled of the daytime and summer, a garden full of flowers and sunshine. I was like cigarette smoke and black coffee.

Astrid let go but was determined to hold me there in conversation. I retreated into the very centre of myself. Our exchange was brittle. It hurt the muscles of my face.

We ran out of things to say. Well, we ran out of chit chat. There were plenty of unsaid things lurking but neither of us said them. We stood in silence, despite everything, reluctant to walk away from each other. Then, simultaneously, we saw her cousin approaching. We hated her cousin. On seeing our old enemy, I couldn't resist making a little joke. We laughed and it was like we once were. Then something passed between us like the shadow of a bird flickering across a wall and we went back to being cool.

I excused myself and went to get a drink. Astrid looked sad as I turned away. I felt triumphant but it was the kind of triumph that brought me no joy. Even with my back to her, I could feel her standing there and part of me wanted to comfort her. And then I remembered. Actually, I didn't have to remember, for I had never forgotten. My unease and suspicions, the look in their guilty eyes and, finally, the betrayal. I dreamed about it some nights. And even when I could not remember my dreams, I woke up thinking about it. Round and round it went, spinning for all eternity, sucking the life and joy from me. I fought to block it out. All I had to do was stop fighting for a few moments and it would be back.

You want everyone you love to love each other too, or at the very least to like each other. You want life to be like some great solar system, with you as the sun at the centre. You want the people you love to love each other – and how delighted you are, at the beginning, when they do. Their admiration for each other is no more than a compliment to you on your good taste. The problem arises when they begin to love each other more than they love you, when their love gradually pushes you out, until you are a distant star on the very edge of your own galaxy; a star whose light is dimming and no-one even notices.

How like the sun Astrid was. So loved and so adored. I did not begrudge her even one of these people orbiting around her now. But that made what she had done all the more painful. She had so many people; why she did have to take the one person that I loved?

They had said that they never wanted to hurt me. Well, Astrid did, at length. She sat me down and told me with tears in her eyes, as if she was the one whose heart had just been broken. Again and again, she repeated that they had never wanted to hurt me. Perhaps they didn't want to, but they did. The world is full of hurt people and people who never wanted to hurt them.

I thought of the dead mermaid down on the beach and shivered. She had had her gills sliced off and I had had my heart hacked out.

Their love for each other diminished me. I was insignificant, incapable of inspiring passion or love. All I could muster from others was fondness. And pity, of course. They couldn't help it. They were swept away by it. As Astrid said this, she smiled. She could not help it; it was that powerful.

My mother had rolled her eyes. 'These things never last,' she said. 'Passion burns itself out quickly.'

Certainly, the passion which I had inspired had spluttered and died pretty quickly. And the person I had been spluttered and died along with it.

Cassiopeia fussed round me and fed me cake. 'You'll find someone else,' she said.

But I didn't want anyone else. Which was just as well, as she was wrong, and I didn't find anyone else.

But surprisingly, my mother was right about him. He and Astrid didn't last long.

I said I didn't care but inside I was very, very happy. It turned out to be a hollow victory, though: a cheap piece of nickel masquerading as gold; the kind of victory which quickly buckled and finally broke. Although it was over with Astrid, it didn't mean that he came back to me. The problem had never been Astrid, the problem had been me. Maybe that is why I forgave her. Well, I had not completely forgiven her, but I was willing to keep up some sort of pretence. The problem was that he had never loved me.

Chapter 5

Anything that is empty on the inside will always be filled with darkness, no matter how intricate the outside is.

from *Coffee and Cigarettes* Maud Leslie

I sat on one of the turquoise chairs beneath a large beech tree (*Fagus Sylvatica*, as the sign told me). It was right on the edge of where the party stopped, and the park began: a hair's breadth away from not being there at all. It made me feel like I could easily just disappear into my surroundings at any moment.

The evening had relaxed and softened out. It had become something warm and malleable. But I could not join it. I hated parties. I never used to, but I did now. Or maybe it was only this party. No one wanted to talk to me, and I didn't want to talk to anyone either.

The band started to play. A couple of people clapped, and somewhere someone cheered. I sat smiling my brittle, fake smile, wishing that I could fade away. Although it felt awkward that no-one was talking to me, part of me prayed that no-one would.

All my memories were simmering inside me: the night we met; the first night that we kissed; the nights we lay beside each other, naked and talking until dawn. Love had flowed through me then like a current of electricity. I never felt tired in those days; now I was always weary. We had talked for so long. It seemed inconceivable that we would ever run out of things to say. So, that made the silences, when they came, seem all the more incomprehensible. I rehearsed clever things to say, desperate for the spark that would reignite the flare of connection. It was only at the end that I understood that it wasn't that he had run out of things to say or that he didn't want to speak. He had lots of things to say; he just didn't want to say them. Well, he didn't want to say them to me. As I later found out, he was saying them to other people.

I had assumed that he would always tell me everything. I had assumed that he would always want me. Actually, I had assumed quite a lot. I had assumed that someone who talked about hurt and betrayal would never, himself, become a betrayer. I still struggled to accept that he had. I suppose it was because he did not love me. The anguish of that realisation swept over me like a great icy wave. It felt as if a blade sliced through my stomach. I thought again of the dead mermaid.

I comforted myself by imagining that we were still together. Sipping our drinks and gossiping about the other guests, he would lean in close to me and stroke my hand and ask me about my day. I would tell him about Lina, even though I probably shouldn't. But I trusted him, so it would be all right. That is what I missed more than the passion and the sex. And, believe me, I missed those a lot. But what I missed most was having someone who was interested in the minutiae of my day. Someone who could make me laugh and whom I could make laugh in return. I missed having someone that was mine.

I tried to pull myself back into the present. The past and the world of my imagination were much sweeter places to be, but I paid a heavy price for lingering in them. I decided I would count to ten and then get up and mingle. But I reached eleven and retreated back into the safe little world inside me.

The park stretched out behind me, and it felt as if it went

on forever – a lush green version of the Milky Way. It ran down the edge of the City, starting in the high ground in the north, until it reached the sea. It wasn't a straight line but bent sharply, moulding itself around the shape of the City. We were in the part just after it changed its direction of travel. Or just before, I suppose, depending on which direction you were moving.

It was well into the evening now and the daylight was gradually disappearing. The candles in the trees were burning brightly. Occasionally, the flare of a match twinkled like a firefly, as someone lit up a cigarette. Two great lanterns illuminated the dancefloor like a stage. New Park was one of the first places in the City to get electric lighting. I watched as a great moth flew into one and fizzled against it.

I thought about light and darkness. Is darkness just a lack of light or is it an entity in its own right? Shadows were beginning to pool. The edges of things were becoming less distinct. The boundaries were dissolving as individual things smudged into one another.

Gradually, it became harder to make out the true shape of things in the distance. The shadows played with the colour of objects too, repainting them in different shades. As if by magic, green became brown, daubed with occasional flecks of red. The evening flowers opened up and released their scent, seductive, both sweet and peppery, a mix of what was left over from the day and what was promised by the night.

Sounds bled into one another too. The distant murmur of voices mixed with the band and the hum of insects and rustle of nocturnal animals as they moved through the shrubs and trees. Even in the City there was wildness and for a moment I thought of Madame Martinet's garden. I imagined that it must be darker there than anywhere else. Night-time did not bring sleep to the park, just a different kind of wakefulness. It brought alive something that was hidden during the day.

The air felt as if it had substance, a consistency somewhere between solid and liquid, like a fine mist made from silk. I could feel it brush against my neck and caress my bare shoulders.

I jumped as someone said my name. A friend had come over to say hello. Pulling myself out of my thoughts and back into the real world was like swimming up from the depths to reach the surface. Misery clung to me like water, trying to drag me back down again.

My friend was happy, and I let her chatter away. She had a new job and a new boyfriend. They were going away for a few days' holiday. Had I tried one of the little pies? They were delicious. Of course, they were, I thought; everything that Astrid did was delicious.

I felt like I was becoming a shadow of myself. What was left of me was just a facade. Like one of those half-demolished buildings that you see around the City, where only the front and a fraction of the roof remains.

My friend drifted away. I was not surprised. I did not belong with happy people. It was as if they belonged to a club of which I was not a member. And if I did manage to sneak in, someone would soon realise and I would be ejected.

I felt so disconnected from everyone. It was as if there was a thin pane of glass between us.

I longed for a partner, a partner in crime. Well, not exactly in crime, I thought, bearing Uncle Timeon and the detective agency in mind. Just someone who understood me. All I wanted was to be someone special and to be special to that someone too.

I tried to think of something to distract myself and my mind went to the mermaid with her gills sliced off. I wondered: did whoever did that, do it first or last or somewhere in the middle? Is that how they killed her? I pictured her lying dying on the shore, gasping, and bleeding. It made me shiver and feel queasy. Pull yourself together, I told myself, you're at a party.

Everyone was laughing and dancing. I should mingle. I could go and talk to Astrid. No, not Astrid. I should stick with other people: nice, normal, neutral people. I should have a nice, normal, neutral conversation about nice, normal, neutral things. I should avoid topics such as betrayal, abandonment and dead mermaids.

No-one had ever lied to me before. Of course, I'd been told white lies as a child – if I threw litter on the ground, the City of Light would sink; if I cried too much, I would shatter all the windows – but I had never been properly deceived. Never been told one thing that wasn't true. And not told other things that were. Lies of omission are like a magician using smoke and mirrors: getting you to look one way while the real action is going on elsewhere. Leading you on a wild goose chase. When you have been lied to in that way, nothing seems truthful anymore.

I gave myself a little shake and made a deal with myself. I would get a drink and mingle, and when I had finished my drink, then I could go. I would say my goodbyes or maybe I wouldn't. I might just slip away into the night like a ghost.

There was a crowd round the table under the willow. There were now three waiters, all wearing different-coloured bow ties. One was shaking drinks. Another was pouring wine and the third was opening bottles of champagne. Each time he popped a cork, someone would cheer. Now that I had a plan, I wanted to implement it. As Uncle Timeon liked to say, 'My advice is: if you have to walk through hell, run.' I joined the crowd, half-pushed and half-carried by the press of people behind.

Near the front, a man had pulled a chair up to the table and was reading a book. I noticed his reflection first, in the bottles stacked behind the makeshift bar. Occasionally, he would look up and make a comment to the waiter with the dark-purple bow tie, the colour of a bruise. How stupid, I thought, to sit there; how selfish. He was blocking the way. The crowd surged, another wave breaking. I kicked his chair: half by accident and half on purpose. He lowered his book and looked straight at me.

Afterwards, we would argue about who had smiled first. It was him; I am sure of it. Why would I smile at him if he had not smiled first at me? He looked up and smiled at me and I smiled back. It was automatic, a reflex. I would not have smiled first.

He insisted that he only smiled at me because I had smiled at him. Why on earth would he smile at someone who had kicked his chair? He was reading his book, minding his business. He was just sitting quietly, doing no harm, when someone kicked his chair and he looked up. Then he saw my smiling face. 'And what a face it was,' he would say. It took his breath away, and he smiled back. And that, he would insist, was the order in which things had happened.

Chapter 6

'And just like that, the world was well again,' said Lavender.

from *The Syllables of Love* Hyacinth Harper

I took my drink back to my chair under the beech tree. Suddenly, I was a little more awake, a little more alive. It was as if I had moved into a world of colour. Something inside me had started to sparkle. When I reached my seat, I was still smiling. I sat there smiling to myself as I sipped my champagne and watched the scene around me. Darkness had crept like an inkblot across the sky making all the lights in the trees twinkle like stars. The thin pane of glass between me and the rest of the party shattered.

Two other friends joined me. 'See the difference it can make when you smile,' my mother had said and she was right, as she often was. They had just returned from a trip and were full of excitement. As they talked, I became aware of something nearby. I looked around. There he was, with his book and his drink, sitting at an empty table. He was smoking and watching me. The smoke from his cigarette furled upwards into the branches of the trees and dissolved into the darkness.

I turned back to give my friends my full attention. Well... some of my attention. I knew that he was watching me. I knew he was watching me even when I was not looking. I knew he was watching me even when he was not looking.

Quite suddenly, the evening opened up. I began to tingle. It was as if every bit of me was waking up. Every single muscle, bone and nerve, like a hundred thousand lights had been turned on, sending a shock through my body, a great jolt that shook me from my somnolent state.

I turned to see him chatting to one of the waiters. And I felt myself crash back down to earth. Something was sucked out of me. I felt the tide go out, leaving a beach littered with debris. The fine thread that connected us had been broken.

I returned to the conversation with my friends. I tried to join in. But I couldn't help it. I looked back again. And I saw it, the sidelong glance in my direction. The dizzying sense of relief was overwhelming.

My friends and I continued to talk. Someone else walked past and said hello. I allowed myself another sly glance, and then, out of the corner of my eye, I saw him move. He pushed his chair back and, slowly and deliberately, up he stood. He lifted his drink and finished the last few drops and then tapped the empty glass a couple of times on the table.

I felt a little sick. My friends were talking – 'great view, great food, a little ornamental train called the Puffer that looked like something from a children's story.' On and on they went. They had no idea.

I was only a little sick though. Because deep inside, I already knew. I just knew because it was meant to be; it was fate flexing her muscles and reminding me of her existence. Later, much later, when I told my mother that, she just rolled her eyes. And Cassiopeia sighed and gave me a little hug and said, 'Oh, darling,' in a sad little voice with just a hint of bitterness. Like in a cocktail, but a serious, sophisticated kind of cocktail; one that is sipped elegantly and comes in a heavy glass.

He looked across at me and, for a moment, everything slowed. It didn't stop, it just slowed, fractionally. Time seemed to become both solid and elastic. The space between the notes that the band was playing became marginally longer. The dancers elongated their movements in response. The bubbles in my champagne took a little more time to reach the surface. High in the sky, a flock of sea birds, their undersides lit up by the lights from the party, hovered like paper bags lifted up by the wind. Even the air seemed to move more slowly.

I sat there and did nothing. I offered him no encouragement. For the second time that evening, I let someone come to me. But I couldn't resist one last little look. I turned myself fractionally so that I could just make him out in the corner of my vision.

He threw his cigarette down and ground it out. Neither Astrid nor the park authorities would be happy about that. There were signs telling you to dispose of such things in the bin. He put his book into his back pocket and made his way towards me.

I returned my gaze to my friends, smiling and nodding enthusiastically at an interminable story about a train journey and a lady with a cat in a basket. The cat was trying to get at the cheese my friends had just bought. As they went through a tunnel it managed to escape and demolish the Brie.

I laughed. It wasn't because of the story. It was because he was now very close.

'Then,' she continued, 'there was a lady with earrings like great hoops...'

'Hello,' he smiled at me. 'Do you mind if I join you?'

'Not at all,' I answered. One of my friends fussed round looking for a cushion for the spare chair.

For a few moments, no-one said anything. Despite Uncle Timeon's training, I didn't like this silence. It might work on getting information out of reluctant clients but there was much more at stake here.

Getting him here had been the easy part. Experience had taught me that holding on to people was the hard part. I needed to do my best to keep him here. If I failed, I would lose him. And I would have only myself to blame.

I needed to fill the silence and fill it well. I needed to fill it with clever, entertaining words. If not, I ran the risk of him wandering off to find someone more entertaining or interesting or clever. Wandering off to find someone beautiful. Astrid, stealer of men, flitted across my mind.

'Great party,' he said.

One of my friends agreed. They talked about the night, the weather, the band. Then the silence crept back. My other friend opened her mouth. I feared the start of another long story about trains or earrings, and I could not take that, so I started talking. I told them a funny story about my day. Of course, it wasn't my actual day. It was a collage of several days, none of them today. But it was amusing, and everyone laughed.

Suddenly she was back. Funny Vulpe, clever Vulpe, witty Vulpe was back. The lassitude that clung to me evaporated. I hadn't been that Vulpe for such a long time. It wasn't until her return that I realised quite how much I had missed her.

Surely, there is nothing better than making people laugh? It was glorious and I felt jubilant. I looked at him and, this time, I smiled first.

I didn't see it then, but something else had crept in. I was too busy laughing and being clever to notice it, or to notice how dangerous it was. Gratitude, that's what it was. I felt grateful to him for bringing back the part of me that I thought that I had lost forever. For the first time in ages, I felt like dancing.

The darkness had fully descended. But it was a shining, sparkling kind of darkness, the sort that shimmers with reflections of the candlelight and the distorted shadows of the night. It was the sort of darkness that feels like the start of things, not the end of things.

My friends disappeared to dance or drink or mingle. Or perhaps to relate the story of the cat and the Brie to another lucky audience. We sat and talked. Or, rather, we danced with our words. Our conversation had a rhythm to it. Back and forth we went. Speeding up and slowing down. Showing off to each other. We matched each other's tempo word for word as we twirled around each other. It was a rhythm that matched the music of the band. A rhythm that matched the night and the City and, beyond that, the sea.

At once I felt connected to something greater than myself. I felt expansive. I felt myself fill up with something light and frothy, as if I could float away at any minute. But, simultaneously, I felt that the world had contracted, to contain just the two of us. The night had closed around us, encasing us in our own little bubble. We were held by that and something else: intimacy, perhaps, or maybe the intensity of our conversation.

Something crackled between us, something combustible. The sky suddenly lit up. For a few seconds it was filled with magenta and golden light. I thought Astrid must have got fireworks for her party. Then it disappeared and I realised that it must have been a ship setting off a flare out at sea.

Chapter 7

Darkness may be monochrome, but it is also fathomless. It can hide a lot of things.

from *Feathering the Crow's Nest* C Morani

We had nearly finished our drinks. I recognised this as a dangerous time, a treacherous time. For when his glass was empty, he could put it down, thank me and bid his farewells. I would never see him again. I did not want the magic to end. Surely, he must feel the magic too.

But I had been fooled before.

His glass was like an hourglass with the sand slowly running out. I tried to sip my champagne in an attempt to stretch out time again. Each sip of my drink was hardly anything at all, just enough to make my tongue tingle.

Hope was all I had left but, to be honest, I did not trust hope – nor luck, for that matter. Both had let me down before.

He finished his drink and looked at my nearly empty glass.

'Would you like another?' he asked, gesturing towards it.

I looked at my glass as if I were surprised to find that I had only about three millimetres of champagne left. I paused for a few seconds, as if trying to decide.

Finally, I nodded. 'That would be lovely.'

As he walked across to the bar, I was relieved, but not out of the woods yet. The acid test would be if he returned. There was nothing that I could do now except wait. Another thing that did not come easily to me.

Despite the darkness, the park was still busy. I could make out groups of people in the penumbra of the party, sitting in the no-man's land between light and dark. I was near the edge but still within the boundaries of brightness. People moved amongst the shadows of the trees.

It was the kind of evening that stirred up mischief and misbehaviour. The type of night that encouraged illicit things.

Then I noticed Lina. She was at the edge of the party, holding the hand of a young man. She looked like something bright reflected in the darkness; like the light from the lanterns down at the shore, shimmering in the sea. Her fingers were linked with his and they were standing very close. Then he let go of Lina's hand and dissolved into the shadows.

I waved and beckoned her over. I am not quite sure why I did this. We weren't friends after all, and until then I had been happy to have my companion's undivided attention. Maybe I just felt open and generous? Or, perhaps, I felt that the earlier intensity was too much. No, not too much; more that it was moving too fast. I wanted it to slow so that I could enjoy the view.

Lina looked behind her and called into the darkness. She walked towards me, hesitant and sweet. She was in a dress the palest shade of pink, the colour of the start of a blush or the sky as the sun begins to rise. As she got closer, I could see tiny, diamond clips sparkling in her hair. I thought that they were in the shape of stars but when she sat down, I realised that they were starfish.

They had been out for a walk, she said, and had been drawn to the lights and the music.

'Like a moth to a flame,' I replied.

She looked puzzled, as if she had never heard the expression.

'It is my friend's party,' I continued. I was surprised I called Astrid a friend without sounding bitter. I wondered if that was due to my new companion or Lina's smiling face or just the magic of the night.

Beyond Lina, I could see my companion returning. He had acquired a tray with a whole bottle of champagne and some fresh glasses. When he realised that I was watching, he smiled at me and balanced the tray on his hand like a waiter. Showing off, he raised it high into the air.

'Have a drink with us,' I said, impetuously, to Lina. I felt a thrill using the word 'us'. It would be easy for her to cross the invisible line from outside to inside and join the party. It was that time of the evening when nobody cared anymore. All kinds of boundaries were melting.

Lina hesitated. She looked behind her and then leaned in close to me. Her perfume smelled like the end of a day spent at the beach: a hint of the sea mixed with sweet ice cream and sunshine.

'Don't say anything about' – she faltered and leaned forward to whisper in my ear – 'you know, about how we know each other.'

It did not surprise me. Everyone keeps secrets. I nodded to reassure Lina as my companion reached us. He set down the tray in the centre of the table with a flourish. Lina's friend appeared and she introduced him as Rufus Klumpe. I poured us all drinks. Lina smiled and blushed as she said his name. She looked at him in that way that people do when they are in love.

Rufus was a tall, thin, young man. He was one of those people who appear a little stooped but actually are not. Later, when he was walking away beside Lina, I realised that he was not as tall as I had first thought. He just gave that impression.

He was smartly dressed but his clothes looked old and well-cared-for rather than brand-new. They had the appearance of having been expensive. He wore dark trousers and a white shirt with gold cufflinks. As he sat down, they caught the light, and I saw that they were engraved with a crest. I wondered what it was. Uncle Timeon had told me to practise observing people by doing it with everyone I met.

Rufus had an old-fashioned, rather elegant air. He looked like a character from a play or a book, the sort of man that would stride rather than walk. Despite his name, his hair was not red but dark. It looked like it wanted to curl but it was not quite long enough. His features gave him a haughty, patrician air, noticeable when he was not speaking. But when he talked or laughed and became animated, he looked quite different.

When Lina said my name, Rufus looked at me with interest.

'Like the artist?' he said. 'Vulpe du Temps.'

I nodded.

'And do you paint? Are you an artist too, Vulpe?'

I felt my insides tighten. This was another place I didn't want to have to go.

I was saved from having to answer by, of all things, a black cat, which appeared, as if by magic, from the darkness.

I like cats, and black cats are lucky, so I reached down to stroke it, but it ignored me and went immediately to Lina. It purred and wound itself around her legs. She gave a little scream.

'Lina hates cats,' laughed Rufus, 'but they love her.' He gallantly scooped the cat up and returned it to the night.

'Isn't that always the way with cats?' I replied. 'Then again, isn't that always the way with men, too?'

My companion replied, 'Actually, I was about to say, isn't that just like a woman?'

We all laughed. But he and I exchanged a look. We were alike, him and me.

'Well,' I said, lifting my glass up in a toast. 'Drink up everyone, the night is short, and we don't want our champagne to get warm.'

'*Vive hodie, cras enim morimur,*' said Rufus, clinking his glass against mine.

Lina looked at him as if he was the cleverest man on earth.

I was feeling clever too, and couldn't resist translating. 'Live today, for tomorrow we die.'

I was Uncle Timeon's niece, after all, and was used to hearing Latin phrases thrown out here and there. I said it ever so casually, as if I went around speaking Latin all the time.

Everyone looked at me with respect.

'Aren't you a woman full of surprises?' my companion said, smiling in amusement.

'Oh, yes,' I replied. 'All sorts of surprises.'

We looked intently at each other, neither of us wanting to break the other's gaze.

'Rufus knows lots of things,' said Lina adoringly.

Rufus said nothing. He neither agreed nor disagreed with this statement.

'What do you do, Rufus?' I asked.

'I am a watch- and clock-maker,' he replied.

'He is very good with his hands,' Lina couldn't help adding.

We all laughed when she said this, and she blushed, but this time it was a deep pink.

'That is a lovely watch you have on,' said my companion, looking at Rufus's wrist. 'Is it a family heirloom?'

'No,' replied Rufus. 'I made it for myself. It is a copy of one I saw in a picture, but I liked it.'

Lina looked at him proudly and reached to hold his hand.

My glass caught the light and I noticed that it had a tiny crack near the rim. I'd better be careful, I thought, I don't want to end up cutting myself.

Chapter 8

The problem with darkness, is that it makes it very hard to tell if you are lost.

from *Unhitched* Sali Vary

Shortly afterwards, Lina and Rufus said goodnight and left, Lina holding onto his hand tightly. We heard her laughter disappear into the night.

Now it was just me and my companion.

'So,' I said to him.

'So,' he imitated me, smiling and raising his eyebrows: something that I do when I want to turn a word into a question.

We sat and looked at each other.

Astrid came over to say goodbye. She was bright but somehow her brightness seemed out of place in our dark little corner: a brashness that didn't quite belong. She smiled at me and hugged me very tight before she left.

'Let's go out soon, Vulpe,' she said. 'Just the two of us.'

I nodded, but I didn't really mean it. For a moment, I forgot about everything, even my new companion. I was aware of something bitter burning at my centre. There would never be just the two of us again; *he* would always be there, unnamed and unspoken of, but between us.

With Astrid gone, the party lost the gravitational pull that had kept us all present. Things began to break up quickly. The band started to pack up their instruments. The music was replaced by the sounds of the night: the ever-present rush of the sea, along with the hushed chatter of the few remaining guests, clustered together, reluctant to leave. The waiters removed their bow ties or let them hang open at their necks, whistling the last tune the band had played, as they packed away the bar and the tables and chairs.

The party disappeared around us. The lights and candles were removed from the trees and the darkness flowed in like the sea at high tide. It lapped at the edges of our table which was marooned in its own tiny pool of candlelight. We hung on, talking, waiting for the waiters to come and take our chairs, for only then would the party be truly over. Then we would have no reason to continue talking to one another. No reason at all. We would just be two people in the park at night.

Finally, they came for our chairs and table, blowing out the remains of the candle as they did so. We moved closer to each other in the darkness. The shadows moved across our faces as if we were wearing masks. For a moment, neither of us said anything. Each stood waiting or perhaps daring the other to speak next. Just like earlier, despite my experience in the detective agency, I was the one that broke.

'So,' I said again.

'So,' he replied. I knew that he was smiling.

'It's late,' he continued.

'It is.'

'Let me walk you home.'

I felt relief and disappointment. Relief that he was not going to leave me to go home alone in the dark. The relief was more about not losing him than not making my own way home. I didn't really need anyone to walk with me, I just wanted him to. But I was also disappointed because I wanted him to kiss me. He might still kiss me, but I couldn't bear waiting any longer. I wanted him to kiss me right there and then. I have a very impatient nature.

Once again, it struck me how alive the park seems at night, in a way that it doesn't during the day. During the day, the park feels as if it belongs to the people, but at night it belongs to itself. I wondered: did it look forward to the darkness? Did it yearn for the time when it could be what it really wanted to be? Did the park feel more real at this time than it did in the day?

The back of my companion's hand brushed against my arm. I felt a shiver run through me, as all the hairs on my arm rose up. I stumbled and grabbed onto him and for a moment he held me to steady me. It was hard to see where the path ended, and the grass and more uneven ground began.

As we walked, the atmosphere became less charged. It flowed around us like a river, and it felt as if we were being carried along by it. As we passed the garden of Madame Martinet, he stopped and turned to look at me. I sensed that smile again in the darkness. He opened the door to the garden and took my hand, leading me in.

He laughed when I protested.

'Madame Martinet is supposed to be the protectress of thieves and swindlers and other people up to no good in the City,' he said. 'I doubt she'd mind. In fact, I imagine that she would approve.'

His comment reminded me that I should leave a gift. I had slipped one of the little wooden cocktail sticks in my bag. It had a tiny, carved bird on the top. I placed it on the wall for her, hoping she would appreciate the gesture. Everything seemed so perfect. Superstitiously, I did not want to run the risk of annoying the gods or other supernatural beings.

The garden felt different from the rest of the park, stiller and quieter. It seemed to be holding its breath, watching to see what would happen next.

We sat on a bench beside a fountain. The garden was very dark, lit only by the moon and stars. We looked at each other but neither of us said anything. The silence felt as if it was being pulled taut, pulled into something almost unbearable. It pulled us closer and closer together. He bent downwards slightly. We were so close now. As close as we could be without actually touching.

It was as if he were kissing me without our lips touching. And then he was kissing me, and I closed my eyes. It felt like I was dissolving.

After we kissed, we walked home. We held hands for a while but it is hard to walk holding hands. We stopped intermittently, as he pulled me into the shadows and kissed me again and again.

When we reached Cassiopeia's house, we stood outside, whispering to each other. I did not want him to go, of course, but I was excited that we had the whole summer ahead of us. I was eager for our lives together to start.

As he turned, I felt a flicker of panic as to when I would see him again. But just before he left, he said he would call me. At that moment, I trusted him.

Uncle Timeon had a telephone in the office and Cassiopeia had recently bought one for the house. I ran inside to find a pen to write down the numbers and the office address. I was still jittery enough to feel relieved that he was there when I returned.

I watched until he disappeared. The cat from next door came over, surprised that someone else was awake at this time. She gave an indignant meow when I tried to stroke her. I thought of Lina and the way cats loved her though she did not like them.

Then I went back to thinking of him.

Chapter 9

'Why not assume it is as it seems?' said Juliette. 'We have to start somewhere.'

from *Stranger than Us* Robbie S Harp

I woke up feeling that something wonderful had just happened. Then I remembered and realised that I was smiling.

The sun streamed through my window and made the shadow of a vase of gerberas, which Cassiopeia had placed in the room, dance across the wall. I dressed quickly. I sang one of the songs from the previous night that had stuck in my head, and I could not stop smiling as I did so.

Cassiopeia looked at me in surprise as I waved goodbye to her. I was not known to be a morning person, so my energy and cheerfulness must have been startling. Everything looked so beautiful in the little square as I walked to work. Still singing, in my head, I bought myself a coffee and a pastry and then went to the office to think up a plan.

The obvious place to start looking for Ruby was in the DT Watch Factory. In fact, it was the only place I knew of to search for her, as that was all the information that Lina had given me, although I was pretty certain Lina had been lying or, at the very least, holding back. And in my book, holding back the truth is still lying. A lie of omission is still a lie, and worse than a blatant lie.

I would speak to Lina again about what she knew. She would no doubt slip up, eventually. That was another thing Uncle Timeon had told me. They take work, those lies of omission. They need to be remembered. The liar is constantly remembering what not to say. And that is harder than remembering a false story.

The factory is on the other side of the canal. It is walking distance, but only if you are happy with sore feet and have a lot of time to waste. As I wasn't, and didn't, I would get one of the waterbuses. I checked the petty cash tin. I was not going to spend my own money, nor wait for Uncle Timeon to reimburse me.

It occurred to me that I could not just walk into the factory and ask for Ruby. I certainly could not walk in and announce that I was a private detective. I was going to need some kind of cover story.

I went over to the props box, which contained a vast array of objects that Uncle Timeon used on surveillance to make him less conspicuous. Amongst them was a peaked cap and a jacket, with matching logos, depicting a whale. I idly wondered if they had been embroidered by Cassiopeia, as I thought I recognised her style. The logo was meaningless. It just created the impression that the wearer worked for or belonged to something or someone. And, as Uncle Timeon says, if people think you belong to someone or something, you can get away with a lot.

Near the waterbus stop is a flower shop called Violetta's. I often looked in as I went past, enticed by the sweet smell. Uncle Timeon sometimes bought flowers from there for his lady friends. I'd see bunches of them in the office, wrapped up in their distinctive, violet-coloured paper and tied with pink and silver twine. I bought a small bunch of gerberas, like the ones Cassiopeia had put in my room. Paid for from petty cash.

I sat at the back of the waterbus and enjoyed the sensation of the breeze ruffling my hair. I saw a couple of women glance over at my flowers. I sometimes looked at women with flowers and wondered where they came from. Had the women bought them themselves or were they a gift from someone who loved them? I held the bunch of flowers and allowed myself to be wondered at.

The DT Watch Factory was close to the waterbus stop. A great sign stood outside it. Along the top it said DT Watch Factory in curly letters. The sign was divided into two halves by a diagonal line. One half had a sunny scene, and the words Day Time were written across it. The D and T were in red whilst the rest of the letters were in black. The other half had the same scene but this time at night with Night Time written across it. The N and T were in black and the other letters in red.

I idly wondered why the factory wasn't called the DTNT factory. Then it occurred to me that maybe, at the beginning, it was, but people had just got lazy and left off the NT part over time. People often plan a lot of things at the beginning, but there is no guarantee that they will get them.

I put on the jacket and the peaked cap. I also took a clipboard out of the bag. Uncle Timeon believes that a clipboard is one of the best disguises of all.

I walked into the DT Watch Factory looking confident.

'Always look confident, no matter how you feel,' Uncle Timeon had told me.

So that's what I did. I even whistled a little. It was the last song that the band had played the previous night. Then I remembered Cassiopeia saying that a whistling woman summons the devil. That spooked me, so I stopped.

The front door opened into a small lobby area. It had chipped tiles in faded red and green arranged in a diamond pattern on the floor. A large clock stood in one corner. Its face looked like the classic DT watch face.

In the other corner there was a dilapidated lift. Beside it was a door, which, on opening, revealed a steep staircase and a long corridor with a marble floor. I decided to try the corridor first.

The walls were lined with old black and white drawings of the sort that no-one ever looks at. No doubt they showed the factory's illustrious history and scenes from the City through the ages. I glanced at one as I went past, and it looked like the street where Uncle Timeon's office was situated. Then again, every old street scene looked like the street where Uncle Timeon's office was situated.

One section of the corridor passed an alcove which displayed a collection of portraits of men with varying different shapes and sizes of moustache and the occasional beard. A plaque on the wall indicated that they were all members of the Zeit family. The Zeits were the wealthiest family in the City and owned a lot of businesses, houses and land.

Just beyond the alcove, the corridor opened into another, similar, one which ran at an angle to it. I was just deliberating which way to go when a man emerged from a door, half-hidden from sight by a plinth which had on it a vase containing a large pot plant.

I jumped in front of him and said that I was from Cetus Florists (*Cetus* is Latin for whale, another Uncle Timeon flourish) and I had flowers for a – at this point I looked down to consult my clipboard – a Miss Ruby Alleck.

'Never heard of her.' The man tried to walk on.

I manoeuvred myself in front of him and, waving the bunch of gerberas in his face, repeated what I had just said.

'Does she work on the factory floor?' he asked.

I was about to say yes when I realised that this was not the kind of information that would be noted on the clipboard.

'I have no idea,' I replied. 'It just says that she works here.'

He shrugged. 'Try the factory floor,' he said, and waved his hand down the corridor in the opposite way from which he was heading. 'Down there, you can't miss it.'

I heard it before I saw it. He was right.

The noise was deafening – a combination of the work involved and the hum of chatter from the workers. I could just about tell that a radio was playing but I could not make out what the song was.

The workshop was overheated. There was a distinctive smell of hot machinery mixed with something else, a cleaning fluid perhaps or maybe even perfume. At the far end, a large clock hung on the wall. Again, it resembled the classic DT watch face. Below it was a sign advising that smoking was strictly prohibited on the shopfloor.

No-one seemed to notice me or, if they did, they didn't care. I approached the woman closest to me. I had to ask for Ruby a couple of times before the woman paid me any attention and a couple more to make myself heard and understood. After all that, the woman shrugged and muttered that she did not know her. At least, I thought that was what she said.

I did not relish the idea of going round everyone in the room, but fortunately I was saved from this onerous task by the arrival of an officious-looking man, also carrying a clipboard and wearing a large pair of headphones.

He demanded to know who I was.

I told him and he yelled that I was to speak up. I shouted at him a few times until it occurred to him to take off the headphones.

'Never heard of her,' he said.

'What about these?' I said, holding up the gerberas.

'Give them to your boyfriend,' he replied.

Defeated, but also secretly pleased that he thought I would

have a boyfriend, I turned back towards the corridors of boring pictures. I was frustrated at the failure of my first attempt to investigate a case. I would have to come up with another plan. Just then, I heard someone call out, 'Excuse me.'

A tall man in overalls and a peaked cap, was leaning on a broom in the alcove of Zeit family portraits.

'You looking for Ruby?'

Remembering to consult my clipboard, I replied that I was indeed looking for a Ruby.

'Reckon that's the Ruby that works the night shift,' he answered.

'There's a night shift?'

He nodded. 'Not always, but when they need to complete a big order, they have one. People like it – the money's much better.'

That sounded right; Ruby would be the sort of person easily drawn by the promise of better money. Lina had not said so in as many words, but the way she described her friend had given me that impression.

'Is there a night shift tonight?' I asked.

The man looked at his broom as if expecting it to reveal something and nodded.

I tried not to look too excited or even interested. I reckoned that there was only so much emotional attachment an employee of Cetus Florists would have in delivering a bunch of flowers.

I thanked him and had turned to go when something crossed my mind.

'How do you know it's the same Ruby that I'm looking for?'

'She looks the kind of girl that would get sent flowers,' he replied.

Chapter 10

Think very carefully about killing time, for it may come back to haunt you.

from *The Ghost of a Slain Dragon* Irving D Golden

I left the DT Watch Factory with no idea what time it was. The irony of this was not lost on me. I walked until I found a church with a clock which told me that it was just after midday.

I had wandered into a square with a garden in the centre, so I sat down on a bench to gather my thoughts. I should go home and come back again later that evening. That felt very irritating, but I could hardly wait around here all afternoon. Such a big, awkward chunk of time to kill, I thought.

The garden was a bit wild and overgrown, but it felt cool. It made me think of last night and being kissed. The memory sent a shiver through me. I was desperate to see him. Or even just to be reassured that I would see him again.

I tried to put my anxious thoughts out of my head and focus on Lina. I was working, I told myself, and I should concentrate.

Something about the whole thing struck me as strange. She had seemed happy last night: happy with her life and happy with her love. In my experience, people rarely go searching for something when they are happy with what they have already got.

This brought me back to my conviction that Lina wasn't telling me something. As Uncle Timeon likes to say, what you are not told frequently tells you so much more than what you are. So, what was the truth? Again, Uncle Timeon popped into my head.

'If we waited to hear the truth, we would never start a case. Just start searching for the answers and the truth might emerge like a figure in the mist. Or it might not. Sometimes we get the answers that are required without the truth. But, more importantly, much more importantly, we also get paid.'

The church clock chimed as I got up to leave. Other clocks joined in. It struck me that they weren't quite coordinated, like the clocks at Cassiopeia's house. Each clock told its own time.

The gerberas were looking a little sad and the violet paper they were wrapped in had lost its crispness. I did not think that they would last to the evening and anyway I didn't feel that the florist delivery story would work on the nightshift. The people of the City are often described as being romantics, but we are not so romantic that we deliver flowers at any time of the day or night. I would have to think up a new cover story.

The trees rustled, and I thought once more about last night and the garden. I would leave the flowers here for Madame Martinet. I felt that it was wise to cover all my bases.

I spent the afternoon in the office. I felt a stab of disappointment as I pushed open the door. I had hoped to find a little note or something. Maybe a note asking me out that evening; it was Saturday night after all. But there was nothing. I tried to comfort myself with the thought that if I did get a note asking me out, I wouldn't be able to go as I had work to do. But this was of little comfort as I knew that I was lying to myself. Given the choice between going out on a date or trudging back to the DT Watch Factory, I knew which I would choose.

All afternoon I hoped the phone would ring. I had hardly paid any attention to the phone before. Now it seemed to dominate the room: a huge, sulking presence, like some kind of malevolent creature crouching in the corner, taunting me with its silence. At one point I even went to check that it was working. It was. He just wasn't calling me on it.

As evening fell, I went back to the house.

Cassiopeia called to me from the kitchen as I opened the door. For a moment, I thought that she was going to tell me that he had phoned, but she only asked if I wanted a drink. I said yes, trying to hide my disappointment.

I couldn't help myself. 'Did anyone phone for me?' I asked, trying to sound as casual as possible.

'No,' she replied, as she handed me a glass.

Of course, I knew it was understood that no-one calls the next day. It is one of those silly rules. I hate these rules; they make no sense to me. Why should women have to wait powerlessly and passively for someone else to do something?

Cassiopeia was looking at me curiously.

'Is everything all right?'

'Yes,' I gave a brittle little smile that did not even come close to reaching my eyes.

She looked unconvinced but did not pursue it. As always, she had cooked too much, but I said I was going out to meet a friend. I sensed that she would not be happy about my visit to the DT Watch Factory, though, really, it was not any concern of hers. I had moved out of home to get away from one mother; I really didn't need someone else acting as one. It seemed easier to lie.

I walked to the waterbus stop for the second time that day. It was dark now and Violetta's was closed. Empty vases sat in the window, and further back in the gloom I could make out the twisted shadows from the selection of ornamental trees in pots.

The factory too would be a different prospect at night:

different rules would apply. I had decided to approach my task, like many things approached under the cover of darkness, by just brazening it out. I would simply walk in and start asking people questions. I felt more confident about doing this by night than by day. And, of course, it was my second visit. If I didn't find Ruby or any helpful information, I would go back to Lina and ask her to tell me what she wasn't saying.

On the waterbus, I took a seat outside, at the back. There was a stiff breeze. I pulled my coat tightly around myself.

Two girls, in flimsy dresses, sat in front of me. I wondered how they were not cold. Good grief, I was sounding like my mother now. Maybe I was just jealous and wanted to be going out, dressed in flimsy clothing. I thought of Astrid and felt a little stab of pain. The girls' different perfumes mixed with the oily smell of the boat and the fishy smell of the canal at low tide. There was something repulsive about it. Like trying to use something sweet to cover up the smell of something that was rotting.

'They say they sliced off her gills and laid them across her eyes,' said one.

'Horrible,' said the other. 'My gran says it's a bad omen of something else to come.'

'Like what?'

The girl did not reply but I could make out her shoulders rising and falling as she shrugged in the darkness.

I watched the reflections of the lights in the black canal and the way the waves broke them up as we moved through the water. In the distance I could just make out what I now realised were the chimneys of the DT Watch Factory.

As I walked towards the factory, the night seemed darker here, somehow, than in the rest of the City. I wondered whether this was what the City had been like in the old days. Although the City is now all glass and light, the darkness has never truly gone away.

I noticed the name of the street: Ghost Walk. I hadn't noticed it during the daytime; some things are more visible in the day and others at night. Or maybe I just had never paid attention before. Attention is one of the skills a detective needs, Uncle Timeon is fond of saying. My old teacher said the same thing about artists.

Many streets in the City are said to be haunted, home to one ghost or another. The City has a long relationship with supernatural beings.

We were even taught ghost stories in our history classes as children. We were told that there was something special about the darkness. It had a particular quality to it. Substance? Solidity? That was it, the substance of the darkness matched the solidity of ghosts or was it the other way around? This created a particular effect, an optical illusion, where the ghosts appeared formed.

This phenomenon enabled ghosts to walk around the City as if they were real. This was very popular with ghosts, apparently, and even drew ghosts from other places. These 'foreign' ghosts flocked to the City and took up residence. That's why the City is supposed to be so haunted. We have other people's ghosts as well as our own.

The factory loomed in front of me in the darkness. It was hard to believe that there were people working inside, in that brightly lit room, surrounded by noise and machinery.

I was surprised that the door opened easily. If I am being honest, I had hoped to find it locked. I was reluctant to enter. I tried to pull myself together. This was my own fault for telling myself ghost stories on the way here.

The corridor was lit by a dim green light that did nothing to reduce my anxiety. I felt all the hairs on my arms rise up.

Don't be so silly, I told myself. Then I thought of all those books where someone walks somewhere sinister at night or goes up into the attic or down to the cellar. And you, the reader, scream at them in your head, 'What are you doing? What is wrong with you? Why are you so stupid?' Now I was one of those people. I was about to walk around a strange factory at night, alone.

Even Uncle Timeon had told me, in some sort of pep talk, never to go somewhere suspicious by myself.

'How will I know what is suspicious?' I had asked.

'Experience,' was the answer.

Well, experience or no experience, I couldn't help but feel that this was suspicious.

So, when a man appeared from the shadows, I screamed. Not just a little squeak to register shock or surprise; no, a great, big, piercing scream. To be fair, the man screamed back just as loudly.

I was sweating and shaking and my heart was thumping. I have no idea how the man felt; he was giving nothing away.

He was quite ordinary-looking. He was wearing a jacket and a peaked cap and carried nothing more sinister than a torch and a clipboard. Then again, many evil killers are supposedly people that you would pass in the street without the slightest suspicion. Nevertheless, my gut told me that he was not an evil killer.

His name badge said Gus Wilde. I deduced that he was the security guard.

'Who are you?' he asked. 'And what are you doing here?'

'I'm looking for Ruby,' I replied. 'Ruby Alleck.'

I decided to stick to my original plan of just brazening things out. Gus did not seem overly interested in the answer to who I was. It was not, perhaps, the kind of attribute one would want in a security guard. But I guessed that being a security guard was more of a job than a calling for many people.

'Ruby with the red hair?' he answered. 'Pretty girl?'

'Maybe,' I said. 'I don't know her; I just have a message for her.'

'There used to be a Ruby,' said Gus, 'but I haven't seen her here for quite a while.'

Well, that was that then. I was about to walk away when he added, 'I saw her somewhere recently, though.'

I waited for him to continue but he said nothing else. We stood in silence for a few minutes.

'Where?' I finally asked.

'Can't say I remember.'

Great, I thought, very helpful.

'Memory comes and goes,' said Gus.

I smiled politely.

'Memory comes and goes, goes and comes,' he repeated, more emphatically this time, staring me right in the eye.

I was about to ask if there was anything that might make the memory come, when the penny dropped. He wanted money. I had seen Uncle Timeon have to do this once or twice. I looked in my purse and, luckily, I had some notes. Nice, new, crisp notes, actually, which rustled in a satisfying manner. I took one out, folded it in half and handed it to Gus.

'Perhaps this will help?'

I got a little kick. I felt like a real private detective.

Equally deliberately, Gus placed the note in his pocket.

'La Sardine,' he said. 'You know La Sardine?'

I had certainly heard of La Sardine; it was one of the best restaurants in the City. I had never been there, for obvious reasons. But, then again, Gus didn't look like one of its usual clientele, either. Unless, of course, an awful lot of people were paying him to remember things.

'Friend of mine works the door there,' he said, 'I help him

out, from time to time, when they are short-staffed. I was there a couple of times last month and I saw her then.'

He looked at me expectantly. I was not giving him any more money. Was he stupid or something? No-one gives someone money after they have shared their information. Even I knew that, and I was a complete novice.

Finally, I said, 'Thank you, Gus,' and turned to leave.

'Goose,' he replied.

'I beg your pardon?'

'Call me Goose,' he answered. 'Everyone calls me Goose on account of I sound like one when I laugh.'

He made a loud honking sound. I gaped at him. There was really nothing to say to this.

When he had finally composed himself, he announced, 'There might be a picture, a photograph of Ruby somewhere, if you're interested? A photographer came and took some photos of the girls for a newspaper.'

He looked pointedly at my bag.

I took out my purse and handed Gus – or should I say Goose? – another note.

'Wait here.'

He opened a door hidden in the shadows of an alcove. I had not noticed it. Behind it was a storeroom of some kind. I hesitated in the doorway. I trusted him, but not that much. Not enough to follow him into a room with potentially no means of escape.

Gus disappeared through another doorway at the back, and I looked over the room. There was a desk with things strewn across it: a cup, a pen and a nameplate.

At the back, there were stacks of old frames which had not made it out onto the corridor of boring pictures. A few were old posters advertising the DT Watch Factory. Actually, I found them more attractive than the pictures outside. At least they were in colour. One showed the inside of a watch, all the wheels and cogs. 'Nothing fits as snugly as a DT Watch' said the caption. That was a saying Uncle Timeon used from time to time, in a sarcastic way when he thought something was too good to be true or if someone was lying to him.

'Mmm, all nice and snug,' he would mutter. 'As snug as a DT watch.'

Another showed the classic DT watch face which displayed the date as well as the time. Date and Time, it said on the poster. The D and T were in red, the other letters in black. Ah, I thought, of course, that's how the watches got their name; that's one mystery solved then. I found this strangely satisfying.

Goose came back, shaking his head.

'Nope,' he said. 'Can't find it.'

I tried to read his expression. I wasn't sure of the etiquette. Was I entitled to ask for my money back? Goose was in no hurry to offer it to me. Had I been an idiot, handing it over before seeing proof? I was reluctant to draw attention to this. I decided I would reimburse myself from petty cash, chalk it up to experience and never mention it to anyone, particularly not Uncle Timeon.

I was trying to think up a way to leave with dignity when I had an idea.

'I know,' I said. 'Let me try to draw her.'

Goose looked confused.

'You describe her, and I will try to draw her,' I persisted.

Goose did not look entirely comfortable but he couldn't refuse. He was bound by some kind of unspoken rule around the money exchange. As he had taken my cash he was, somehow, obliged to help me find an image.

There was some scrap paper in a box and on the table was a glass which contained a few pencils, a screwdriver and an implement that I did not recognise.

'What was the shape of her face?'

Goose looked blank.

'Round, oval, square, heart shaped…?'

He remained impassive.

I started to sketch. From what I could tell, Goose was not a man for paying attention to details. I imagined that if you were his wife, he'd not notice if you were wearing a new dress or had changed your hairstyle.

Finally, I managed to produce something.

'Like this?' I said holding it up.

'Sort of,' said Goose, but he didn't sound convinced.

I wasn't convinced either. It just looked like a generic face.

'Pass me that red pencil,' I said.

As he handed it to me, I glanced down at his watch. It was getting late.

'Nice watch,' I said, conversationally.

Goose pulled his sleeve down to cover it up.

'Did you get it from here?'

'It was a present.'

Ah, I thought. A 'present' that Goose had helped himself to, no doubt. But that was absolutely none of my business, so he really need not have been so evasive.

I coloured in Ruby's hair and held it up.

'Yes,' he said. 'That's it.'

He sounded as if he were just being polite. The drawing was now just a generic face with red hair. Put it this way, I didn't think that I would be able to recognise Ruby from it. Then again, I wasn't that good an artist, I remembered, with a pang.

I stuffed the picture into my bag. As I turned to leave, I had another thought. 'What is the name of your friend?' I asked. 'The one who you help out at La Sardine?'

I reckoned that Goose still owed me something for my money. Obviously so did he, as he answered easily and did not even look in the direction of my pocket.

'Mack, Mack Guffin,' he said, quickly. 'And I know a few of the waiters who work there as well. Go down in the afternoon between lunch and dinner when it's quiet. Say I sent you,' he patted his pocket where he had put the money.

'Make sure to call me Goose, not Gus,' he added, 'because otherwise, they won't know who you are talking about.'

With that he started honking again.

My gaze fell on another framed poster propped up by the door. It said 'Owned by Zeit inc.' in big curly letters, above a picture of a mermaid reflected in a pane of glass. A shiver went down my spine.

It was the old Zeit company sign. Once upon a time these were all over the City. They had earlier in the year brought out a new one and this style had all but vanished. The new sign showed the Zeit building: huge, modern and made almost entirely of glass.

I had the sensation that Goose was watching me as I left. I did not look around until I reached the door, but when I did the corridor was empty. The only people watching me were the portraits of the various Zeits.

Even as I walked along Ghost Walk to get to the waterbus stop, I couldn't shake the feeling that I was being watched. Halfway there, I could stand it no longer so I ran the rest of the way. I jumped aboard the boat without looking back.

Chapter 11

Be careful of echoes, for they are not replies.

from *Love is like the Tide* Magnolia Saint

I was still on edge when I got home. Cassiopeia called out, 'You're early.'

Just goes to show how time moves differently depending on what you are doing. To me, having been roaming around a dark factory, it seemed very late. For Cassiopeia, who had assumed that I was out with friends, the night was still young.

She appeared in the hall. 'Come and have a drink with me.'

She must have read my distraction as reluctance, because she added, 'It is Saturday night, after all. And I am going to visit my sister tomorrow.'

I didn't need any persuading. In fact, I needed – and also deserved – a drink; a very big one at that.

'Did anyone phone for me?' I couldn't stop myself asking again.

I knew that he hadn't called me. If he had, Cassiopeia would have said; she was too nosy not to have remembered. She would have come rushing out, full of curiosity, the moment I opened the door.

'No,' she replied. 'Were you expecting someone to call you?'

'Yes. Astrid.'

I congratulated myself. Cassiopeia would assume my agitation was related to my hope for a reconciliation with Astrid.

Cassiopeia had only bought the telephone after I had fallen out with Astrid and so she had never phoned me on it. Obviously, Astrid had had a phone for some time. Her family was one of the first families in the City to get one. Suddenly this struck me as ridiculous. What was the point of having a phone when no-one else had one?

Cassiopeia gave my hand a little squeeze.

'I'm sure you'll get your call soon.'

'I hope so,' I replied, honestly.

I awoke the next morning with the sense that I had had strange dreams all night. Cassiopeia was bustling round the kitchen, and I went down to join her. The Sunday paper was beside her bag. I glanced at the headline. They had found the body of another mermaid on the beach.

Her name was Dulcie. The picture was grainy but I could still tell that she was beautiful.

She had a mass of wild, curly hair which was described as being in many shades of purple from pale lilac to deepest lavender, shot through with the occasional thread of green. Her skin had been coffee-coloured and her eyes were dark brown, almost black. She wore jewellery of silver and sea glass.

She had been slit open with one long vertical cut and her guts strewn around the beach. As with the previous victim, her gills had been sliced off and placed across her eyes. She had been found in the early hours of the morning, by a barman from a nearby establishment who had gone out for a smoke. His attention had been drawn by a great number of seagulls who were fighting over her entrails. That last detail made my stomach heave.

'Why would anyone want to kill a mermaid?' I asked, again. I still couldn't comprehend it.

'Maybe to spoil all that beauty, because the killers are ugly. Ugly on the outside or,' she added, thoughtfully, 'ugly on the inside, all twisted up and corrupted.'

'What do you mean by corrupted?'

She searched for the right word. 'Altered,' she decided.

'Ah,' I said. 'Someone in disguise, like someone wearing a false moustache. You mean that someone with a false moustache is killing mermaids.'

We laughed.

'I mean someone who started as one thing but has changed into something else,' she went on. 'The thing is, we all change with time. We become weathered, like the statues of the angels of Truth and Knowledge on the bridge. Time and tide and salty air, they rub away at them and us. Sometimes they polish us and produce a patina. Other times they diminish us, erase us completely. The City of Light wears everyone down over time. But' – Cassiopeia passed me a cup of coffee – 'sometimes people get corrupted from the inside out. Something gets in, like a wasp in a fig, and devours a person from the inside out.'

'Or maybe,' I said, thinking aloud, 'it's something that is there from the beginning. Maybe some people are born with a void at their centre instead of a soul.'

Cassiopeia looked at me strangely.

'Like a black hole when a star dies and collapses in on itself,' I continued, 'when it sucks everything else into its nothingness.'

'Maybe it's the City,' said Cassiopeia. 'Maybe the City is killing the mermaids, like a poisoned river kills its fish.'

'No,' I replied. 'The mermaids didn't just die; they were mutilated too. The City didn't do that; a human hand did.'

'Mermaids represent storms and forgotten things, memories that we have buried away.' She picked up her bag. 'Maybe whoever is killing the mermaids doesn't like storms or memories.'

'So,' I said, 'we are talking about someone who has been corrupted from the inside out by a thing like a wasp or, alternatively, has a dark void at their centre where their soul should be. They could look normal on the outside, but their inside is damaged. They don't like beauty or storms, or memories and they may be wearing a false moustache.'

We both laughed again.

'Maybe you should share this information with the police,' Cassiopeia smiled. 'If they know the why, they might be able to figure out the who. But hopefully, they will just catch them and we won't need the why.'

'I would still need the why. That is just the kind of person I am. I always need to know the why of things.'

Cassiopeia pulled on her coat.

'Do you need me to get you anything?' she asked.

'No, no,' I replied. 'Go, or you will miss your train.'

'Are you sure?'

I nodded and she gave me a hug before she left.

I couldn't get the dead mermaid out of my head. Who would do such a thing? And why? The why interested me as much, if not more so, than the who.

I looked at the kitchen clock. On its face, a cat was eternally chasing a mouse. I should focus on work, I thought; focus on the elusive Ruby and formulate a plan.

Immediately, though, my thoughts turned to my companion of Friday night and whether he would phone me. Today seemed a much more reasonable day for him to phone than yesterday. But that only increased the pressure. If he didn't phone today, it would be so much worse. The longer time went on, the less likely it would be that he would make contact.

If only I had a way of contacting him. I could hear my female friends' horror in my head. 'You can't possibly contact a man first,' I heard them shriek. 'You have to wait for him to contact you.'

I made myself another cup of coffee and looked again at the kitchen clock. The cat had still not caught the mouse.

Chapter 12

'The aquarium is a very fishy place,' said the red herring, in such a way that the sardine could not tell if he was joking or saying something important.

from *Fish Tales* JJ Rock

La Sardine was situated on a promontory that stretched out into the water. Once an old sardine factory, now it was famous throughout the City as the place where the very wealthy ate.

The wall nearest the sea was made entirely of glass. It was said that the view inside was breath-taking. It was probably wasted on the regular clientele. Uncle Timeon had once told me that the more money you had, the more it took to take your breath away.

'That is why the very rich often commit stupid or unpleasant crimes,' he said, 'because they are bored and their lives feel pointless.'

In the autumn and winter, opening time was based around the sunset. People would gather for afternoon tea or cocktails and watch as the sky changed colour and the sun disappeared. However, as it was summer, a sign said that it would open at five.

A light sea breeze was battling to keep the temperature just about tolerable. I got off at the nearest waterbus stop, which was very close indeed, although any distance seemed too far to walk in the heat. I bought myself my favourite ice-cream, black cherry, from a nearby stall.

It was as if the heat had melted my brain and it couldn't seem to function except to undertake the most rudimentary of tasks.

More to the point, my mind kept wandering to the memory of the kiss. The more I thought about it, the more I realised how lonely I was. It was as if there was a huge void in my centre. I didn't just want to see him again, I *needed* to see him. We were perfect for each other. He couldn't have been more perfect if I had dreamed him up myself.

La Sardine's courtyard was shady and fractionally cooler than outside. Tables were set under trees festooned in fairy lights and the streamers of silver paper that are so popular in the City. Later, they would be covered in white linen tablecloths and set with the restaurant's famous cutlery which was shaped to look like the tail of a sardine.

The cutlery was made exclusively for the restaurant. People often tried to steal a piece for a souvenir; it had a certain status, especially amongst the wealthiest of the diners. I wondered whether Gus had had to stop people taking cutlery. I imagined him searching in ladies' evening bags for teaspoons or forks.

It was mid-afternoon and the place seemed deserted. A board gave a brief history of the building. In its heyday, it had been the largest sardine factory on the coast. It had been owned by the du Temps family and when they went into decline, it had too. After a long period of dereliction, an enterprising local called Madame Fish (so not her real name) had taken over a corner and started selling fish straight from the fishing boats to the locals.

'Humble food for humble people' was written under a drawing of a woman wearing a bonnet. Now it sold not so humble food to not so humble people. Right at the bottom it said that the current building had been constructed using glass supplied by the Zeit Glass company. Beside it was the Zeit Glass logo: the new one, not the old one of the mermaid.

I looked around the empty courtyard, hoping that someone

would appear. This was the problem of not having a plan; you had to rely on hope, and I had never found hope to be particularly reliable. But amazingly, for once, hoping seemed to work, as a man came around the corner of the building.

He was wearing a navy-and-white striped apron. He sat on a rock facing the sea for a smoke. I supposed, even if he wasn't paying for La Sardine's famous vista, that shouldn't prohibit him from enjoying it.

With no plan, I was just going to have to be direct. Being direct required a degree of confidence that I didn't really feel. However, I had no choice but to go for it.

'Hi,' I said. 'I'm looking for a man called Guffin, Mack Guffin.'

'Never heard of him.'

'Gus Wilde sent me,' I continued.

The man continued to smoke and enjoy the view.

'Goose,' I amended, remembering the piece of advice that the honking one had given me.

The man turned to look at me, blowing smoke in my face.

I gave a little cough, which he ignored.

A silence stretched between us.

In the end, I relented and tapped my pocket. Information was by no means cheap. I might as well cut to the chase. I didn't have time for this nonsense. The heat was making me tetchy.

'I'm looking for a woman,' I said. 'A woman called Ruby. She's got red hair and is very attractive.'

It sounded a bit weak, even to me.

He blew more smoke in my face. Then, with a look that implied that he was bored, he returned to staring out to sea. I followed his gaze, just in case something interesting was happening out there. It wasn't.

He ground the stub of his cigarette into the gravel, then

kicked it to the side. I imagined that the management of La Sardine would take a dim view. Finally, he said, 'Ruby. Pretty girl with red hair?'

I was about to hand him a banknote when I stopped. He hadn't actually told me anything I didn't already know. In fact, he hadn't told me anything that I hadn't just told him.

I had not had one of Uncle Timeon's pep talks on the subject of paying for information but I was learning for myself. Note to self – it is not information if it is something you already know. I gave him a look that I hoped conveyed an 'I wasn't born yesterday; I know what I'm doing' attitude.

'Yes, she's been here a few times,' he said.

'Really?' I said. 'How do you know if it's the Ruby I'm looking for?'

I was getting the hang of this now.

'Everyone knows Ruby or knows her by sight. She's that kind of girl and she's got red hair.'

This did indeed sound like my Ruby. However, it was not really deserving of payment.

He looked pointedly at my pocket.

'Does she have a particular night she comes in?' I asked.

He looked at me with something resembling contempt.

'When was the last time you saw her?' I tried.

He shrugged but did not take his eyes off my pocket.

Think, Vulpe, think, I told myself. What would Uncle Timeon ask at this point? What else would be useful to know? A gull swooped down and began to fight with another one over what looked like a crust of bread. Then I had it. No-one dines alone at a place like La Sardine. And from what I had heard of Ruby, I didn't imagine that she was the sort to pay for her dinner either.

'Does she come with anyone in particular?' I asked.

He smiled and looked at my pocket.

I held out the money.

'Guisse Zeit,' he said. 'The last few times she has been with Mr Zeit. Of course, I have seen them separately but the last couple of times I saw them together. Very cosy.'

He took the note, folded it in half and pocketed it. Then he took out another cigarette and resumed his study of the sea.

As I walked back, even the breeze seemed to have taken a siesta.

My informant (I felt like a proper detective now) had promised to contact me if he saw Ruby. I was not quite sure about that. Ruby seemed the kind of person to go out at night; was I supposed to wait by the phone all evening for him to call? As he had offered to report back to me, he had looked at my pocket. Undoubtedly, he would want payment for that kind of information. I was getting fed up with these people. I had the niggling sensation that they were taking me for a ride. Well, I wasn't a fool, or not that much of a fool, anyway.

I felt a stab of anxiety. I was getting through a lot of the petty cash, and I didn't feel as if I was getting my money's worth. Worse still, I suspected that Uncle Timeon would be of the same opinion. Maybe I was that much of a fool.

On the waterbus, I could make out the Zeit building in the distance. The way it shimmered in the afternoon sun made it look almost unreal, like a mirage. It was known as a 'modern classic', whose beauty rivalled some of the more traditional buildings such as the Cathedral of Two Crosses and the Bridge of Truth and Knowledge. At the time of its construction, there had been some outcry amongst traditionalists, claiming that it ruined the appearance and character of the City. But Mr Zeit got his way, in the way that very wealthy men usually can.

The Zeit family had not always been wealthy or famous, unlike the du Temps family, who had been amongst those first settlers, and who were, for a time, the most powerful family here. Legend has it that the City is not built just on flotsam and jetsam but also on the bones of murdered men, and that the du Temps knew where to find the bodies because they buried them.

They were a big, colourful family. A streak of madness ran through them.

The Zeits were not like that. They were not old money.

But now the du Temps had disappeared, whereas, the Zeit name seemed to be everywhere. How had this happened? I would have to go and look it up. That was me: as soon as something piqued my interest, I always wanted to know the why of it.

But, never mind the past. Here in the present, I had to work out a way to speak to Guisse Zeit. He was my only lead.

Chapter 13

Even the most honest people can take to crime like a mallard to water.

from *The Cat That Curiosity Killed* Angel River

I awoke the next morning with dread lodged like a great stone in my stomach. He still hadn't contacted me. There had been no little note pushed under the door, no telephone call. I had gone home via the office the evening before, telling myself it was to check that there was no business that needed attending to. Then I had reminded myself that it was Sunday. Then I told myself that it was to check up on the plant that never seemed to need watering, just to make sure that it still didn't. Even I thought that was pathetic.

I had spent the whole night praying for Cassiopeia's phone to ring. At one point, I thought that I heard a gentle rap on the door and jumped up to answer it. But there was no-one there. It must have been my imagination playing cruel tricks on me.

It was three days since I had seen him. One school of thought amongst my friends is that if someone hasn't contacted you by day three, then forget it. Confusingly, another school of thought says that day three is the optimum time to contact someone. Any earlier than that and you look too keen. And being keen is the worst thing you could be. Clearly, day three had a lot riding on it.

Miraculously, in amongst all the emotional turmoil of the previous night, I had somehow come up with a plan to get in to see Guisse Zeit. And it was, in my opinion, pretty ingenious.

Uncle Timeon, however, was suspicious of ingenious plans.

'Don't overcomplicate things,' he would say. 'The more complicated an idea is, the more places it can go wrong.'

Well, this plan had a lot of places where it could go wrong, but I was determined not to let it.

I had realised that the delivery person idea would not work. The Zeit building, no doubt, had a whole army of people between the front door and Mr Zeit himself. The waving around of a clipboard and demanding his personal signature would get me nowhere except escorted out of the building. I considered a variety of personas that would get me past Mr Zeit's secretary but none seemed right. I imagined her as a fearsome woman, sitting in a glass box, guarding him like a tiger. A bit like my mother might be if she got a job.

Then it struck me that it was not *what* I was but *who* I was. Rich and powerful people were always happy to meet other rich and powerful people. I just had to pretend to be worth knowing. I would need different clothes to begin with. Expensive clothes.

That's what made me think of Astrid.

Astrid's father was rich and powerful. Astrid carried that glossy quality around with her too. I was certain that Guisse Zeit would be happy to talk to her.

But I did not want to take Astrid with me. It wasn't that I didn't trust her – well, obviously, I didn't trust her with men that I was in love with – but I just didn't want to share anything with her. It might make her think that we were back to being friends again and I didn't want that. I imagined that she would be happy to be involved, delighted even, but I did not want her to be happy.

At first, I thought I would steal Astrid's identity. But Guisse Zeit could easily have met her at one of the places where rich people go. And let's face it, I don't look anything like Astrid.

Then it came to me. I could pretend to be a cousin of Astrid's, a student. I would pretend to be a business student. I would say I was doing a project and that Astrid's father had suggested that I go and speak to him as he was, obviously, the most successful man in the City.

Uncle Timeon had told me that a little flattery will get you a long way. The rich and powerful are particularly vulnerable to it. I was surprised by this as I would have thought that they did not need it.

'Oh no,' Uncle Timeon had said. 'That's the problem with being rich and powerful. There is always someone richer and more powerful coming up, right behind you. It makes you incredibly insecure.'

I shoved a few things into a bag. No clipboards this time, for this plan was all my own design.

The office was not my intended destination, but I could not resist going that way to check it was okay. As always, I crossed the road to avoid the glass scissors outside du Trims barbers.

There were no messages pushed under the door for me.

The air in the office felt old and stale. For a moment, I thought about watering the plant. I glanced up at it; it looked like it always did, sitting on top of the bookcase beside the picture of the red fish.

I walked down to the waterbus stop and waited for my boat. Finally, one came, and I got my favourite seat, outside at the back. This journey took me to a very different part of town than the one which took me to the watch factory. It took me to a part of town where the streets were wider and, somehow, cooler. The houses were bigger, and everything seemed cleaner and brighter. Even the air was different. Fresher. It was strange being back.

Once it had been so familiar, but I had not been here for ages. There it was, Palazzo Paradiso. Astrid's house.

I went into the tiny garden opposite. It was one of those private gardens. Once upon a time, they were all kept locked, and only the residents had keys. That was a long time ago and now most of the keys were lost. Apparently, according to Astrid, one had sold for a lot of money at an auction. I smiled at the memory of this. We wanted money to do something, and we had searched through drawers and other such places in her house to see if we could find the key and sell it ourselves. It suddenly occurred to me that Astrid rarely needed money; she just asked her father for it. She used to offer to pay for things for me as well but I always declined and so she stopped. She must have been looking for the key for me.

The garden was surrounded by a railing and a high hedge which meant that what lay inside was hidden from without. I found a position from which I could see the front door of Astrid's house and settled down to wait. At the party, I had heard Astrid arrange to meet her aunt for lunch today, so I reckoned that she would leave the house soon. I was pretty confident that she would not come into the garden. Astrid and I had sat there, many times, our heads close together as we shared our secrets and plans for the future. We had laughed and cried together there. But I had never known her cut through the garden to reach somewhere else.

Just in case, I took from my bag an object that I had prepared earlier. It was a pad of blank paper, not quite a sketch pad, but it looked like one. On it, I had roughly drawn the fountain that sat in the middle of the garden. If Astrid did see me, I would say that I had decided to take some art classes, and this was for a project called 'What is Now Lost to Us,' or something like that.

I had prepared it last night, as I did not want to be

concentrating on drawing in case I missed Astrid. I would just pretend to be working on it. I wondered what I would do if Astrid did find me and ask me why I had not visited.

Then I realised that I didn't need a reason. I would just look at her in a way that said, 'Why would I want to do that?' The thought brought me some satisfaction.

I waited for what seemed like a very long time. That is the way with time: sometimes it can stretch itself out like elastic and seem never-ending. I added a few flowers and a bird into my drawing. I found some sour cherry sweets in my bag and sucked slowly on one.

I began to lose confidence. What if Astrid didn't come out at all? What if her lunch had been cancelled? Her aunt could have something wrong with her. Shingles, perhaps? I wasn't entirely sure what shingles were, but people seemed to come down with them quite suddenly and have to cancel things.

At what point should I just give up and go home? The longer you wait for something the harder it is to give up. Then I had a worse thought. What if Astrid had left already? What if I waited for ages, only to see her returning instead of leaving?

How could I not have taken that into consideration in all my careful planning? I was furious with myself. I thought that I had been so clever, so meticulous with my drawings of fountains and the like. And I had missed something so crucial. Uncle Timeon was right with his warning about over-elaborate plans.

The front door opened and Astrid emerged, dressed as if she was going out to lunch. She did not so much glance towards the garden but hurried off in the direction of the waterbus stop.

My satisfaction that things had turned out just as I had imagined was marred by the realisation that this was down to luck rather than my good planning. I never took luck for granted nor did I assume that it would be on my side. That made me think of Madame Martinet; I was in a garden after all. Who knew if this was one of hers? I left the remainder of my sour cherry sweets, just in case. I was taking no chances.

I gave myself a little shake, checked the street to make sure that Astrid was gone, then, satisfied that the coast was clear, I walked up to her front door and rang the bell.

The door was opened by Maud, the family's maid. She had had her hair cut since the last time I had visited, and it was now in a fashionable, short, pixie cut, which did, in fact, make her look a bit like a pixie. I was unsure whether telling someone that they looked like a pixie was a compliment. She looked very pretty.

'Is Astrid home?'

'You have just missed her. She isn't expected back until later this afternoon.' Maud looked disappointed at having to deliver bad news.

'Oh no, that is such a shame.' I pretended I was coming to terms with this information.

'Perhaps she could phone me?' I tried to perform the role of someone just having an idea. 'She could phone me at my uncle's office or even at my home. My landlady has recently got a phone and she is very happy for me to receive calls on it.'

Astrid had actually been banned from calling me at the office phone. It was for business, and not for young ladies to gossip on. We had, of course, ignored this until he had answered the phone to Astrid one day and shouted at her. Astrid, understandably, was very unwilling to phone the office after that. But I didn't think that I needed to go into any of this with Maud. I was keeping it simple; Uncle Timeon would be pleased.

'Do you have a pen for me to write the numbers down?' I added, ever so casually.

'I will just go and fetch one.'

I couldn't help smiling as I watched Maud disappear down the stairs. The hall smelled of polish mixed with the scent of flowers; lilies, I think. The drawing room door was open, and I could see the end of the piano. Samson, the big, ginger cat, watched me suspiciously from his seat on the piano stool, as well he might, for what I was about to do was not entirely honest.

I turned my attention to a small, wooden table just inside the front door. It had on it a large, green vase full of peacock feathers, beside which was an oblong, silver tray, with a stack of cards upon it. Astrid's father's business cards.

I reached out for them. Something flickered at the corner of my eye. It was only the shadow of a bird quivering across the wall as it fluttered past the window, but I took a moment to control my breathing. I seized a few of the cards and shoved them into my bag.

Samson mewed. He knew I was up to no good. Thank goodness he wasn't a dog.

I let out a huge breath. Then I noticed the blue glass bowl beside the vase. I was hoping that it might contain some little boiled sweets. That was exactly the sort of thing Astrid's family would have for guests. And I needed a sugar rush.

But it was, in fact, more cards; other people's cards, that they had signed on the back. I felt my brain whirr into action as I realised their potential. Was it too great a risk to try and take them?

I was sweating now. I grabbed a handful of the cards and threw them into my bag. I heard another mew. Samson was right beside me, flicking his tail in my direction, as if he were trying to point out my crime. I briefly wondered if cats ever spontaneously attacked humans.

At that moment, Maud reappeared. Maybe I looked guilty or maybe it was the way Samson's tail was pointing at me, or maybe it was just my imagination, but I thought she looked at me suspiciously. My hand shook as I took the pen, and I fumbled as I wrote down Cassiopeia's number. Cheekily, I picked up one of the business cards to write it on.

I said goodbye, and as soon as Maud had shut the door, I practically leapt down the steps. I glanced back to see Samson glaring at me, his face pressed against the window, his whiskers quivering with indignation.

A waterbus was waiting at the stop. I felt a great wave of relief wash over me. I had done it.

I had a twinge of guilt as I realised that I had deceived Astrid's family and, in a small way, stolen from them. Then I remembered what Astrid had stolen from me and I was unrepentant. In fact, I experienced a frisson at the idea that I couldn't be trusted.

Chapter 14

Love is a gift of a sharp pair of scissors; be careful or it will cut your heart out.

from *Apricots Rot in the Sun* Lady Mariana du Temps

The office was intolerably hot. It was that type of heat that meant it was best to close all the windows and pull down the blinds. I turned both fans on and positioned them at either side of me. I had bought myself an icy drink and held it up to my face.

When I had cooled down enough, I had a look at the cards. Astrid's father's cards could be useful, but it was the others that were the real find. They were all printed on expensive card. They were from a selection of what Uncle Timeon would describe as the great and the good and the great and the not-so-good of the City. Many of them had signatures on the back and a couple even had a little message.

Then I hit the jackpot: a card that belonged to Alicia du Pont, owner and editor of *Jolie* magazine, a popular read in the City for modern, young women. It had fashion tips, recipes for cocktails and advice on things like getting stains out of dresses and how to stop your lipstick smudging. It also carried interviews with famous people and notable citizens.

I could pretend to be Alicia's niece, with ambitions to be a journalist. She had given me a job for the summer and sent me to interview Guisse Zeit about the inspiration for the new sign. That was exactly the sort of thing *Jolie* readers would want to know about. That, and his favourite song.

She had even written on the back, 'Thanks for your assistance.' It was impossible to know if this was thanks for something that had already been done or something that would be done but that was immaterial. I leaned back feeling very proud of myself.

I checked if the plant needed watering. As I approached the bookcase, a title caught my eye: *The History of the City in the Sea; Part 1 – The Dark City* by Professor Justin Lambe. It might be worth learning a few facts about the Zeit family before I pretended to be an aspiring reporter.

I looked under Z for Zeit but there was nothing. I looked under G for Guisse but there was nothing there either. I was disappointed and also surprised. This was supposedly the definitive history of the City. However, a quick look at the index of *Part 2* showed me that the Zeits did, indeed, feature.

I lugged the book back to the desk: it was a weighty beast. I turned the fans on again and sat down to read.

According to Professor Lambe, no-one, including the Zeits themselves, had any idea of how long they had been in the City. To begin with, they were the kind of family that were not important enough to write about. They had simply appeared at some point in the City's history; set up home, lived and worked here. It would be unfair to say that no-one cared about the Zeits. But nobody cared enough about them to record the details of their life. They were, like many families, part of the cogs that kept the machine of the City turning.

That is, until Guisse Zeit came along. Not the Guisse Zeit of today but the first Guisse Zeit – or the first recorded Guisse Zeit. He had lived in the City two hundred years or so ago.

He was the kind of young man who wanted more than life or fate seemed willing to offer him. He was also the kind of young man who was not inclined to listen to life or fate. His first job was down at the port in one of the du Temps warehouses. There, as he watched the ships come in and go out, he handled wealth. Other people's wealth. He packed and unpacked it for them. Guisse wanted some of that kind of wealth for himself. He wanted wealth and power and, more than that, he wanted to be remembered.

He made his money and wrote himself into history because of glass. For many centuries, glass had been considered too dangerous to make here, for a variety of reasons. People just lived without it. You don't miss what you have never had. However, on an island close to the City, they had begun to manufacture it. It was exquisite too, of the finest quality and colour. Zeit saw his opportunity. Helped by a mermaid called Melusina, he became the first importer of glass to the City. Some say that it was Melusina who told him about it in the first place, and it is certainly true that without her input the enterprise would have failed. The island was surrounded by a treacherous ring of rocks known as the Devil's Teeth. Melusina enlisted her mermaid sisters to guide Guisse's ships through the rocks.

Some sources say that Melusina and Guisse were lovers. Others, that Melusina was inspired not by love but by hatred, and a desire to get revenge on Rufus du Temps, a previous lover who had rejected her. Records show that the du Temps had tried and failed to import the glass themselves. Their ships had perished on the Devil's Teeth during a storm, and they had abandoned the idea. A few sources suggest that Melusina had somehow called up the storm herself, but this has been discounted as fantasy.

The importing of glass marked the beginning of the Zeits' ascendancy in the City, and this coincided with the decline of the du Temps family.

The next chapter was about how Guisse Zeit had expanded the business. This was exactly the kind of thing that I should read before my interview with the current Guisse. But it looked boring, and I was beginning to feel hungry.

Time to go home. I picked up my bag and collection of cards, and remembered the plant. The room might have cooled down fractionally, but I did not have the energy to climb up there. The plant looked fine. It could wait.

The street had that early evening feeling. As I opened the front door, the cuckoo clock and the grandfather clock greeted me in unison. Whoever had fixed the cuckoo clock had done a good job as it now kept perfect time and the cuckoo had not crept back into his old, tardy ways; it did make a real racket, though. It was possible his lateness was preferable.

I was pondering what I might have for dinner. My mother's darkest fear, that I might not have anything to eat now that I lived on my own, might be about to be realised.

As I stepped into the hall, my foot kicked against something. It was a piece of paper, folded perfectly in half. It took a few seconds for me to register what it was, but when I did, I started smiling. I couldn't stop myself. The smile exploded inside me like the sun coming out from behind a cloud. I just stood there smiling inside and out.

It had arrived.

It was all right; everything was all right. He had contacted me. He had contacted me and on day three, neither too early nor too late. None of my friends could look grave and find something to disapprove of in that.

How foolish I had been to doubt things. I always feared that there was something defective about me. I had feared that I was unlovable. But no, I was the kind of person that a man would meet and want to take out on a date.

Hi Vulpe, will you meet me tomorrow at 7.30 at La Lumière? I am going out of the City today and so will not be contactable, but I will turn up tomorrow night and wait for you and hope that you come.

I read the note three times and felt like doing a little dance. I don't think that I had ever been so happy. Not only did he want to see me again, but he was prepared to wait for me. He felt the same way as I did. I imagined him writing it, coming here, and putting it under the door.

Previously, this was the sort of thing that Astrid and I would have pored over. We would have studied it like an ancient scripture. We would have read it and re-read it looking for all kinds of hidden meanings and messages.

The thought felt like a shadow momentarily dimming the light. I pushed the feeling away. I was going to read the note again, feel happy and enjoy it.

I went out onto the porch and watched the evening light settle in. The square was full of cooking smells and the occasional sounds of laughter. It was a beautiful evening. Perfect, in fact. Everything looked perfect and felt perfect to me.

I was no longer hungry. Love always does that to me. That fluttery, dancing feeling inside allows no room for anything else. When love arrives, I'm overflowing with joy and when it goes, it takes all that is joyful with it. Either way, it robs me of my appetite and makes me too excited or distressed to eat.

I could drink, though. I fixed myself a cocktail from Cassiopeia's drinks' cabinet. I had no idea that she had so many bottles of brightly coloured alcohol. Clearly, Cassiopeia took cocktails very seriously. She had a long-twisted stick to stir them with, made out of strands of red- and orange-coloured glass.

As I drank my cocktail, I checked half-heartedly to see if

she had a copy of *The History of the City in the Sea*. Cassiopeia had a sizeable selection of paperbacks. There were romances and crime novels and a few of the classics. She also had several poetry books, which surprised me. Uncle Timeon had lots of poetry books. In fact, a couple of them were the same as those on Cassiopeia's shelf. Uncle Timeon reading poetry did not surprise me as much, as he liked to quote things.

I couldn't see a copy of *The History of the City in the Sea* but a book entitled *Scandals and the City* caught my eye. I recognised the painting on the cover. It was a famous portrait of Mariana, Penelope, and Vivian du Temps. The original hung in the City Art Gallery, but reproductions appeared all over the City on things like biscuit tins and cigarette boxes. The three du Temps sisters were the most famous members of a famous family. They lived around about a hundred years before the time of my namesake, Vulpe du Temps.

They had all been writers and poets and led scandalous lives. Mariana had had a relationship with the poet, Lord Percy. They had ended up hating each other and writing angry poems about it. That reminded me of what I had read about Rufus du Temps and the mermaid, Melusina.

I made myself another drink. What Cassiopeia didn't know wouldn't hurt her. She had a box of little salty crackers and sometimes poured a few into a bowl to have with her drink. I took a handful, my appetite slightly restored, and settled down on the sofa to read *Scandals and the City*.

Each chapter was dedicated to a different scandal. *The Affair at Mosaic House*, *The Murder of Madame La Clef*, *Madame Martinet and the School of Thieves* were among the titles. Some were stories that I knew and some I didn't. I turned to Chapter

Seven: *Debauchery and the du Temps.* It was, basically, a description of the bad behaviour of the du Temps family from the birth of the City to the time of writing.

In the early days, the du Temps had an unbeatable combination of ruthlessness, cunning and opportunism. They easily acquired wealth, which they then used to acquire more wealth. They bought and owned everything they could: houses, streets and also people. In the very early days, they were slavers. But when that abomination was outlawed, they found other ways of owning people. If everyone has their price, one of talents of the du Temps was knowing not just what that price was but, also, the currency in which people desired to be paid.

They accumulated not just wealth but power. They loved power more than anything. Everyone in the du Temps family loved being 'someone'. They loved that they held so many people's fates and fortunes in their grasp. One of their early crests was a gloved hand clasped around the outline of the City.

Wealth did not just bring them power but also all the excesses and corruptions that are found in those kinds of families: excesses that descended into decadence and, finally, debauchery. They were fond of throwing lavish, masked balls, complete with exotic entertainments and all sorts of bad deeds. Disappointingly, *Scandals and the City* was, despite its name, quite prudish and did not go into any details at all. It used terms such as 'unnatural behaviours' and 'dissolute goings on'. One party, celebrating the arrival of spring, degenerated into an orgy which resulted in several high-profile attendees being excommunicated.

There was also a long list of maids who had been de-flowered (the book's term) and made pregnant by a du Temps scoundrel. On the whole, the du Temps appeared generous to these women.

No doubt they were pragmatic enough to know that paying for silence was money well spent. Numerous milliners, cake shops and florists were opened by fallen women and funded by the du Temps. I was interested to read that some of these businesses still exist today. These include Violetta's florist and Lita's Sweet-and-Sours. Sweet-and-Sours are a favourite of mine; they come in a variety of fruit flavours, and the novelty is that you do not know if it is a sweet version or a sour version until you put it in your mouth. A bit like life, their creator, Melusita, had apparently joked. It took me a moment to realise that Lita was a diminutive of Melusita.

Others, however, fared less well. *Scandals* cited one unfortunate maid who drowned herself out of shame. Or did she? According to the book she may have been drowned by her du Temps lover to prevent the shame. This was based on very flimsy evidence: she had bought a new hat and what woman buys a new hat before killing herself? Also, the case against this was that the du Temps were famously shameless. Whatever happened, her ghost still haunts the path near where her body was found. But the City is full of ghosts.

There was a whole section dedicated to Mariana, Penelope and Vivian. The sisters seemed to spend a huge amount of time attending parties, for which they came up with increasingly extravagant and risqué costumes. This culminated in Vivian appearing, at a fancy dress ball, totally naked except for a string of pearls and shoes made from seashells, as the Birth of Aphrodite.

The du Temps definitely had a wild streak. However, this wildness had a dark side, and that dark side was madness. The kind of madness that some call wickedness. This was most pronounced in Rufus du Temps, twin of Vulpe.

Vulpe was relatively normal, at least by du Temps standards. As a young woman, she exhibited classic du Temps behaviour, running away with an undesirable and having to be brought home. She went to parties, wore outlandish clothes and swam naked in fountains. But her behaviour was harmless and she seemed to grow out of it.

I felt relieved to read this. I did not want to be named after someone wicked. Wild, yes, but not wicked.

In a family renowned for their delinquents and deviants, Rufus stood out, even as a child. There was a particularly horrible story about him killing a cat when he was seven. Unlike Vulpe, the older Rufus got, the more pronounced his behaviour became. By the time he reached adulthood, he was a totally immoral young man.

The following chapter was all about him. Before reading it, I went to make myself some coffee. I even considered another cocktail. Perhaps reading about the du Temps was making me feel louche. Then, with a shiver of excitement, I remembered my date the next evening. I decided against the cocktail. I wanted to look my best.

I wondered if there was something small and simple to eat. Something that I did not need to cook. Luckily there was a loaf of fresh bread still in its wrapper. To my surprise, I also found cheese, fruit and a box of almond biscuits. It was almost as if Cassiopeia had stocked the pantry for me before she left. Honestly, she was beginning to behave like my mother. I had not moved away from home to live with another mother.

But it looked very nice so I took some back into the room with me, got comfortable and began to read about the wicked ways of Rufus du Temps.

Chapter 15

Much has been written about Rufus du Temps, but not much has been verified, and so it is hard to separate fact from fiction.

from *A History of the City in the Sea, Part 2 – The City of Light*
Professor Justin Lambe

Rufus grew up a wild, young man who enjoyed drinking, gambling, and easy sex, like many of the sons of the wealthy did and still do. If he was caught, his family would pay his way out of trouble, like the wealthy did and still do.

He was easily bored. As a child he enjoyed taking things like clocks, watches and other pieces of machinery apart, although he could never be bothered putting them back together again. Then he began to break things just for the sheer joy of it. When there was nothing left to break except the law, he turned to crime.

To begin with, it was thieving: objects like works of art from the galleries, the gold cross from the altar of the Cathedral of the Two Crosses. Initially, these objects would reappear in unexpected and, at times, funny places, for, at the start, it was about the daring and not about the value. But when his father had had enough and refused to pay off his gambling debts, Rufus began to see it as a way to keep his head above water.

Then came the violence. Violence towards those who stood in his way. Then against those he believed had slighted him. And finally, violence just for the sport of it. There was something dark and twisted inside Rufus and, as he got older, it began to unravel.

He began to look around for what other boundaries he could push against. He experimented with the breaking of the natural laws: the laws of the universe, the laws of this world and, more importantly, the laws that govern the edges of this world and keep it separate from all the other worlds that flow around and through it like currents in the sea.

The City has a long history of inhabitants famous for dabbling in the dark arts, obsessed with crossing over or calling through to that which lies beyond. The City was full of all kinds of secret societies which met in taverns, salons or people's houses for this purpose. The myths and legends of the City abound with creatures who settled here amongst the human inhabitants. Many of them were harmless, of course; others, not so much. The most infamous of these was the mermaid known as Melusina.

She was – predictably – very beautiful and, like the sea, had depth as well as beauty. Melusina preferred the world of men to the world of the sea and so she came and lived in the City. *Scandals and the City* phrased this in such a way as to imply that there was something suspicious about it. Something 'fishy', I thought; I laughed at my own little pun. That was exactly the kind of thing that Uncle Timeon would say.

Melusina performed as a dancer. She danced in human form and then flung herself into a great tank and danced as her mermaid self. The book implied that the dance routine was more risqué than it described.

Rufus never lacked lovers. He was certainly handsome – all the du Temps were blessed with good looks – and he could also be charming. However, there was something cruel about his features. In the young, cruel features can appear beautiful; it is only in old age that they start to look ugly.

For a time, Rufus and Melusina became the most beautiful

and the most fashionable couple in the City. He turned her from a cold-blooded creature into a very hot-blooded one. It is rumoured that Vulpe du Temps painted a wonderful portrait of them, a painting which has long since vanished.

The book did have an illustration of a portrait painted of Melusina at around this time. There was something familiar about it and I realised that the mermaid was similar to the one in the old Zeit sign. I wondered if they had used that image when they were designing it.

I couldn't help but feel that *Scandals and the City* had oversold itself. It promised so much more than it actually delivered.

Rufus and Melusina were inseparable. Together, they managed to belong to high society, low society, and the demi-monde. They had a shared interest in the esoteric and the occult and they regularly attended salons and soirées with the weird and wonderful Madame Grise, who read tarot cards and tea leaves. She had a black cat with different-coloured eyes, and claimed that she had a spirit guide who could see to the beginning and the end of time. He sometimes came to her in the form of a raven.

Inevitably, Melusina and Rufus du Temps' love affair did not last. Theirs was the kind of relationship which burns brightly but quickly. Rufus had discovered being hurt by someone you loved was exquisitely painful, and this made it particularly satisfying. He was also quick to discard a beloved for someone new. And that is what he did with Melusina.

Melusina was the kind of creature in whom heartbreak quickly turned to anger – an anger that soon cooled her hot blood. Before long, that anger turned to hatred.

According to *Scandals and the City*, Melusina swore vengeance on Rufus, cursed him, jumped into the sea and was never seen again. I knew, from my earlier research, that that wasn't strictly true. She remained in the City for a time, met Guisse Zeit (may have fallen in love with him) and helped him import glass. However, I don't imagine many people read *Scandals and the City* for the facts.

Rufus began to dabble seriously in the dark arts. He frequented societies dedicated to alchemy, sorcery, necromancy and other nefarious rituals and around this time he became involved with the mysterious Dr Dorridorri. It is unclear if Dr Dorridorri was ever really a doctor, but he was a famous practitioner of the dark arts. *Scandals and the City* described him as a scourge: a twisted, corrupted necromancer of the vilest kind and an abomination whose very presence defiled the City.

After he died, his diaries were found and they revealed a plan to trap the ghosts of the City and to turn them into slaves. Dr Dorridorri had, apparently, designed a machine to do this. I couldn't help wondering what such a thing would look like.

Rufus's diaries have long since disappeared. One theory is that the City fathers and the bishop of the Cathedral of the Two Crosses burned them at a secret service.

Eagerly, I turned the page. Chapter Nine: *Fakes and Forgeries – What is Real and What is Not?* No! How could the book do this to me? I wanted to know more about Rufus and the evil-sounding Dr Dorridorri.

A loud crash came from outside. A cat meowed and hissed. I checked the clocks. I had become so engrossed in reading that it was later than I had realised.

I should go to bed; I wanted to look my best for the next day. The thought of this did not fill me with as much excitement as it had earlier. It was as if the book had tainted me. Some of the darkness had escaped and cast a shadow over me. Maybe it was reading about Melusina and Rufus and how their passion had burned itself out. I could not understand how passion could ever burn itself out or disappear. Deep down, I believed that it must not have been real passion to begin with. Or, even worse, only one person had felt the passion and the other had not. That was my greatest fear: that I had been deluded in what I felt. People say that hatred is the opposite of love but it's more likely the opposite of passion.

But what is the opposite of love, in that case? Maybe it's friendship, I thought. I remembered my previous lover and Astrid. He valued me as a friend. I laughed bitterly. How insulting that was. I would have preferred it if he had said that he hated me. For at least there would have been some passion there. I would have known that I could inspire emotion. But no. I was a mere friend whilst Astrid was the beloved one, the object of desire. The memory of those words stabbed me in the stomach.

An image of the eviscerated mermaids dying on the sand popped into my head. The cuckoo clock and the grandfather clock chimed in harmony. I really was twitchy now; I should just go to bed and get a good night's sleep. But I could not shake off my dark thoughts and memories and I had the sense that they followed me into my dreams.

Chapter 16

If you look for something hard enough, you often think you've found it.

from *Is it Sham or is it Real?* Rosemary Shade

I had moved in with Cassiopeia to gain some independence, but this was, in fact, the first night I had spent in a house on my own. I imagined all kinds of things: someone scraping at the windows and rapping at the door. On occasions, I thought I heard or sensed the sound of someone moving around downstairs. The noises of the night were magnified. The ticking of Cassiopeia's many clocks sounded monstrous.

I fell into a fitful sleep at dawn and woke with my head full of bizarre images, fractured and jagged and making no sense. They melted away like ice on a bright morning, leaving me with a fleeting sensation of a mermaid cut open with a giant pair of scissors and a blade, lying amongst dead plants, whilst her blood turned the sea, and all the fish in it, red.

With no Cassiopeia moving round the house, I did not wake at my usual time. I even managed to sleep through the racket caused by the grandfather clock and the cuckoo. I ate a late breakfast – a peach and several of the almond biscuits – in my dressing gown, which made me feel slovenly. Perhaps my mother's anxieties about me living alone were well-founded.

I had planned to go and see Guisse Zeit, but it was already much later than I had intended to leave. The Zeit building took a while to get to. The building was becoming a bit of an attraction, but it wasn't popular enough for a frequent waterbus service. For a time, there had been talk of building a bridge out to it. It was to be made of glass, predictably enough. The thought of a glass bridge over the sea made me shiver.

I wanted to give myself plenty of time later to get ready for my date. I needed to look beautiful. Well, as beautiful as I could be, which wasn't that beautiful. I thought of Astrid and felt a pang of envy. Well, if not beautiful, I could aim to look something else. I could look bewitching. I liked that idea. But I still needed time to look bewitching.

I felt nervous about going to see Mr Zeit. This would not be as easy as my previous deceptions. Perhaps I needed to do some more research. If I walked in with a notebook full of facts, I would look more impressive. Even better, I would feel more impressive.

That seemed like a good compromise, a good way to spend the day. I would go to the library.

First, I went back to the office. I told myself that it was to check that everything was all right and that the plant didn't need watering. It was only when I arrived that I remembered, with a little shiver of pleasure, that I didn't actually need to. I hadn't forgotten about the note; it was just that checking constantly had become so ingrained over the last few days. I felt the relief wash over me and then a shiver-sliver of excitement, quickly replaced by nervousness.

A History of the City in the Sea, Volume 2, was still on the desk. I had a quick look at the next chapter on Guisse Zeit, but it told me nothing new or interesting. Or if it did, I did not recognise it. I looked up Melusina in the index to see if I could discover any more about her, particularly her relationship with Rufus du Temps, but she only featured in the chapter I had already read. Finally, out of curiosity, I looked up Dr Dorridorri, but he wasn't mentioned at all. I was heading out of the door when I remembered about the plant. It would just have to wait another day.

I walked down towards the library. As I passed du Trims, I heard a fearful creaking sound. The rotating display of glass scissors and razors had stopped, and was just starting up again.

The Vulpe du Temps Library was at the corner of the street. Honestly the du Temps were everywhere in the City. I had always known about them but had never before realised quite how prolific they were. Often you do not really notice what lies in the familiar until your attention is drawn to it and then you can't stop seeing it.

The entrance was via a porch. It had terracotta tiles on the floor and a huge sign reminding everyone that they were now entering a library and that they MUST be quiet, not eat sweets, nor bring in drinks. The library proper was a great, open room. A plaque informed me that the building had belonged to the du Temps family for generations and had been many things including a slaughterhouse, a grain store, and a factory. Now that I knew this, I could see remnants of its industrial past. It had high ceilings which now had a row of fans attached. Just below the ceiling was a row of small windows which let the sunlight in, in shafts which illuminated the dust particles dancing round the fans. There were a couple of skylights too and this was the main source of light in the room. The gloominess was soothing in a way that reminded me of a cathedral. There was something sacred about the place.

At one end, a desk stood on a raised platform. It reminded me a little of a pulpit. I could not shake the church-like impression. Behind the desk stood a thin woman with a pinched face. I recognised her, but hadn't known that she worked here. A man with small, round glasses was whispering earnestly to her. He had the look of an academic. He had a very long list which I assumed was a list of book titles. The librarian was checking them and then consulting a box of cards beside her.

I had my own, much shorter, list: just one book. Is that even a list? I wondered. I was looking for the unimaginatively titled *The Zeit Family – the Definitive History*, by Jeremiah Finn, referenced by Professor Lambe.

I noticed a box of cards on a nearby table, similar to the one the librarian had. This was promising; perhaps I could bypass her altogether. I looked up Zeit; the library had a list of titles, including the one by Jeremiah Finn. Beside it was a green tick, but unfortunately there was also a sequence of numbers and letters. I was not sure what they meant, except that I would not be able to avoid queuing after all. I made a note of them.

I looked up Melusina to see if the library had any books about her, but no. The librarian was still busy with Mr Academic. I flicked to D to see if there was anything about Dr Dorridorri. There was only one book – *A Life Lived in Darkness: the story of Dr Dorridorri* – by the improbably named MM Mystery. It had an orange tick and more letters and numbers. I wrote them down, too.

I was about to see what books they had on Rufus du Temps – I couldn't imagine them not having any – but glanced up to see Mr Academic folding up his list. I hurried to the desk. The librarian's name badge said: Miss Mercy. She looked forbidding, as if she had also recognised me and had not liked what she had seen.

I asked for the Zeit book.

'That is in the basement, and it will take me some time to have it fetched as the boy is on a break,' she said, in a way that suggested that she disapproved of breaks or the boy or both.

'That's fine,' I said, brightly. 'I am happy to wait.'

'And,' she added, 'you can't take it out; you are only allowed to look at it here.'

Miss no-Mercy, more like, I thought.

'That's fine,' I said, smiling even more.

I then requested the Dr Dorridorri book.

At this she looked even more disapproving.

'We do not keep such a book,' she said.

I bit my tongue. Uncle Timeon had taught me never to antagonise someone who has something you want. I forced a further smile and said, 'But in that box over there, it says you have it; the number is EX 7 YF8D.'

She consulted her cards.

'It has an orange tick. That means it is stored remotely.'

She said the word 'remotely' like it was the ends of the earth. I said nothing; the old power-of-silence trick again.

'You will have to order it.'

'That's fine,' I replied, smiling until it hurt.

'It's, it's' – she looked at me – 'a very unsuitable book.'

I heard the unspoken addendum 'for young ladies'. Even Miss no-Mercy had the sense not to say it. Nothing piques a young lady's interest like being told that something is unsuitable.

'It's for work,' I replied.

'It cannot leave the library; you will have to read it here.'

I produced another smile. 'That's fine.'

It was a last-ditch attempt on Miss Mercy's part, but I had already shown that I was prepared to read a book in the library.

'I will have your other book fetched for you,' she said. 'Where will you be?'

I was going to say in the Z (for Zeit) section, but I noticed a sign that indicated that XYZ were in another room.

'In the G section,' I said. I could look at books on glass. There were plenty. But they all looked pretty boring, and, as I feared I was also waiting for a boring book, none of them tempted me. There were only so many boring things that I could read in a day.

Then I noticed the section on Ghosts. I remembered that the unsuitable Dr Dorridorri had been interested in ghosts so I went to take a closer look.

I lifted down a book called *The Evolution of Ghosts, Birds and Humans* by Sister Assumpta, noting that she was also the author of *Ghosts – Parasites or Epiphytes?* According to Sister Assumpta, ghosts are the spirits of dead people who were determined to hold onto their life. Some just didn't want to let go of the people or places that they loved. Others felt angry that they had been robbed of reaching their full potential and were still trying to achieve that. Many were driven by a desire to finish things, in order to feel complete.

But, as Sister Assumpta warned, finishing is not the same as completion. Completion will not be found at the conclusion of tasks: it is more than just finishing of external things. In fact, completion is a sense of wholeness, an ability to feel whole even when some parts are missing. Completion is acceptance. Ghosts are spirits who cannot accept that they have to let go and move on. And that is what spirits are supposed to do. For life is a game and they are out.

I jumped as I felt a tapping on my shoulder. It was not a ghost; Miss no-Mercy was trying to attract my attention. She placed a large block-like object down on the table. It was the definitive history of the Zeit family. Her fears that anyone would take the book out of the library were unfounded. I could hardly hold it, never mind sneak it anywhere. I tried to lift it up but it was so heavy that I set it down again with a loud thump. I couldn't help it. This earned me glares from three people nearby and a disapproving stare from the departing Miss no-Mercy.

Not only was the book huge, but the writing was tiny. And the pages were very thin, like the pages of a bible or prayer book. Jeremiah Finn must have really loved the Zeit family. It looked like it would take a lifetime to read. I thought about Jeremiah spending all that time working on it. What drives a person to write a book that, perhaps, no-one else will read?

I skipped to the end to see if I could learn anything about the current Mr Zeit. Almost unbelievably, he was barely mentioned. The last sentence merely said, 'The business has now passed to a new Guisse Zeit, named after his illustrious ancestor.'

Great.

I turned back to the beginning to see what I could learn about the start of the business. There were several chapters about the original Guisse Zeit's early days working in the docks. Jeremiah Finn could make anything sound boring.

'It was here that he noticed glass, of a high quality, on a couple of the ships that came from an Island on the edge of a lagoon... blah, blah, blah... they mainly came to sell fish and other local produce ... blah, blah, blah...' I skimmed the tiny writing.

Then there were two – yes, two – exceptionally boring chapters about the rules and laws around buying a ship versus renting one and/or leasing one. Renting and leasing a ship appeared to be two different processes. I couldn't take any more of this. It was actually worse than school.

Anyway, the readers of *Jolie* magazine wouldn't care about this either. I just had to ask the current Mr Zeit something like why he decided to change the sign, who designed the new one and what his favourite food was.

It was time, I felt, to go home and get ready to go out. I suffered a little pang of guilt that I had wasted the day and had not really done anything to look for Ruby. In a last-ditch attempt to find anything, I looked at the index to see if there was any reference to Melusina. There was only one. It was back in the section that I had just skimmed through.

Jeremiah described Melusina as a mermaid and performer of some renown. Although she had chosen to live in the world of men, the sea still called to her from time to time. Some nights she would go down to the beach and take on her mermaid form. It was here she met Guisse Zeit, for he liked to walk down to the shore and look out to the world beyond the City. One account stated that she had become entangled in some fisherman's nets, and he cut her free.

According to Jeremiah they fell in love and Melusina helped Guisse in his business interests. He made it sound very boring. A calculating kind of love, nothing like the fiery passion that she had shared with Rufus du Temps. But that could have just been Jeremiah's writing style.

I closed the book as quietly as I could and struggled up to Miss no-Mercy's desk, where, despite my best efforts, I dropped it with a bang, earning myself another disapproving stare.

Then I hurried out of the library to attend to the task of making myself look bewitching.

Chapter 17

Someone will always appear when you need them, but also when you don't.

from *Let's Meet Under the Clock (the Type of Clock that People Meet Under)*
Heidi Edmundson

I felt edgy, getting ready for my date. It was vital that I looked the best that I could. My whole future happiness might depend on this. I had to look almost impossibly good but in a way that did not look as if I had tried too hard. No-one likes someone who tries too hard.

This is where things get complicated. As with many of these things, my friends broadly fall into two different camps. Some are of the very strong opinion that no man will like you if they feel that you have not put enough effort into how you look. It is important to make them feel special. You also have to look like you care about yourself and your appearance.

'Nooooo,' the other camp squeals. This is the last thing you should do. Men like women who look like they hadn't put in too much effort. The trick is to look like you have just thrown your clothes and make-up on. This is by no means the easier option, as looking like you have just thrown your clothes and makeup on is very different from the way you look when you have actually just thrown your clothes and makeup on. It is like the difference between the taste of real cherries and the taste of cherry sweets.

Also, looking like you are trying too hard may make some men anxious that you like them too much. Men panic when they think that a woman likes them too much. In fact, men just don't like women who are 'too much' in any way. Some of my friends are firm believers that you have to make men feel that they are pursuing you. You have to make them do the running. If you do not do this, they quickly lose interest. So, you have to be able to run very fast to keep that little bit ahead.

Obviously, you do not want to get too far ahead, or they might then begin to think that *you* aren't interested. I can never seem to find the right balance between looking interested but not too interested; the balance between being too good and not good enough.

Even knowing what time to start getting ready was tricky. I obviously didn't want to leave it too late as I needed lots of time. But I didn't want to finish too early either. Then the effects of my efforts would be beginning to wear off at the moment when I needed to look most impactful.

In the past, I would have phoned Astrid to discuss a strategy. She might even have come over to help me, to sit giggling on my bed, offering advice, telling me that I looked lovely and had such beautiful eyes. It is easy to tell someone that they are so pretty when you look like Astrid.

I made myself a cocktail. I was sure Cassiopeia would have offered me one. I tried to decide what to wear. I had a new red dress but felt that that perhaps was 'too much', so in the end, I settled for green. My hand shook as I made up my eyes and I had to restart three times. Finally, I was ready.

I took the waterbus. It was only one stop, and I could have walked but I didn't want to end up looking hot and bothered. I took the seat I had taken a few nights ago on my way to the DT Watch Factory. With a jolt, I realised that I hadn't really thought about Ruby all day. I had been too engrossed in my date and reading about the past.

La Lumière was famous. It was one of several places which claimed that it was the first to get glass. It had been a tavern in the old days. A small plaque on the door said that back then it was known as The Broken Bed, and had hosted female boxing events very popular in that era.

La Lumière paid homage to its history. Around the circumference of the main room was a series of raised booths. These were designed to look like boxing rings with glittery ropes strung with glass beads. You could reserve one for a small amount of money. If you did, they wrote your name on a card, like it was a boxing match. In the middle, there was a raised platform where the band played. On nights when there was no music, you could hire it and have your own little party there.

Three huge chandeliers hung from the ceiling, and all around them hung numerous smaller lamps and other glass ornaments. Many were shaped like sea creatures. Others were like the moon, stars and planets. All the tables were covered in little squares of glass. The huge bar at the far end of the room was made of glass. And behind it was a great mirror, the length of the wall. Every surface reflected other surfaces back. And the mirror at the back reflected all the reflections back out again. The effect was dazzling. It was indeed like being in the centre of a giant lumière.

Suddenly, I felt anxious. La Lumière was a popular place. Although it was a weeknight, it was still busy. Did I just stand here and hope we would see each other? I hated leaving things to chance. Especially something so important.

What if he didn't come? Or what if he did and we just missed each other? That would be worse. All the reflections seemed confusing and disorientating, so dazzling they were blinding.

And then I saw him. Well, not him, but his reflection in the mirror, darting in and out of all the other reflections. There one minute, gone the next, just a flash. Then he was beside me, smiling. And everything was okay.

'Hello, Vulpe,' he said.

We sat in one of the corners, at a table decorated with squares of glass in different shades of blue and green, from the palest aqua through turquoise and indigo, jade and dark green the colour of wine bottles. It felt as if the sea had flowed in and swallowed us up. We created a little world for ourselves. But I also felt that we were the centre of things. We exerted a pull, a centre of gravity, which drew all things into our orbit. It felt as if we were the brightest thing in that room of light.

A group of girls sat near us in one of the booths, celebrating a birthday. They wore crowns of silver paper and the waitress brought a cake alight with candles. Happiness radiated from them. One of them looked at us, glanced at me. I had done that before, looked longingly and a little enviously at people in love. Did we light up the room in the way that people in love do?

The waitress came bearing a silver tray with our drinks, which she held aloft on one hand. She sashayed towards us, moving in time to the music, through the crowd of people dancing.

Conversation flowed, full of glimmering things darting like fish just below the surface of water, full of hidden little treasures for us to find. The atmosphere changed between us from light and frothy to golden. Then it became stickier, like honey, and then amber, trapping us like flies, and, finally, something darker.

How can anyone ever explain falling in love? For it is just magnificent. Falling in love is of the senses and the spirit, not of the mind. It is transcendent. Love allows you to be you and something higher. You cannot think, or reason or categorise love. Love crashes in and sweeps away all before it like the sea does to a city of sandcastles when the tide turns. That is what love does; it turns everything else to sand and knocks it down and drags it away in its undertow as it goes out again. All that magic and power condensed down to two people looking at each other across a table, their fingertips brushing together as they long to touch. They sit down below when, for those brief few hours, they should be high up, just beneath the angels. And even after all this time and a canal's worth of water under the bridge, I still do not think that it should be any other way.

The band was in full swing. The singer was dressed in a costume of glittering shells. It fitted tight across her body and flared out at the bottom to give the impression of a mermaid's tail. But I felt too full of joy to dwell on disturbing things.

She sang of love and lust and loss in a sultry voice that growled like a tiger and purred like a cat. And I felt that I possessed those passions too. I belonged to the music and it to me. In one direction, time rushed by but in the other it seemed almost to stop.

I was told a story as a child, about a man given a magic watch. If he stepped on it, he could stop time forever, at that exact point. I often think back to that evening and wonder, if I had owned such a watch, would I have stopped time then? It is pointless to think such things. Not just because of the chaos stopping time would bring, but because, in my heart of hearts, I know that whatever magic I might have possessed, I would not have stopped time that night in La Lumière. I was too eager for more. I wanted the evening never to end but I also was desperate to get to the next part. Moments of sublime happiness seem as if they must go on for ever; they are so bright that they seem like the start of things and not something that is already beginning to end.

We moved closer. So close and straining to be closer yet. I caught a glimpse of myself in the mirror, all lit up by the lights and reflections, and how radiant I looked. Like I had been polished by the hand of God. The edge of the table dug into my ribs and yet I pushed further into it, just to be nearer to him. Our heads touched whilst he caressed my hand as he talked. Sometimes it is hard to tell the difference between intimacy and intensity.

La Lumière had its own rhythms and tides. It filled up, emptied out and filled up again. The lights dimmed, the shine contracting into scattered sparkles. But we clung on, steadfast, as others came and went around us.

We shared the sort of conversation that dances along, that has its own rhythm and movement. Fast and funny, sharp, and staccato and then slow-moving. The kind of conversation that feels as if you will never run out of things to say.

We talked about what made us laugh and what made us cry, what scared us at night. What we were doing and what we hoped to do in the future. How our lives had been blown off course and how we wanted more. I could admit this to him when I had not even been able to admit it to myself.

Like many people in the City, he was born to a family of sailors, men who walked more steadily on a surface that moved beneath them. I asked if he was planning on going to sea, but he shook his head.

'My mother called me Finn and joked that I would grow up to swim like a fish,' he said. 'Funny how wrong a name can be.'

'Exactly,' I replied. 'My mother named me after an artist and, in the end, I couldn't draw.'

Whilst we talked, I realised that I had always felt that something was missing: that inside me there lay an emptiness so vast that I was, in fact, hollow. I was nothing more than a thin veneer in danger of collapsing in on itself like a dying star. And now it was as if he filled up that emptiness, filled it up to overflowing.

The tide was going out on the evening. It thinned out the crowd, leaving behind isolated pools of people. The waitresses had stopped serving and so Finn had gone to the bar to buy us some drinks. The band had stopped playing, but there was still music coming from a big gramophone in the corner. The band members were all sitting round a large table near the front. The female singer sat amongst them in her shiny, slinky costume. She was very attractive. It was more than just her beauty; something radiated off her, something hot and pulsating. I could not take my eyes off her. However, the band around her did not seem to notice her at all. They were laughing raucously, and someone had brought out a pack of cards.

Only the very rowdy and the very quiet remained now. In the big mirror above the bar, I watched Finn order our drinks. Even his reflection seemed more vivid than the others. The diminishing evening had an undertow. I could sense it pulling at me, trying to drag me out to other places.

Soon the staff began to wash the tables and stack chairs. They turned the music off and the lights on. But still we clung on, making our drinks last, like we had done in the park. I felt anxious again. Life is a series of thresholds waiting to be crossed, and crossing them takes you to somewhere different, somewhere that you can never come back from. It's not as simple as just crossing the canal.

What would happen next? Would he walk me home, hold my hand, kiss me? Would he...? I could not think about it. I was a little scared about what might happen, but, more than that, I was terrified that nothing would.

A waitress yawned. The staff no longer looked so shiny and glossy; now they just looked tired. Someone came up and pointedly asked if she could take our glasses. The time had come.

I swayed as I rose. I had had more to drink than I realised. Helping me into my coat, Finn said, 'I suppose we'd better get you home, then.' The word 'we' warmed me up inside and I felt a little shiver of delight.

Chapter 18

She fell and fell and fell in love.

from *Untitled* Mary Longhurst

The door closed behind us and a bolt was shot home.

'Let's walk,' he said.

The City at night seems more like the true City, as if the day is a disguise, a veneer of respectability in which it dresses itself every morning. But it is more than that. They seem like two different Cities which inhabit the same space.

We set off down the dark, twisty streets, alone except for the occasional cat. It was as if we were stretching out the night as we had done our drinks. We spoke in whispers, unwilling to disturb the silence.

Although it was late, I didn't feel tired. I felt like I could walk like this all night. I could walk like this forever. We paid no attention to where we were going; we trusted that we were moving in the right direction.

Turning the corner, I was surprised to see that we were at the bridge that crosses the canal into Fibonacci Street. When I told Finn it was one of my favourite places, he stopped. He turned and faced me. We stood there, saying nothing, just listening to the night. The only sound was something unseen, creaking down near the water. Then, silently, he took me by the hand and led me into the middle of the bridge. It felt as if we were high up, higher than we really were. To one side was the street; to the other, darkness where the bridge turned the corner. Then, still saying nothing, he bent down and kissed me. A dizzying feeling that nearly knocked me over rushed through me. I kissed him back. I would never tire of kissing him, I thought.

Then he led me back into the street. Walking hand in hand, we crossed an invisible line, another threshold. Things would never be quite the same again. I was no longer just Vulpe. Now it was us. And I was so happy to not have to be just Vulpe anymore.

Eventually, we reached my house. Cassiopeia's house, not my mother's – that would have been too awful.

Here we were on the edge of another threshold, an obvious one this time. As usual, there are a lot of rules about how to behave at this point. And a lot of very different opinions on what to do next.

However, no matter what camp people are in, they all agree on one thing. You should wait until the man does something. How you react is the crucial bit. One group staunchly advocates that, no matter what he says or does, you are, on no condition, to allow him to come into the house. As soon as you do that, then it is over.

He might stay for the night but then I might never see him again. By giving him what he wanted too quickly he would lose all interest and respect for me. And I would only have myself to blame.

The other camp says that this is old-fashioned nonsense. If you don't let him in, he might even think that you aren't interested.

Then I would never see him again and it would be my fault for getting it wrong.

'Could I ask him?' I had once asked my friends.

'No,' they said in unison. 'Then he'll think you're crazy.'

I breathed in the scent of jasmine. Next door's cat regarded us from a safe distance, curious as to why other creatures were up at this time of night.

I desperately searched for a thread of conversation and, finding nothing clever or funny to say, said, 'Here we are then, this is where I live. But you know that.'

He struck a match and lit a cigarette. For one moment, I saw his face illuminated, looking at me intently. I tried to read his expression, but the flame flickered and died. But the cigarette had bought us more time. I had until he smoked it to do something.

'Cassiopeia, my landlady, is away. Why don't you come in?'

It was easier said in the dark. It made me feel braver. I sensed him smile. He threw his half-smoked cigarette onto the porch and ground it out with his foot.

Entering the house, I felt something shift. We were in a different territory now and I had become the leader. I was reluctant to turn on the hall light. It felt like I was signalling to everyone what I was doing. I liked having the darkness to hide in. I led Finn into the living room and turned on the little table lamp. We rarely used it, as Cassiopeia sewed most evenings and needed lots of light for that. My hands shook as I fumbled with the unfamiliar switch. We were cast into a tiny pool of light. I indicated the drinks cabinet with both hands.

'Ta da!' I said, like a magician performing a trick.

I had planned to make us both a cocktail. But now my hands were shaking, and I was unsure if I could remember the exact ingredients. Instead, I poured us both a large measure of cherry liqueur. I downed my whole drink in one mouthful. Finn looked at his dubiously and sniffed it. My heart began to pound. At this point, rejection of anything was a rejection of me.

A soft click and the quiet of the house was ripped apart by a cacophony of sounds. It was the stupid grandfather and cuckoo clocks. They sounded even louder than ever, as if they were taunting us, letting me know that they knew exactly what I was up to. A little of Finn's cherry liqueur sloshed over the rim of his glass and onto the floor.

'What the –?' said Finn, and we both started laughing.

Oh, how I preferred the laughing to the silence. I never wanted it to stop. It was something we were doing in unison, together. A shared thing between us. How I loved the grandfather clock and the cuckoo clock for bringing us together like this. Finn placed his glass on the table He pulled me towards him and kissed me. He tasted of cigarette smoke and something salty like the sea.

'You taste like cherries,' he said.

I would never forget that. It just seemed perfect to me. That moment seemed perfect to me. And whilst I was in it, I seemed perfect to me. I've done it, I thought, I've really done it.

'I need to lie down,' I said.

This was not some sort of seduction technique; I really did. The excitement was making me lightheaded.

'Show me where,' whispered Finn, his mouth pressed against my ear. Then he kissed it.

I led him upstairs. Then I heard a familiar click.

'Be careful,' I said. 'The clocks are about to go again.'

We both started laughing. Laughing, laughing, laughing. That's how we entered my bedroom, just laughing. This is what sex should be like, I thought. Lots and lots of laughter. Finn pushed me onto the bed with surprising force. I felt a little thrill.

Suddenly our clothes were too much. I have read in books about people ripping off each other's clothes. I have never been quite sure how that worked. We took off our own clothes but very, very quickly. We kept our underwear on. I'm not sure why. Finn lay on top of me. He was trembling and I felt the pounding of his heart above mine.

Very gently, he swept his index finger across my clavicle. I found a scar on his shoulder. My fingers traced the outline of it as if I were trying to read its story. It felt like he had shared a secret with me; a secret about his vulnerability.

He ran his hand down my body until he reached my hip bone. Then he ran his finger across the lace band at the top of my pants, pressing the lace into my flesh. Then he slipped his finger under my underwear. I gave a little sigh of pleasure and arched my back and pushed myself further into him. I dug my fingernails into his back and scratched him as hard as I could. A long scratch that ran the length of him. I had a wild urge to draw blood. I wanted to leave my own scar. Or at least a scrape that would take several days to heal. Something that would sting and throb from time to time and remind him of me.

Then he took my hand and pressed it down on top of his pants. I felt the thick cotton under my fingers. I did not need much encouragement. He felt hard. Next, he ran my hand down the length of his penis, pressing my fingers into it. I felt it grow under my touch as if I had a kind of magic.

'Harder,' he whispered. 'Harder.'

A cloud must have moved across the moon and a weak silvery light filled the room and I could see his face silhouetted above me. I felt bold and reckless. I liked this idea of me.

We were both totally naked now. I felt him press against me and I kissed him. I couldn't stop now, even if I wanted to. I deserve this, I thought. I could feel his weight on me, but I also sensed him hesitate.

'Yes,' I whispered. 'Yes.'

He kissed me very gently.

'Don't be too gentle,' I whispered.

I felt him pushing into me. I put my feet flat on the bed and lifted my body up to meet him. When he was inside me, I curled myself into a ball trying to force him deeper. I wrapped my legs around him. I felt myself start to go hot and loosen up inside. He gave a few little grunts. There was something animalistic about the noise, which excited me. Then he gave a great shudder and a sigh, and it was all over. And I couldn't help feeling a little disappointed.

He threw himself back onto the bed. I curled into him, trying to get as close as I could. I wanted us to be melded together. To be an us rather than a him and me. In spite of feeling disappointed, this was often my favourite time, the most intimate. All I wanted was to love and be loved.

'You are so wonderful,' I whispered, pressing my mouth as close to his ear as I could.

He stroked the top of my arm and kissed my forehead. I repeated it and he squeezed me closer. I wanted him to say the same thing back to me. There will be plenty more times, I comforted myself, and kissed him back.

Later, when we had both gone to sleep, I dreamed that I woke up. Finn was standing looking out of the window. He turned and I saw that he was crying. When I really did wake, I was relieved to feel the heaviness of his arm across me.

I listened to his breathing, enjoying the feeling of the length of his body against mine. The rhythm of his breathing made me feel safe. Then I felt him stir. There is something intimate about being with someone as they wake up. It is a moment you share with so very few people.

He kissed my shoulder a couple of times. I turned and kissed him on the mouth. Gently at first, then harder and deeper. I stretched out beneath him to shake the sleep from my bones. In the morning light I could see his face above me. I noticed little details that I had not seen before. Faint freckles and a tiny, faded scar beside his left eye.

Our kissing became more urgent. I bit him on the shoulder and to my delight he bit me back. I laughed. Then, quite suddenly and unexpectedly, he put his hands under my back and spun me round so that I was now on top of him. I clenched my thighs tightly around him, both for the sensation and to keep my balance.

Below me, I heard him groan and so I clenched them even tighter. And he groaned again. The sense of power was exhilarating. I could make him forget everything but me. All he could think of was me and my body and what it was doing to him.

Then he was inside me. I squeezed even harder and felt everything inside me squeeze back in response. A wave passed through me, and I screamed as loudly as I could. I felt wild. I felt something savage deep inside me. When it was over, he gently rolled me back to the bed beside him. I was sticky with sweat and sex, my hair was damp. I gave his hand a little squeeze.

'You're wonderful,' I whispered.

He kissed me on the head for an answer.

I repeated it, in the hope that he would say it back to me.

'You make me feel alive again,' he replied. 'So alive.'

Then I understood it all; he made me feel alive too. All summer I had felt bored, trapped, merely existing. He had brought me back to life again and I had done the same for him. We had saved each other. That is why we were meant to be together.

We lay and chatted about those little but important things,

the glue that binds relationships together. I told him my favourite flavour was cherry. His was lime. He liked the sourness. I gave his hand another little squeeze. I wanted to tell him that he was wonderful again. I wanted him to tell me that I was wonderful. But before I could speak, he let go of my hand and I felt something icy come between us.

'My life is complicated,' he said.

I kissed him. I was not scared of complicated. I could manage complicated. I thought of Lina and the search for Ruby. That was complicated, but I was managing that all right. Not perfectly, but I was managing it. His life could not be more complicated than that, I thought.

I offered to make him breakfast, but he declined. I had a little moment of anxiety. But he lingered to kiss me in the doorway and I felt reassured again.

As he walked away, I comforted myself that this was the start to something and not the end. Last night had been the perfect start to something.

Chapter 19

As soon as you get what you want, you worry about what you're going to get next.

from *New Boots and Blisters* Sukie Garfield

After he left, I lay in bed. Neither sleeping nor entirely awake. All the energy had been drained from me. Getting up would signal that last night was well and truly over. If I could lie in bed for a little longer, then I could hold onto some of it.

Hoping to see him again had consumed me; now that it had happened, I didn't really know what to think about. The idea that I could start to hope that I would see him again popped into my head. I did not like this one little bit. Surely, I shouldn't have to hope to see him again. Surely, it would just happen. Surely, now, we had become people who just saw each other, and didn't really have to hope for it. Like Astrid and I had once been. The thought of Astrid made me feel worse. Stop this, I told myself. You are just being silly and fanciful. You got what you wanted. It was a lovely evening. The first of many lovely evenings, I added in my head.

But I couldn't shake that feeling. When he had left, I had trusted completely that I would see him again. I had not raised the question of when we would see each other again. I had assumed, as he had held me and kissed me goodbye so passionately, that he too would be counting the minutes until he saw me again. But, already, doubt was beginning to creep in.

The problem was, I told myself, that needed to get up and think about something else. And, conveniently, I had the case to consider. I went downstairs and made myself a cup of coffee, but I found it hard to focus.

I decided that being in the office would help and I needed to water the plant. I could write a list of everything I needed to do. In fact, I could write a list of everything I had done and then everything I needed to do. There is nothing so satisfying as ticking things off a list, my mother always said. Outside, it was already hot and the air was sticky. It seemed to wrap itself around me, holding me back.

The door to the office pushed against something as I opened it, but it was only the morning paper. I set it on the desk and got out my notebook. The plant still looked fine, up in its spot beside the drawing of the red fish. It could wait.

I looked at the headlines. Another mermaid had been found dead on the beach. My stomach tightened.

The body had been seen glinting in the moonlight by some patrons leaving Frutti di Mer, an exclusive club near the beach. One of the men went to take a closer look and told the women to stay back. Then he had sent one of his friends to call the police. 'We were all a little tipsy,' the friend told the newspapers, 'but we sobered up pretty quickly, I can tell you.'

She was silver from her hair to her tail. Her skin would have had a glow to it when she was alive, but the man who found her described it as a dull grey. She had been sliced down the middle and the killer had cut her hair off and wound it round her mouth like a gag. She had not been mutilated in any other way. The police suggested that her killer may have been disturbed.

I needed to focus on Ruby. I took another look at Uncle Timeon's bookcase to see if there was anything else that I could possibly read in the name of research. .

Uncle Timeon has a vast and eclectic selection of books: fact, fiction and reference books all jumbled together. Eventually my eyes settled on *The City – the People and Places Who Shaped It*. It sounded promising, and it had the added advantage of being at eye level so there was no need to climb up to get it.

It was a slim volume and full of illustrations. Naturally, there was a chapter on Guisse Zeit, although it did not really tell me anything that I did not know already, except that he was a tough but fair boss who believed in paying off his debts early. There were a couple of chapters on the du Temps family, but again I did not really learn anything new. It amused me that I could now consider myself an expert on the du Temps and the Zeits.

Rufus was only mentioned as a very brief aside as the twin brother of Vulpe. I imagine that this would have enraged Rufus were he still alive. Unsurprisingly, neither Dr Dorridorri nor Melusina merited an entry.

However, I did notice the name Madame Grise, whose soirées Rufus and Melusina had attended together. She featured in a section called *Images of the City*. It appeared that her unique gift was the ability to instil magical properties into images such as paintings and other works of art. Some brought luck in money or love and others brought protection. Some people whispered that yet others were cursed, but Madame Grise insisted that she abhorred the dark arts and despised all that was driven by evil and greed. I couldn't help wondering what she thought of Rufus and why on earth she had let him enter her house.

'I am not an occultist,' she frequently asserted. 'I use the power of light to fight against the powers of darkness,' she said. 'It is my life's work. Never underestimate light, for though it can be soft and gentle, that does not mean that it cannot be strong and, when necessary, terrifying.'

At her salon, she offered many services including light baths to cleanse people of the darkness that had seeped into their lives. I recalled how *Scandals and the City* said that Melusina had visited Madame Grise frequently after Rufus left her. She must have needed a tremendous number of light baths.

Madame Grise claimed she drew her magic from the light and joy that is all around. She valued ritual and her ceremonies always followed the same pattern. She believed in the power of music. It was said that she employed a string quartet who played, hidden and invisible, in a next-door room. One woman wrote, in a letter to her sister, that she had taken part in a ceremony during which the room was filled with the scent of flowers and the sound of ringing bells. She described it as 'a most soothing experience'.

Madame Grise, herself, did not paint, she declared that her powers only worked on paintings by artists who were good of heart and drew from the fiery cauldron of creativity that exists inside of us all. 'For creativity and light are similar and they are the enemies of destruction,' she said.

How these powers actually worked seemed unclear. There was a story about two thieves who tried to steal a painting protected by Madame Grise from one of the grand houses. When they tried to lift it off the wall, they were dragged across the room by an unseen hand and thrown straight through the window by a great force. One broke his neck and did not survive the fall. Some claim that this story is apocryphal, and no-one knows what the picture was and where exactly it had hung.

The book also featured a painting of the moon reflected in the sea. A young lady had apparently commissioned it, as she was in love with a man. She hung it in the drawing room when he came to visit and three months later, they were wed. Madame

Grise, however, pointed out, that her pictures could not bewitch someone to act against their heart's desire. The book suggested that, as the picture now hung in the City Art Gallery, young ladies could consider paying a visit to it with their beloved, for who knew what might happen? I thought that I could pay a visit there with Finn.

The chapter finished by saying that perhaps many of Madame Grise's pictures still existed today in galleries and even respectable houses. In all probability, their provenance had long been forgotten and their magic powers lay hidden, unknown to their owners. I glanced at the drawing of the red fish beside the plant. Madame Grise had said that even when she would cease to be and was no more in body, her work would persist, as her magic had woven itself into the very fabric of the City itself. As for Madame Grise's former salon in Martinet Street, it had now attained the utmost respectability as it was currently one of the City's largest police stations.

I wondered what Madame Martinet, protector of the demimonde, would think of having a police station on her territory.

Chapter 20

Are you ready for what you might find if you take the long way home?

from *Haunted* Amethyst Philips

The day had already slipped into the afternoon. It was yet again that annoying time of day: too late to visit Guisse Zeit, too early to go home.

This wasn't strictly true, of course; I could easily go and see him if I hurried, but meeting him at the end of the day wasn't a good idea. Also, I really did not feel quite right, and I would need my wits about me. I would go tomorrow, I promised myself.

Suddenly I had an intense craving for something sweet. Ice-cream maybe, something that would slip down easily and require very little effort to eat. I could go to the beach and buy myself one. I felt a little guilty; I should be looking for Ruby. Yet again, I had hardly done anything, except for a small amount of 'research'. Which, to be honest, was hardly real research. It was just reading about a subject that was not really related to anything relevant.

But I had very little to go on. How was I supposed to look for someone when I didn't even know what they looked like? Lina had told me next to nothing. She hadn't even brought me a photograph of Ruby.

That's it, I decided. I would pay Lina a visit and ask her what she was hiding. I looked for her address and realised that the street was close to the shore. I would be able to buy myself an ice-cream whilst I was there.

I felt as smug with this plan as if I had done a hard day's work. Before I left, I took another look at *The City – the People and Places Who Shaped It*. I wanted to remember the details about Madame Grise's love painting in the City Art Gallery. I would suggest to Finn that we go there when he contacted me. I shook away the little worried voice that asked, 'but when will that be?'

I took my favourite seat at the back of the waterbus, feeling strange and disconnected. I felt as if I wasn't really there. I curled myself up into the corner of the seat. I remember Uncle Timeon telling me that standing out is as much about mental presence as it is about physical. If you believe you are invisible, people will be less likely to notice you. I must have been doing the opposite of standing out, because another passenger nearly sat on top of me.

'Excuse me,' I exclaimed, making him jump.

Lina lived in one of the oldest parts of the City. It had had a chequered past. The City had generally had a chequered past and so, the older an area, the more opportunity it had had to be chequered. It had certainly been home to many of the City's more infamous and notorious residents. These were both human – famous gangs, murderers, and pirates – and otherworldly. Many of the fantastical creatures who lived in the City also took up residence there.

The street that faced the shore was cheerful enough, though. It had a row of small shops and cafés painted in bright colours. I bought myself an ice-cream. Disappointingly, they had no cherry flavour so I settled for coffee.

The tangle of streets grew darker as they climbed away from the sea. Predictably, Lina's building was at the top of a steep hill. Even accounting for the incline, it seemed to be leaning – as if it were trying to escape the City and get closer to the sea.

Equally predictably, Lina's flat was at the top of the building, up a staircase that was worn to a treacherous slipperiness. I was trembling by the time I reached the top. Lina's door was on one side of a narrow corridor, facing an identical one opposite. Near it was a small table with a plant. There was no bell, so I rapped on Lina's door. There was no actual knocker, so I had to use my knuckles. I knocked again, in case she hadn't heard, although I had the impression that inside wasn't that big.

It always gives me the chills, rapping on doors when I don't know if anyone is inside or not. I imagine empty rooms, full of things, just waiting.

I was irritated. I had come all this way and now I was going to have to go all the way back. What a complete waste of time. I started to cry. Perhaps it was tiredness. That was always my mother's explanation for crying for no reason. I banged the door again, harder this time.

'Can I help you?' a voice behind me made me jump. It belonged to a small woman, with grey hair in a bun. She had sharp features and tiny eyes like currants. She reminded me of a little bird wearing a pink apron.

'I'm looking for Lina.' I wiped my eyes, hurriedly.

'She's at work.'

She said this in a way that made me feel disreputable for not knowing it.

'Where does she work now?' I asked. 'Is she still at the same place, at…?'

I put on a little performance of trying to remember the name.

'She's a waitress, but I can't remember where.'

I was trying to think of how to encourage her to remember, when we were interrupted by a grey cat who shot out from behind her and began to scratch frantically at the door to Lina's flat.

'Perdita!' shouted the woman. 'Come here! That cat is always trying to get at Lina, and she hates cats, she's scared of them. But that's cats, I suppose.'

'It certainly is,' I replied.

The woman carried a squirming, reluctant Perdita inside.

Now that we had bonded over our shared views on feline behaviour, I felt confident enough to call after the woman, 'If you see Lina, can you say that Vulpe called?' I scribbled a quick note and pushed it under Lina's door.

It took an age to get back home; the waterbus kept stopping and starting. For a while, it just seemed to float about in the lagoon, doing nothing and going nowhere. When I eventually got off, it took forever to walk back to the house. I have a theory that the City expands and contracts. Some days, the streets seem to grow longer and twist and turn about themselves like writhing snakes. And this was one of those days.

The first thing I noticed, on opening the door, was Cassiopeia's bag. I was surprised to find that I felt happy, relieved even. Perhaps I liked the idea of her fussing around me and calling me in to have a drink with her. I really wanted a drink but, more than that, I really wanted to be petted over.

But Cassiopeia did not call out. I opened the door to the little sitting room. She was sewing, concentrating intently. She didn't even look up when I came in. I was almost beside her but still she didn't seem to notice me, and I had to call out her name. This made her scream and she jumped, pricking her finger on the needle. A drop of blood fell onto the white fabric.

'Oh, Vulpe,' she said. 'You gave me a fright creeping round like that.'

'I wasn't creeping,' I said, grumpily. 'There was no creeping involved. I was just walking in, in a perfectly normal way. It was you; you were lost in a world of your own.'

There was something strange about the way Cassiopeia looked at me.

'You're right,' she said. 'Sorry.'

'Can I have a drink?' I asked.

'Of course, of course,' she replied. 'Here, let me get you one.'

'No, no, it's fine, I'll get it myself. Would you like one?'

She waved a nearly full glass at me and shook her head.

It would have been churlish to make Cassiopeia get up and make me a drink, but I was disappointed that she didn't. Tonight, I felt a real need to be fussed over: fussed over in the way that on other days often left me feeling suffocated. Tonight, I wanted the cosy familiarity.

I felt out of sorts, disjointed, nothing seemed quite right. I had wasted the last two days; I really was going to have to do something about the case tomorrow. I looked up to find that Cassiopeia was looking intently at me but when I caught her eye, she looked down at her embroidery.

I finished my drink and watched the ice cubes melt in the bottom of the glass. I wanted another but felt that Cassiopeia would disapprove. The feeling that had been gnawing at me all day was getting worse. And now I could do nothing to distract myself from it. I wanted to get up and pace around. Panic burned at the edge of my brain, in the way that a match singes paper when held close to it. Working from the outside in. When would I hear from Finn? Would I ever hear from him again?

I listened to the silence, willing the phone to ring.

He was probably tired and would contact me tomorrow. But what if he didn't? Then he would contact me the next day. But what if he didn't? What if I never saw him again? The idea was like a knife had been stuck into my stomach and twisted.

I gave a little gasp of pain. Cassiopeia looked at me.

'You're very pale, Vulpe, would you like me to get you something to eat?'

I shook my head. I wasn't hungry. Last night had been perfect. It felt as if he had shared his secrets with me, bared his soul. It almost felt like a dream now. What had seemed so real, now seemed flimsy and without substance.

Whenever I think of that night, I struggle to remember what Finn looked like. The most I can manage is the sensation of us.

Looking at him was like staring into the sun. The thing is, it is as hard to see clearly in too bright a light as it is in the dark. Sometimes too bright a light can make you go blind. Or maybe it was because when I was with him, I was overwhelmed. Dragged under by a strong undertow of desire. Pulled into a whirlpool. Spun round until I was so dizzy that it was like being drunk and I could not focus on his features. After all, when you eat a piece of cake you don't focus on the individual ingredients. You just enjoy the richness and the sweetness and let yourself feel high on the sugar rush.

Trying to describe Finn is like trying to focus on smoke or mist or something that looks substantial but is not. It is like looking into one of those lakes so smooth and clear that they reflect the clouds. They look like they contain the sky, they are full up with sky. In order to see clearly you have to get to get closer and closer to the edge until you fall in. Then you discover that there is no sky and clouds there at all, only icy water.

Being able to describe people is an important aspect of my job, though, so if I really had to describe him in some significant way, I would say that he was tall, properly tall.

I can say that his hair was brown but with a touch of red

in it when the light caught it in certain ways. His face was just a pleasant face. But that made me like it more. I was tired of those too-handsome men, the sort that look like gods that walk amongst us; the kind of men whom other women were always looking at. I was tired of all beautiful people, actually. Let them all go and be beautiful together, the god-men and the Astrids of this world. They belonged in the light of the party, dancing and drinking and being dazzling together, whereas I belonged out in the edges, in the indeterminate places.

I am certainly not beautiful. I have an unusual face, a different face, but not a beautiful face. It is all angles and shadows. I felt as if both me and my face never quite belonged anywhere.

There was something about him that felt as if he did not quite belong either. He was also from the very edge of things. We were two people who didn't quite belong but somehow had found each other. And to me that was the most glorious thing of all. Because by finding each other, we had somehow found belonging. Or at least the start of belonging. For now, we could belong to each other.

I never attempted to try and explain any of that to my mother or even my friends. I did tell Cassiopeia once, one night. She didn't say anything, she just held me very tight.

His eyes were blue. Just a normal blue like many other people's. Not the kind of blue that invites comparison to the sky or sea or anything like that. But his eyes had a way of crinkling when he smiled. When they did that, they made me smile too.

And when he looked at me, I felt as if I was the only person in the room.

It was hard to pin him down, like trying to pin down a shadow. When I tried to remember him, even just a few hours after seeing him, all I could remember was how I felt. There seemed to be nothing solid to hold on to. No solid facts like where he lived or how to contact him. No plans. Just feelings washing over me, like choppy waves that were throwing me around and leaving me feeling seasick.

For a moment, I didn't feel real either. I was obviously just tired. I should go to bed and tomorrow everything would feel normal again. That great, gaping hole opened up inside me again, and I felt myself start to fall into it. Then I was quite literally saved by the bell: the telephone ringing, loud and urgent.

'Yes, I'll get her now,' I heard Cassiopeia say.

He had rung just in the nick of time to save me. It was going to be all right.

'Vulpe.' Cassiopeia was smiling as she entered the room; she looked happy, excited even. 'It's Astrid, she wants to talk to you.'

No, not Astrid; I couldn't even begin to take this in. It was too cruel. I didn't want to talk to anyone else, but I most particularly didn't want to talk to Astrid. Why was Astrid even phoning me?

'Hello.' My voice seemed dull, like an echo coming up from the void inside me.

'Hello, Vulpe.'

Astrid sounded happy. Astrid was always happy. She sounded a little breathless; no doubt she was running from one lovely thing to another. Fitting me in when she had a few moments. She was a beautiful social butterfly, flitting here and there.

'Maud told me that you had called and left your number.'

I wanted to kick myself. That carefully thought-out plan – here was another flaw in it. I was nowhere near as clever as I thought I was. Stupidity was another thing I ignored in myself. I should have left the wrong number. I was too tired to think up some plausible lie.

'I was doing an art thing,' I muttered. It didn't really matter, though. Astrid was not that interested. She chattered on about stuff, stuff that she was doing. I didn't even really need to be there at all. The cuckoo and grandfather clocks sang out, mercifully drowning her out for a few seconds.

I had hated her before but now I really hated her. Hated her for not being Finn. As if she had, somehow, stolen his call. And she wanted to see me.

'I'm a little busy with work at the moment. Uncle Timeon is away, and has left me in charge.'

'Oh, that sounds very important.'

'I'll phone you.'

'Soon,' she made me promise.

I had to lie to get rid of her. As I hung up, my heart sank. Is that what Finn had done to me. Had he lied to get rid of me?

Chapter 21

It's as if I'm unravelling. Everything feels frayed.

from *Cogs, Wheels and Spirals* Vincent Hare

I had no sooner hung up than the phone rang again. Was fate playing with me? Fate could play with me as much as she liked, as long as I got to see Finn.

Again, the voice was female. It was Miss no-Mercy from the library, calling to tell me that my Dr Dorridorri book had arrived. She still sounded disapproving on the phone. I could hardly speak through my disappointment. How much more of this could I bear? It was exhausting. I felt weak and shaky and sank down onto the stairs.

'I do feel a little tired,' I called to Cassiopeia. 'Maybe I should just get an early night.'

She came out and when she saw me, she looked worried and offered to bring me up something to eat, but I wasn't hungry. I lay in bed for a long time trying not to worry about when Finn would call me.

The next morning was sunny. Maybe today will be a better day, I thought. But somehow, I didn't think so. I had a really bad feeling about Finn. The feeling that I would never see him again was like a certainty. The thought of waiting made me feel sick. How could he just vanish? Did he not want to see me again? Was I not even worth an explanation? I began to cry and had to take some deep breaths. Focus, I thought, focus.

I forced myself to think about the day's work. What should I wear to look like a young socialite on her first journalistic assignment? This was not that hard to figure out as I only had one outfit that would possibly fit the bill. My mother had bought it so that I could wear it to smart occasions. It was a very pretty violet-coloured dress, trimmed in dark green piping. I had a pair of dark green shoes that matched it.

As I never went to smart occasions, the outfit had only been worn once, when I went to my interview at art college. Great, I thought. Just when I feel like a failure, I have to walk around wearing a dress that I've also failed in. The shoes felt stiff as I slipped my feet into them.

I told myself I needed to go to the office to 'check' on things. I didn't have the energy to try and pretend to myself that I was going to water the plant. I wasn't climbing up there in this dress. I really was going to look for a note. I felt like a drowning man clutching a straw. Maybe a splinter would be a better analogy, as holding on was not without pain. Obviously, there was no note, and I didn't even bother to go into the office.

I bought a coffee on the way to the waterbus stop. They had just set out a tray of fresh pastries, but I had no appetite. Even the cherry ones could not tempt me.

I took my seat at the back of the waterbus. There was a slight breeze that felt as if it blew straight through me. Occasionally, I caught sight of my reflection in the choppy water. It was fractured, breaking up and coming back together again.

The Zeit building was located on a small island in the lagoon. Once upon a time there had been a fort there, but it had been completely destroyed by an earthquake so that nothing had remained except for some piles of bricks and stones, which the Zeit building now covered.

It had only opened a few years ago but it was already becoming a place that people visited to marvel at. As well as housing the glass factory, it was also Guisse Zeit's headquarters. A large sign at the front welcomed me and told me how many people were employed there. I can't remember the number except that it was large. It was the design of the building that made it special; it was in the modern style – all sharp angles and geometric forms – and it was made entirely of glass. It was designed to represent the ship that Guisse Zeit used to bring glass back to the City.

I noted, with interest, that the ship was called the Melusina and, according to the sign, had been named after a famous mermaid. Apparently, the mermaid on the original sign was based on the figurehead of the original ship, which in turn was based on Melusina. The sign described the building as a modern cathedral of industry and innovation.

A glass walkway led to the nearest building, which was constructed of large panes of glass: some tinted, some clear, some mirrored. The building in the distance seemed to be constructed in the same way, though it was hard to tell. Surrounded by so much glass, it was hard to tell what anything really was. I was constantly walking through light and shade and reflection.

It was hard to know what was real, what was a reflection and what was a reflection of a reflection. Sometimes two panes of mirrored glass reflected back onto each other. An entire corridor of reflections stretching into infinity. Out of the corner of my eye I glimpsed two long lines of me, in my violet dress, like a string of paper dolls, stretching out into forever.

Also, nothing was entirely still and steady; everything shimmered and shook around me. Finally, I had to ascend and descend a glass stairway which formed a bridge across a narrow channel of water. It was full of the reflections of clouds and sea and the reflections of the clouds in the sea. I could not tell if it felt like floating, swimming or drowning. The effect made me giddy.

Inside the building was an atrium which stretched up through all the floors. A great chandelier hung from the ceiling. It was made mostly of clear glass but interspersed with occasional shards of different colours. Their reflections cast numerous rainbows which danced around me as I approached the long, curved desk in the centre. Behind it stood a young woman about my age, dressed in white. She was very thin and looked like she was made of angles. Her hair was dyed platinum blond, almost silver, and swept up onto her head. Her skin was pale, and she too looked like she was made of glass. I could almost have believed that she was a glass statue until she spoke.

'Can I help you?'

I took a deep breath and channelled an inner, confident person. It felt like I was dragging a shipwreck up from the ocean depths to the surface.

'I'm looking for Guisse Zeit's office.'

'You do realise that Mr Zeit is away?' she said, but I noticed that she glanced towards a corridor to her right.

She had a little note of superiority as she said this.

Damn, damn, damn, I thought.

'But I have an appointment with him.'

I gave my voice an irritated, impatient air. We both stared fixedly at each other as if we were in some kind of competition. Neither of us moved a muscle, not a flicker.

The glass statue made a little tutting sound and disappeared into an office at the back. Then I realised we were trying to see who could make the other one doubt themselves first. And I had won. Except it wasn't me. It was a pretend me who knew that she was lying. But that creation was more confident than the glass statue who, let's face it, was confident enough to go out wearing all white.

There was a big crystal bowl on the desk. It was full of Lita's Sweet-and-Sours. I took a big handful and then another and shoved them into my bag.

Glass Statue returned.

'I have checked, and Mr Zeit is, indeed, away at present.'

But I did make you doubt yourself, I thought triumphantly. Inside, I gave a little smile. The character I was playing, however, gave a little frown.

'Well, that is most inconvenient, most inconvenient, indeed,' I said. 'My aunt's secretary or his secretary must have made a mistake.'

I tapped my index finger irritably on the desk in such a way that implied that words were going to be had. I suddenly wondered if Uncle Timeon had used me in a similar way when he tried to bluff other people. Did he tap his silver cane on the ground and mutter, 'Vulpe assured me that she had done this or that or the other'? Were there people all over the City who had never met me but believed that I was an idiot, or felt sorry for me, or both?

'Would you like to speak to Mr Zeit's secretary?'

'No, no.' I waved my hand around in the airy manner of someone who left such tasks to others. 'I will get my aunt's secretary to do that.'

The last thing I wanted to do was draw attention to myself with Mr Zeit's secretary. The less she knew of me, the less opportunity she had to start making phone calls and discover that I was a fake. I was confident that Glass Statue would not go out of her way to get her anyway. This was an advantage of being so unpleasant; no-one wanted to help me and so no-one interfered too much.

'I don't suppose you know when he will be back.'

I chose my tone, and indeed my whole demeanour, carefully. Glass Statue would not want to help me and so her natural inclination would be to not tell me even if she knew. But if I acted in such a way as to imply that someone like her would probably not know the answer to this, then she might reveal it. I had made her doubt herself and so she would now be keen to prove herself. Or, then again, she might not know.

'There is a very important meeting here tomorrow. He will have to be in attendance at that.'

She said this in such a way as to imply her superior knowledge and understanding of the workings of the glass business and the Zeit empire. Internally, I applauded my reasoning. I would definitely be using that tactic again.

I looked at the bowl of Sweet-and-Sours. Despite the fact that I had two large handfuls of them in my bag, I slowly sifted through until I found the bright pink cherry one. Very slowly and deliberately, I untwisted the little wire and opened the wrapper. Then I carelessly tossed the packaging on the desk for Glass Statue to tidy up. I have absolutely no idea what came over me to make me want to behave like that. I just suddenly had the overwhelming desire to be the kind of person who behaves badly, rather than the sort of person that is always left dealing with other people's bad behaviour. I popped the sweet in my mouth and gave a little grimace. It was a sour one.

On the way home, I shivered at the back of the waterbus. The whole experience had given me a massive adrenaline rush but now it was fading. I felt tired, shaky, insubstantial almost. I thought about what to do next. I could try to see Lina again and ask her if she had a picture of Ruby. But the idea of climbing all those stairs in my smart dress and, worse, my smart shoes, was not an appealing one. I should go home and change first.

That's the thing about certain shoes, I thought, looking at my feet. They look so beautiful, calling out to you from the shop window or your wardrobe. They seduce you. Then you put them on and everything's lovely to start with, but you always end up hobbled, blistered and bleeding. Every step becomes an agony. Then you put them away and vow never to wear them again. But in time you forget about the pain and put them on and hurt yourself all over again.

Chapter 22

'I didn't steal it; I absentmindedly took it home with me,' she said, defiantly.

from *The Scales of Justice and Other Rare Fish* V Pyke

I could hear Cassiopeia moving around as I came into the house. I really didn't want to have to speak to her. There was a certain intensity or watchfulness whenever she was talking to me. I had noticed it last night. I had the oddest feeling that she was able to look right into me or through me when she spoke to me.

Miraculously, I managed to get in and up to my room without her hearing me. I was aided and abetted by the grandfather clock and the cuckoo clock which still seemed to be working harmoniously together. After I had changed, I lay down on my bed and closed my eyes. I was exhausted. I really couldn't bear the thought of going to see Lina and climbing all those stairs.

I really didn't feel altogether myself. I could see Lina tomorrow after I had visited Guisse Zeit. But no, that wouldn't work, as I would have the same clothes problem that I had today.

It occurred to me that perhaps tomorrow would be a bad day to see Guisse Zeit. If he had an important meeting, he probably wouldn't want to talk to a trainee journalist from *Jolie*. I should go the next day. But what if he was gone again? Maybe I should try my luck tomorrow. Then again, I didn't want to hang around the Zeit building so much that I began to draw attention to myself. That would increase the chances of someone checking me out.

I would go and see Guisse Zeit the day after tomorrow and

Lina tomorrow. Anyway, that made sense: I needed time and energy to visit Lina. Mrs Bird, as I had come to think of the bird-like woman who lived opposite, had suggested that Lina worked as a waitress. So, if she wasn't in, I could take a look at the row of cafés in the street closest to the shore, and try and speak to a few people to see if they knew her. I could even speak to Mrs Bird, although I had the distinct impression that she did not like me.

I had a pang of guilt; I really wasn't handling this case very well. I shuddered to think what Uncle Timeon would say if he discovered that I was now having to search for my actual client. Maybe I should just do nothing and wait for Lina to come to me.

I felt my whole stomach clench at the idea. If I took that approach, then endless empty days stretched out before me. I was looking for Ruby as much for myself as I was for Lina. I was looking for Ruby because I needed to fill my time and avoid thinking of Finn.

I jumped up. I had to do something, anything, to occupy myself. I remembered that the library had phoned last night. It took me a few minutes to remember what book I had even ordered. Then I remembered that it was the one on Dr Dorridorri, that had so scandalised the librarian. I couldn't really remember why I had ordered it. It was just on a whim, really. And because the librarian had implied that I wouldn't be able to see it, that had made me all the more determined to try. I could spend the afternoon in the library. That would at least give me something to do. And, who knows? I might find out something useful.

Then I could check the office and make sure that Finn hadn't decided to leave me a message there. Realistically, I knew that that was a ridiculous idea. But I could not give up hope.

Miss no-Mercy was at her desk at the front of the library. She ignored me for a few moments; at one point, it seemed as if she looked straight through me.

'Excuse me,' I said, making her jump. 'You phoned to say that the book I ordered has arrived.'

'Name?' she said.

'Mine or the book's?'

The book was in a large brown envelope with my name written across it in red ink.

'You are –'

'Not allowed to take it out of the library, I know.' Unlike the Guisse Zeit book, the Dr Dorridorri was small, and I could easily have slipped it into my bag.

I tucked myself into one of the corners of the Reading Room. I felt a shiver of excitement as I opened the envelope. What did a truly scurrilous book look like? Disappointingly, it looked just the same as a normal one. It was bound in dark green leather and had the title picked out in faded gold letters. As the book was not long, I started at the beginning.

Dr Dorridorri was a figure shrouded in mystery who had simply appeared in the City out of nowhere. Some sources say that he was born in one of the villages in the north. He was reported to be the son of a miner. According to the book, people from the north were very superstitious. Even more superstitious than the people from the City of Light. We were mostly descended from sailors so that was our excuse. In the north, the reason appeared to be witchcraft. The villages of the north were full of witches who spent their days causing cows to die, crops to fail and milk to curdle.

Other sources claim that Dr Dorridorri was born poor in the City and re-invented himself. He was the son of a sailor or a tanner. And, of course, as happened with anything or anyone disreputable, some rumours claim that he was the illegitimate child of a member of the du Temps family. That would have meant that he was related to Rufus, I thought.

So, Dr Dorridorri appeared in history fully formed. According to the book, he 'cut quite a dash'. Initially, he was described as a practitioner of the esoteric arts: a wizard and an alchemist. He could light candles with a click of his fingers. This was particularly risqué as fire was banned at the time. He also made three homunculi. Two of these he kept in glass jars in his office. The third was very small and he carried this one around with him at all times, in a pocket watch, specially made by a master watch-maker called Reynardo who worked at the du Temps watch- and clock-makers. I hadn't realised that the du Temps were associated with watch- and clock-making. Reynardo was also interested in magic. Together, he and Dr Dorridorri were supposed to have made a watch which could stop time. Several accounts from the City, written at this time, are from people who say that they saw the watch. However, many historians believe that this is nonsense. They claim that Dr Dorridorri and Reynardo were, at best, fantasists; at worst, charlatans. Other sources argue that the watch never existed in any form, real or fake.

It must certainly have been the inspiration for a children's fable in which a man has a watch which can stop time, but he never uses it. He lives his whole life waiting for the right moment, only to discover, as he is dying, that it never came. Where had I heard that story recently? Then, I remembered that I had thought about it myself the night I met Finn in La Lumière. The memory caught me off guard and I had to take three deep breaths to steady myself.

'Are you feeling all right?' asked a man sitting nearby. 'You have gone very pale; you're almost translucent.' He gave a little chuckle.

I replied that I was fine, but I needed some air. I hoped that Miss no-Mercy did not see me, as I was sure that she would think that I was getting what I deserved for reading such wicked material. Thankfully, she did not seem to notice as I walked past.

Outside, I leaned against the wall, taking a few deep breaths. The library was quite stuffy; that must have been what made me feel so strange. I thought about going to check in on the office. But I got as far as du Trims, and decided against it. I couldn't face climbing all the stairs to it any more than I could face climbing the stairs to Lina's. Anyway, I was only going to check for a note from Finn.

I bought myself a drink which I finished in a few large gulps, and returned to the library and the book. I gave the man a bright smile as I sat down, to signify that I was fine.

It was through his association with Reynardo that Dr Dorridorri had met Rufus du Temps. The book described Rufus as a handsome young man with a devilish streak. He had not shown himself to be interested in any of the many du Temps businesses, but he did have a bond with Reynardo that had started in boyhood. Rufus had a childhood fascination with watches and clocks and would visit the watch-maker at his workshop.

Rufus, Dr Dorridorri and Reynardo would regularly dabble in the dark arts at their meetings. They drew the attention of several notable people within the City. The Bishop condemned them from the pulpit one Easter. There was no mention of Melusina but the book did feature Madame Grise, who was described as a practitioner in 'white' magic.

None of this seemed to bother the three men and there were accounts of them holding ceremonies, sacrificing goats and attending black masses. There was a particularly gruesome account of a sacrificial ceremony which I had to skip as I was still queasy. At some point, the trio started working on the 'plan'.

Dr Dorridorri was also a necromancer. There were numerous accounts of him communicating with the dead. He had a number of spirit guides. These included a cat, one of the founding fathers of the City, and a wild rider from the east.

According to Reynardo's diaries, which were seized by the City after his death, the three of them came up with a plan to enslave the spirits – or, as the book put it, to harness the power of the City ghosts – in order to have them carry out their nefarious bidding. They constructed a device called a ghost harvester that combined Reynardo's mechanical expertise with Dr Dorridorri's dark powers and was bankrolled by Rufus.

By this time, Reynardo no longer worked for the du Temps; the book suggested that he may have been fired and that Rufus had been disowned. However, the trio managed to take possession of an upstairs room in one of the many du Temps-owned buildings, which they converted into a workshop.

Turning the page, I gave a shudder. There was Reynardo's sketch of the harvester. It consisted of three great blades attached to a rotary device which, in turn, was attached to a large chamber. Inside, the outlines of many ghosts were squashed together. The great blades were designed to cut through the fabric of time to get at the ghosts. The chamber was built not just to hold the ghosts but to suck them in, so that escape was impossible once they had been drawn toward the device.

At the time of the machine's construction, there were even more ghosts than usual. The plague had swept through the City, leaving lives cut short and potentials unrealised. According to the book, the ghosts were able to take a solid form, walk unnoticed amongst humans, and even have relationships with them. Some sources suggested that this could turn living people into gho–

A loud ringing made my heart race. It seemed to have the same effect on the other occupant of the room, the man who had told me I was so pale that I was translucent. Miss no-Mercy would not be pleased about this. Then the culprit walked into the Reading Room. And it turned out to be Miss no-Mercy herself.

'Attention please, the library will close in fifteen minutes.'

She repeated this twice and then, without saying another word, walked out, still ringing the bell. It took me a few moments to gather my things and then myself. Out in the main library, Miss no-Mercy was back at her desk at the front. Thankfully she was no longer ringing the bell.

I wanted to ask her how long the library would keep the Dorridorri book and if I could come back and read it another day. She pretended that she didn't see me. In fact, she looked straight ahead as if I didn't exist. At the desk, someone else rudely pushed in front of me. Miss no-Mercy just smiled and answered their query. I was so angry that I put the book into my bag and walked straight out of the library. No-one noticed or, if they did, they didn't care.

Chapter 23

Sometimes silence can be the cruellest thing.

from *Rebellious* Lucy Lemon

I walked home with the satisfaction of having done a hard day's work. Then I realised that I had accomplished very little other than one failed trip to the Zeit building and an afternoon spent reading. I had almost forgotten why I had started to read about Dr Dorridorri in the first place. I was trying to find out more about the history of the Zeit family but I had gone way off track.

The truth was, I was just doing it to keep my mind occupied. To stop myself thinking about Finn. I sighed. I had battled hard not to dwell on him all day. But now, in the evening, I had no choice. That is another thing about heartache. It is always so much worse at night. Sometimes it can be just about bearable in the day. But, at night, it becomes overwhelming.

Maybe there was a plausible reason why he hadn't been in touch. Something unpredictable. One day we would sit together, laughing about where he had been, happy, like we were the other night. I tried to delude myself a little more. Of course, he would contact me. I imagined him out there, leading his life. Could he just disappear, and I would never see him again? I felt that familiar emptiness in my stomach and that awful, sucking feeling that threatened to drag me under. In that emptiness, I felt that the truth was that he would not contact me again.

If I ever did see him again, I could never let him know how I had really felt. That was another of those tedious rules. You had to let people know that you missed them but not too much.

What on earth was wrong with me? Why was I never enough for anyone or anything, my previous lover, art school?

Finn was probably off with someone better now.

Hot tears stung my eyes. Someone barged right into me, their elbow catching me in my stomach.

'Careful!' I screamed, unnecessarily loudly, releasing all my pain and frustration. 'Watch where you're going!'

The clocks were making their usual racket when I entered the house. I had the feeling that Cassiopeia was waiting for me, though she did give a little start as I came in.

'Vulpe, hello.'

Her voice was bright but there was something hard about it, as if it could shatter at any moment.

'Sit down. Would you like a drink?'

I was afraid that Cassiopeia wanted to talk to me about something. What if she was going to ask me to move out? When one person doesn't want you, it often seems that nobody else does either. And she had been acting oddly since her return.

'Let me make you a cup of tea.'

Tea? Why was she making me tea? Maybe she was angry that I had drunk some of the alcohol whilst she was away. Maybe that was why she was going to ask me to leave.

'Can't I have a cocktail? One of those you make so well.'

That was another piece of Uncle Timeon's advice. Flatter people, then they are more likely to want to help you.

'I can make you a cocktail. I just thought you are looking so pale that you might like a nice, restorative cup of tea made with herbs from my village.'

No, I wanted a nice, restorative cocktail made with alcohol from the drinks' cabinet.

'Have you seen your mother recently?' she asked, as she mixed the cocktails.

'My mother?'

'I thought you might want to spend some time with her.'

'Why would I want to spend time with my mother?'

'I thought you might be bored or lonely with your uncle away.'

'No, I want to stay here.'

She turned and smiled at me, and, for a moment, she seemed relieved, happy almost.

'Anyway, I'm working on a case.'

'Oh, anything interesting?'

I shook my head. As she handed me my drink, she touched my arm gently. I had a strange sensation as if all my insides were agitated. I felt a dragging inside, as if something was being pulled to the surface. I tried not to react to it, in case Cassiopeia noticed and started fussing. She might take away the cocktails and insist that I have tea instead.

We drank but the atmosphere was strained. I felt very sad.

I overslept again the next morning. Lethargy pinned me to the bed. It took a lot of effort to leave the house.

I sat at the back of the waterbus, shivering despite the heat of the morning. Perhaps I was coming down with something. I might let Cassiopeia make me a cup of restorative tea tonight.

I got off at the stop nearest to Lina's address and looked up and down the street. I had not really thought up a particular plan for today. I was relying on luck, and luck was something I did not really trust. Unable to face the walk up the hill, I went into the nearest café and bought a coffee and a sticky pastry with apricot jam. I asked the waitress if she knew Lina, but she shook her head. I drank my coffee and ate my pastry and commended myself for an efficient use of time.

The street was pretty, lined with cafés and shops with different coloured awnings in ice-cream shades. It was not glitzy like the streets along the shore or in more fashionable areas but there was something cheerful about it. Remarkably, luck decided to grace me with her presence. The assistant at a shop that sold straw hats and silk scarves knew Lina, and directed me to a café called the Jelly Fish.

It had a primrose-yellow-and-white striped awning. Its sign had a picture of a fish made out of jelly, not an actual jellyfish. It sold ice-cream and cakes but, rather disappointingly, no jelly. Lina stood behind the ice-cream counter. She wore an apron of primrose-yellow-and-white stripes.

'Hello, Lina,' I said, brightly.

She blushed the colour of the strawberry ice-cream and immediately declared her intention to come and see me. That was a sure sign that she had not and felt guilty about it. But why? And why did she not want to see me, when she had hired me in the first place?

'We need to talk,' I said. I was very firm. I didn't want to give Lina the opportunity to make some sort of excuse and arrange to see me later. I was tired of waiting around for people who did not show up. I also did not want to have to go home and come back again. I had wasted too much time already.

At that point, a woman came out of the back wearing a similar yellow and white striped apron. She jumped when she saw me and then looked from me to Lina and back again. She must have assumed that we were friends, as she asked Lina if she wanted to take her first break. I looked pointedly at Lina until she said yes.

At the back of the Jelly Fish was a tiny courtyard with broken paving slabs and weeds like flowers growing up through the cracks. There was a table and chairs with a parasol striped in the now familiar colours. One of the table legs was shorter than the others. Someone had wedged paper under it, but it still wobbled annoyingly.

I was tempted to ask for an ice-cream but felt that it would not make me look very professional, especially as I was planning on being stern with Lina. I settled for another cup of coffee. I was drinking a lot of coffee recently and not eating so much; perhaps that was why I was feeling so jittery, I thought.

I waited for her to ask me how the case was going, so that I could say that it wasn't, as I needed a photograph. But she didn't; she just sat, waiting for me to take the lead.

'I went to look for Ruby,' I finally said, 'at the DT Watch Factory.'

'Did you find her?' asked Lina

I nearly laughed but stopped myself; that wouldn't look very professional either.

'Of course, not,' I said. 'If she was that easy to find, you could find her yourself.'

Lina looked away.

'She would also be much easier to find if I had a photograph. You said you were going to bring me one.'

'I will, I will,' said Lina. 'I have just been busy, I will...'

I was fed up with this, all of this. And I didn't just mean Lina. It was a whole lot of other people too. I could sense them stretching out in a line, stretching out back in time. It reminded me of my never-ending reflections at the Zeit building.

'What's this really about, Lina?' I asked sharply. 'What's going on? Tell me the truth.'

Lina bit her lip. 'I don't know Ruby. I've never even met her, let alone have a photograph of her.'

'What?'

'I'm sorry.'

Lina's big blue eyes filled up with tears. In that moment she reminded me of Astrid. A cold fury came over me. Then I remembered that Lina was not my friend, but a client. This was professional, not personal. As she was paying me for my time she could, up to a point, pay me to do whatever she wanted. I had to settle for asking, 'Why on earth have you been sending me on a wild goose chase?' As I said it, something pulled at the edges of my consciousness.

'Oh,' said a startled voice. 'I, I thought you were alone. I didn't notice anyone else out here.'

The voice belonged to a boy who looked to be in his late teens. He was tall and gawky with sandy hair. Lina smiled at him, and he began to blush. I deduced that he had a crush on Lina.

'I'm sorry,' he muttered, as he backed away.

I looked at Lina but this time I didn't have to prompt her. Now that she had started talking, she was eager to continue. 'The trick is to get people to start talking,' Uncle Timeon always said. 'It's like opening a jar. Once you overcome the initial resistance, it's easy.'

'Rufus knew Ruby,' Lina said.

'Rufus?'

I had to drag my mind from the past and the world of books to realise that she meant the man she was with at the party. At the memory of the party, I felt a little bit more of myself being sucked away.

'Ruby and Rufus were lovers.'

I saw the pain in her eyes. I felt sympathetic towards her again.

'And you think that he is still seeing her?' I said, gently.

'No.'

Lina sounded appalled. Rufus wouldn't do that to her. From my experience, people will do anything to anyone, particularly if they think that they can get away with it. And there definitely was a naïveté about Lina. Or maybe love turns us all into idiots. I felt the little twist inside again.

'Ruby conned Rufus.'

'What?'

Neither of them looked like they had the sort of money that would be worth conning each other for. In fact, I was beginning to wonder if Lina could really afford to pay for my services. She had only given me a deposit so far. Then again, did it matter? I wasn't doing this solely for her. I was doing it as much for myself, to keep myself occupied.

'So, Ruby conned Rufus out of some money?'

'They both conned a wealthy man out of some money and then Ruby double-crossed Rufus. But the man deserved it,' Lina added quickly. 'He wasn't a good man. He deserved it,' she repeated firmly.

That was not what I was expecting. I could almost see Uncle Timeon shaking his head. 'Of course, not,' he would say. 'You believed the fanciful story of wanting to find a lost friend. No-one pays that much money for friendship. Maybe they should, but they don't. They only pay it for more money, power, vengeance and maybe, occasionally, lust.'

'He had destroyed Rufus's family. Rufus tried to get the money back via the usual ways but couldn't. It's so unfair. It was his money; he was just getting back what was rightfully his.'

There was a high-pitched intensity to her voice. Maybe she needed to convince me because she had had to convince herself.

'Ruby was very beautiful and good at things like that.'

'Like what?'

Lina shrugged. 'Getting money out of people.'

'Why didn't Rufus come to me himself?'

She looked away again.

'Lina, does Rufus know I'm doing this?'

'He does now, I didn't tell him to begin with, but I had to do something. He was desperate; I had to help him somehow. I had a little money,' she continued. 'I had come here to find my father and had saved up for that.'

'Did you find him?'

I couldn't help thinking that Lina had lost a lot of people in her life. Then I thought of myself. I supposed I had, too.

'Sort of,' said Lina. 'He didn't want to...'

Her voice tailed off. I touched her hand. She hardly noticed.

'But I found Rufus and that is all that matters. I love him so much. You will help us, won't you, Vulpe? If you need more money, I will find a way to get it. I will do anything.'

I didn't like the sound of that. I waved my hand.

'No, no, it's fine.'

I could see Uncle Timeon shaking his head in horror. Well, he wasn't here, so what he didn't know wouldn't hurt him. And, anyway, I wasn't doing this for the money.

'This rich man – could it have been Guisse Zeit?'

I was thinking out loud rather than speaking, so when Lina said 'No,' sharply, it gave me a jolt.

'You know Guisse Zeit?' I asked in surprise.

'I have just read about him. And I visited the Zeit building when I first arrived in the City.'

Lina must have noticed something suspicious in the way I looked at her.

'I think it's pretty,' she said, defensively, 'I visited lots of places when I first came here.'

There was nothing wrong with this but still something about it did not sit right.

'So, who was the wealthy man then?'

'I can't remember.'

'Oh, for goodness' sake, Lina.'

'I can find out; I will ask Rufus tonight.'

So now the name was going to be like the photograph: something else important that I was stuck waiting for.

'You will help me, won't you?' said Lina, panic in her voice.

'You have a couple of days left from what you paid me; I'll see what I can do. But without an image of the person I'm searching for, or the name of the man they conned, I will be rather constrained,' I added, pointedly.

It was a lie. I was working for free already, but not working was even less appealing. A great lonely world stretched out ahead of me and I could not bring myself to start the process of having to come to terms with it just yet. Better to keep myself busy. I was going to have to deal with things soon, but I wasn't up for it today.

Anyway, I was curious. Despite Lina's protestations – actually, more so because of them – I couldn't help feeling that Guisse Zeit was linked to this somehow. Lina had shown that she could lie, so whatever she said had to be taken with a drop of seawater, as my granny used to say. It was definitely worth talking to Guisse Zeit tomorrow.

Chapter 24

There's nothing worse than having your hopes constantly raised and then dashed. It's like seasickness of the heart.

from *Sugar Arabesque* Dahlia Argon

I bought an ice-cream from the shop nearest the waterbus stop. I couldn't resist. I had thought it not a good look to buy one in the Jelly Fish as I was leaving. I felt it might diminish the slight authority which I had managed to achieve.

I had to wait for ages before the waitress noticed me. I took two scoops: one cherry and one hazelnut.

I spent the next few hours in the office. I felt the slightest pang on finding there was still no message from Finn. I was beginning to accept that I would never hear from him again. To take my mind off him, I concentrated on writing down everything I knew about the case and what I needed to do next. Although the day had thrown up more questions than answers, and I had committed to working for no payment, I couldn't help feeling a little satisfied. My instincts had been right about Lina not telling me the whole truth.

Somehow, the story made more sense now. Ruby made more sense. She had an elusive quality; I could never seem to fix onto her. There was something about her that was like moonlight; as soon as I tried to grasp her, she disappeared, and I was left clutching at nothing.

I was convinced that Guisse Zeit must have something to

do with it. 'Pay attention to things that keep repeating,' is what Uncle Timeon would say if he were here.

I locked up the office and walked home. I was in the street before I remembered that I hadn't watered the plant again. I really should do it as the first thing I do when I come into the office. I made a mental note to do better next time.

I had eaten hardly anything all day, except for the ice-cream, and I had drunk a lot of coffee. But I didn't feel hungry; just empty and queasy. People pushed past me in the street, rushing home or elsewhere, happy that the working day was done. I envied them. I realised that I had nowhere or no-one to rush to. I started to cry and hurriedly tried to wipe the tears away. But no-one seemed to notice. In fact, no one seemed to notice me at all.

Cassiopeia was on the phone when I opened the front door.

'...call you. Oh, here she is now.'

'It's for you,' she said, and then mouthed, 'It's a man.' Curiosity sparkled in her eyes.

I nearly laughed out loud in delight. It was true then. Some people said that in order to get something you want you have to truly let go of it. And I had let go of Finn, let go of all hope that I would ever see him again. And now he had come back to me.

'Hello,' I practically sang into the phone. 'How are you?'

'I've got something that might interest you.'

It was the tone of the voice that confused me at first. It wasn't that it sounded cold but abrasive. Like walking barefoot along a stony path. The voice was incongruous. Then I realised that it wasn't Finn.

'Who is this?'

It was the waiter from La Sardine. I could hardly speak. I was having to recalibrate myself and adjust to the fact that the surge of hope and joy that was currently flowing through me was misplaced. I had to return to where I was before, though with a renewed feeling of disappointment.

'Oh, okay.' My voice sounded hollow. 'What is it?'

'Not so fast, you will need to come to get it.'

And pay for it, I thought bitterly.

'Come to La Sardine, at three tomorrow, if you want to find out. And I mean at three. Don't come any earlier or later.'

'What if I can't?' I said, thinking of my trip to Guisse Zeit.

'Then you clearly don't want it enough.' The line went dead.

That reminded me of Finn telling me he would be at La Lumière and that he would wait for me. It was all too much. I started to cry and sank down to the floor. Cassiopeia came out into the hall. She didn't see me and nearly tripped over me.

'Oh, Vulpe!' she cried.

'I'm fine, I'm fine.'

'Who was on the phone?' she asked.

'Work,' I said, and looked the other way as I did not want to discuss it anymore.

I let her make me a cup of the restorative tea. I didn't have the strength to argue.

The next morning, I could have stayed in bed a lot longer, but I forced myself to get up. I was determined to attack the day. I put on my smart, violet-coloured dress and green shoes. Then I promptly took the shoes off again. They were just too painful. I put on my normal shoes. They didn't look nearly as good but at least I could walk in them. Anyway, I didn't imagine that Guisse Zeit would be interested in female footwear. A little voice in my head whispered that Astrid would have worn the smart shoes. Amongst the many advantages that nature had given Astrid was the ability not just to wear but to walk easily in beautiful shoes.

Cassiopeia was in the kitchen. I had the distinct feeling that she was waiting for me.

'Oh, Vulpe, are you sure that you should go to work today? Maybe you should take the day off.'

'I'm fine, I'm fine.'

She wanted to make me breakfast, but I declined. I wanted to get away as quickly as possible.

'You're so pale.' She stared at me intently.

I remembered the man in the library who told me that I was so pale that I was translucent. I reassured Cassiopeia about three times that I was well enough to go to work.

'Well, if you're sure.'

She was wrestling with something else that she wanted to say. I had a moment of apprehension, but it turned out that all she wanted was for me to take her broken watch to the new clock-maker's that was close to the office. The clock-maker was the one responsible for the cuckoo clock. As if on cue, the cuckoo started his usual argument with the grandfather clock. I threw the little packet with the watch in it into my bag and used the noise as an excuse to escape without having to have another round of reassurances that I was well enough to leave the house.

At the back of the waterbus, the two women in front of me were talking about the mermaids. For a moment, I feared there had been another murder but then, with a great sense of relief realised that they were just talking about the previous deaths.

I mentally rehearsed my plan. I would reveal to Guisse Zeit early on in our conversation, that I was not in fact a reporter for *Jolie* magazine but a private detective. Remembering Uncle Timeon's advice, I would do this confidently and then briskly move on. I had thought a lot about when exactly I should tell him. I had the feeling that Guisse Zeit might not be too happy to speak to a private detective. He most certainly would not be happy speaking to someone who wasn't really a private detective, but was merely someone who worked in a private detective's office. However, I also felt that he would be the type of man who would not deal well with being fooled, therefore it was best not to keep the deception going for too long. I would say that Ruby was a person of interest in a current investigation, and I had reason to believe that he might know her. I was very proud of the phrase 'person of interest' and pleased that I had remembered Uncle Timeon using it from time to time.

Now I knew the way, the route to the Zeit Building did not seem quite as confusing. I was familiar with what was reflection and shadow. I could tell what was real and what was not.

Inside the atrium, Glass Statue was not behind the desk. Instead, it was another girl, about my age, with a mass of dark curls. She was talking to someone whom I took for a delivery boy. The way she was leaning towards him, laughing, and waving her hands about, made me think that she was probably flirting. She did not even look in my direction.

It was a few moments before she even noticed me. She glanced at my business card, wrote my name down in a ledger, then pointed towards the same door that Glass Statue had indicated yesterday. Then she got back to the more important business of flirting.

The door led to a long corridor, of which one side was a curved glass window which looked out over the sea. The reflection of the sea flickered and danced on the opposite white wall. The glare made me squint.

The corridor took me to an area with two chairs, a selection of plants and a large painting in the modern style. It was a swirl of blues and greens with a yellow line running through it. It made me think of the sea. That's the thing about modern paintings; they can be whatever you see in them. There was something pleasant about it.

'Guisse Zeit's office?' I asked a tall man carrying a huge pile of files.

He pointed without even slowing down. I took a deep breath and walked down the next corridor. It opened into a wider area with a thick carpet. At one end was a door with Mr Guisse Zeit painted on it in gold letters. Sitting at a desk in front of this, as if she were guarding the door, was a thin, angular woman. She wore her glasses on a chain round her neck. She reminded me of Miss no-Mercy from the library. A little sign on the desk said, 'Miss Hope'. Let's hope that she's not Miss no-Hope, I thought.

I took a deep breath and walked up to Miss Hope's desk.

'I'm here to see Mr Zeit.'

'Do you have an appointment?'

'Yes,' I replied.

I didn't say the words 'of course' but I mentally added them onto the end of the sentence.

'Name?'

'From *Jolie* magazine.'

'Name?' repeated Miss Hope impatiently.

'Violetta.'

Uncle Timeon was not in favour of using false names.

'It's very hard to maintain, and you always slip up eventually,' he said.

In those situations when it was unavoidable, he suggested always using the same name. It should be similar to your own – for example, start with the same letter – and have something else memorable about it. I felt that Violetta worked. My dress was the same colour as the paper that Violetta used to wrap her flowers in. I was going to say that my second name was Storm when Miss Hope said, 'You're not in the book.'

'There must be some mistake.'

Miss Hope looked like she didn't care.

'My aunt's secretary made the appointment.' I handed over the little card that I had stolen from Astrid's house.

Miss Hope glanced at it without much interest and handed it back to me.

'You're not in the book.'

'Well, this is most inconvenient.'

Miss Hope kept her gaze level. Glass Statue had been one of the most intimidatingly impressive-looking females that I had ever seen. Yet I had made her doubt herself. But I couldn't seem to work the same magic on Miss Hope. I felt a mixture of awe and frustration. What was her secret?

'I'm here to write a piece about Mr Zeit for *Jolie* magazine,' I explained. 'A nice piece.'

I implied that I was here to do Mr Zeit a favour, and that I had power, because I could just as easily write a nasty piece. Miss Hope was unmoved.

'You're not in the book; you will have to make another appointment.'

I had the feeling that Miss Hope would happily guard Guisse Zeit until the end of time if need be. Then the door to his office opened.

Chapter 25

And he changed into something quite terrifying.

from *The Eel* HR Bond

'Miss Hope, can you – oh, and who do we have here?'

He was a tall man with a great shock of wavy, silvery grey hair. He was one of those men who seemed to fill up the room. Uncle Timeon was like that too.

'I'm from *Jolie* magazine, my aunt sent me to get an interview with you for our next edition, her secretary made an appointment but there must be a mistake for this lady is telling me there isn't one and...'

I gulped in a breath. I had spoken quickly and in one long sentence, before Miss no-Hope could get in. Guisse Zeit looked faintly amused.

'And my aunt told me that it was very important that I spoke to you today as we need to get it ready for the next print.'

I thrust the stolen business card at him.

'And if we don't?'

I tried to think of some terrible fate that would befall me if I failed in my task. It occurred to me that I should try and look upset. I didn't have to try very hard. I was perpetually close to tears these days. I could feel them, all dammed up behind my eyes, held back by the flimsiest of barriers.

Guisse Zeit looked at Miss Hope.

'The young lady isn't in the book,' she said.

He looked down at the card.

'So, you're Alicia's niece.'

I nodded. I felt uncomfortable telling such a direct lie. Since I'd started searching for Ruby, I had misled a lot of people and pretended that I was a lot of things, but this felt different. Perhaps it was because I was pretending to be a specific person and using a stolen business card as a prop. It felt worse than pretending to be a delivery person, wearing a fake uniform, and holding a clipboard. I felt myself redden.

Guisse Zeit slipped the card into his pocket. I felt a pang of disappointment as I had rather hoped that he would hand it back to me. But I had plenty more at home and I could hardly ask for it back. I had a slight feeling of anxiety that it might come back to haunt me.

'Well,' said Guisse Zeit, 'I couldn't possibly let down Alicia or all the lady readers of *Jolie* magazine for that matter. I'm sure I can give...'

He raised his eyebrows.

'Vulp –' I stopped myself just in time and changed to Violetta but it came out as Vulpietta. Uncle Timeon was right. This false name thing was harder than you might imagine.

Thankfully, Miss Hope did not seem to notice.

'Violetta,' I corrected.

'I'm sure I can give Violetta a few minutes of my time.'

'But she isn't in the book.'

Guisse Zeit smiled and beckoned me to his inner sanctum.

I couldn't resist giving Miss Hope a small smile of triumph. She regarded me impassively. I noted her writing something. No doubt adjusting the book, as if it were some holy document.

Guisse Zeit's office was huge. The walls, carpet and chairs were all a tasteful cream. One entire wall was a window that looked directly out to sea. It gave me the sensation that I was on a ship. Despite the fact that it was a very calm day, I felt a little seasick.

He invited me to sit in one of the cream armchairs. Their backs were shaped to represent clam shells. They looked like ordinary chairs but something about the proportions was off. They were slightly bigger than normal chairs. This had the effect of making me feel smaller and suddenly intimidated. For the first time since I started this, I wondered if I might be out of my depth.

'So, what would the readers of *Jolie* magazine like to know?'

A wave of panic swept over me. Gone was my 'I'll just walk in there and tell him I'm a private investigator' swagger. My mind went blank. I felt like I was being swallowed up by a giant clam.

'Don't you have a notebook?' Guisse Zeit asked.

I started fumbling around in my bag. I don't think that this made him suspicious. It just made him think that I was not very good and had probably been given the job by my aunt as a favour to my father. I was constructing this fictional scenario in my head when I sensed his impatience. He was a busy man after all. I glanced down at my notebook and my eye fell on some of the 'research' that I had written there earlier.

'Do you believe in being a firm but fair boss?' I squeaked.

Guisse Zeit smiled and began to hold forth. I pretended to take notes. I doubted that he read *Jolie* magazine, so he would not be looking out for the article. I had an overwhelming urge to abandon the whole thing. I would ask him just a few more questions and then go.

But something stopped me. Something pressed me to ask the man what I had come to ask him. It wasn't loyalty to Lina. She had lied to me and was, perhaps, still lying to me. No; it was the idea that if I didn't, I would have failed somehow. And I knew that if this happened, then that would be it. The case would dry up. Those long, empty days would lap around me like the sea outside the window. The loneliness scared me more than Guisse Zeit. He finished droning on about enlightened company practices.

'So,' I said, 'do you know a Miss Ruby Alleck?'

Guisse Zeit had been wearing his professional face as he told me about his views on firmness and fairness. It radiated calmness and benevolence and remained in place after he had finished talking. No doubt he expected the next question to be about something like women in the workplace.

I could almost see the wheels and cogs of his brain whirr into life as he began to register what I had said. A frown passed across his face like a cloud across the sun. For a moment, the facade started to crumble before righting itself.

'I beg your pardon?'

'Ruby Alleck. I believe you may be acquainted with her?'

Guisse Zeit crashed both his fists on the table and leapt to his feet. He was red in the face.

'Who are you, who are you?' he roared. 'You don't work for *Jolie* magazine! What rag do you work for?'

I felt a flash of pride that he thought I was a proper journalist. He smashed his fist on the desk again. He seemed to grow larger as he loomed over me.

'Get out, get out!' He rang a small bell on this desk. 'Miss Hope?' he bellowed, and she appeared almost instantly. She silently observed the scene. I could almost see the sentence 'I told you so, she wasn't in the book' form in her head. I had to hand it to her; she showed remarkable restraint in not saying it.

'Get this person out of here immediately!' he thundered.

Without a word, Miss Hope grabbed me roughly by the arm, pulled me to my feet and marched me out of the room.

Chapter 26

Don't choose your shoes to make an entrance; choose them to ensure that you can make a speedy exit.

from *The Secret Code of Womanhood* Roxie de Light

Outside the office stood two large men in uniforms. Guisse Zeit had seemed huge, and his presence had filled the room. Part of that was due to his authority. These men were absolutely huge and filled the room with themselves. And there were two of them.

'Problem?' asked one.

Miss Hope pushed me towards him. He took my arm, albeit more gently than Miss Hope.

'Come along, then,' he said. 'No need to make a fuss.'

I found that totally unnecessary as I was not making a fuss. I also had enough sense not to point that out. As he marched me briskly from the office, flanked by the other guard, I stumbled. Miss Hope caught my eye, and gave me a small smile of triumph.

We did not go out the way I had come in. Suddenly I felt embarrassed, humiliated even. Thinking of Ruby, I asked, 'So do you remove young ladies from Guisse Zeit's office often, then?'

Silence.

'Is this a regular occurrence?'

We came to a door. The other guard unlocked it. The guard who had my arm gave me a little shove on my back. There was one step and I tripped and fell out of the building. As I lay, sprawled on the ground, I heard the sound of the door locking behind me.

I was too shocked to move. Gradually, I realised that I could not lie here forever. One of my shoes had come off and I scrambled to retrieve it.

I was at the back or at the side of the Zeit building. The front had been like a vast expanse of wide-open beach made of glass. Round here was all glass blocks of differing shapes and sizes, all stacked on top of each other before disappearing abruptly into the sea. They were like jagged rocks, on the very edge of things, where the land stops and the sea begins.

I had torn a hole in my stocking and cut my knee. I hadn't grazed my knees since childhood. The thin film that had been holding back my tears broke. I cried in great, noisy, gulpy sobs that made my nose run. I wasn't crying about being thrown out of Guisse Zeit's office. I was crying over everything, all my losses: Finn and Astrid; my hopes and dreams; the life I had wanted to lead. I had tried to make the most of the life that I had been forced to settle for and now I had failed at that, too. My tears ran over the glass rocks and into the sea. The sound of my crying mixed with the cry of the gulls and the slapping of the waves.

Finally, I got up. I needed to find my way back. The glass rocks were slippery and not easy to walk on. I was very relieved that I had not worn my good shoes. They might have looked better, but they would have been impossible out here. And, as I had predicted, Guisse Zeit had not been in the slightest bit interested in my footwear.

I clambered across the glass until I came to a corner. I rounded it hoping that it would take me to the front of the building. Instead, it led to a small promontory jutting out into the sea and the pathway curved back again. At this point it was only a narrow ledge. I slipped and nearly fell but just managed to keep my balance. Eventually the path entered a tunnel of glass.

One side was the building and the other the glass rocks. It was very disorientating and, being hot and tearful further confused things.

I was sure that I could hear voices. The front of the building must be close, I reassured myself. I became aware of reflections of figures flickering around me.

Then I started, for I was sure that I could see Lina amongst them. I watched her reflection dancing amongst the others. Suddenly, I was sure that I saw Finn. I blinked to get rid of the tears and squinted close to the image. It reminded me of the night that I had met him in La Lumière and watched his reflection in the big mirror. I reached out my hand to touch him. But even as I did the image seemed to flicker and die.

I turned a sharp corner and came out in the middle of the glass walkway that led to the front which was busy with people. I scanned them for Finn or Lina but neither was evident. I stood still, not going one way or another, torn as to what to do next.

Probably I had imagined them. I was just seeing illusions. It would be a wild goose chase. I just wanted to get away from the Zeit building. I'd had enough of it for one day. Actually, I had had enough of it for a lifetime. A waterbus was approaching the stop and I walked briskly towards it, breaking into a run – well as much of a run as I could manage – as it drew close to the pier.

I took up my favourite position, feeling utterly defeated. Thinking that I had seen Finn had shaken me and I found myself once again full of desperate longing and rejection. I had tried to fill my days, but the place that I had created to hide in – the search for Ruby – had utterly failed me. The game was up now. I was as useless at private detecting as I was at everything else. I had spent my whole life deluding myself: that I could draw, that Astrid was my friend and that people loved me. And now this: I had nursed the delusion that I could be a private detective.

I had believed that if I could get in to see Guisse Zeit, he would tell me something useful. I had come away with nothing. Uncle Timeon popped into my head. He said that people are always telling you things: sometimes not directly, with their words, but with their actions and with what they leave unsaid. They tell you with their pauses and hesitations. Often, he said, we miss this as we don't pay close enough attention or, sometimes, we just don't want to hear what they are saying. He had told me this around the time my previous lover had left me for Astrid.

I had ignored him because the very idea had made me uncomfortable. I was worried that I had been told a lot of things that I didn't want to hear. That my former lover had been telling me that he did not feel the same about me as I felt about him. Or that he did not take our relationship as seriously. I had not wanted to hear any of that. But now it occurred to me that what Uncle Timeon had said had some truth in it. And, in the light of that, Guisse Zeit had actually told me quite a lot.

His reaction had been extreme, to say the least. Moreover, he did not question who I was or accuse me of lying. He assumed that I was a journalist from a newspaper. And, let's be honest, I didn't think my acting had been that convincing. So why had he believed me?

He was behaving like a man with a guilty secret. But what? And what did it have to do with Ruby? According to Lina, Ruby had double-crossed Rufus. Had she also double-crossed Guisse Zeit? That seemed preposterous.

If she had, why hadn't he just gone to the police? I'm sure they would have bent over backwards to help a man like him. Perhaps he and Ruby had been up to something illegal together? That seemed unlikely. Maybe Guisse Zeit did not have as much money as he pretended. I was always reading about wealthy men going bankrupt. Or maybe he had got Ruby to spy on his competitors for him. But that did not sound very plausible either.

There was something else about the way Guisse Zeit had behaved. There had been something else there, behind his rage. Then I got it: fear. Guisse Zeit had been afraid.

Of course, I had been blind. Ruby was beautiful; they could have been lovers. That was so much more likely than that they had been working together. They were lovers and he thought that I was going to publish a piece about it in the papers. That must be it.

Uncle Timeon popped into my head again. 'It's always a temptation to settle for your first theory,' he would say, 'because you like it. But does it really fit?' Wealthy men have affairs all the time. Would Guisse Zeit really have behaved like that, in front of a journalist, if he was having an affair? Surely, he would have denied everything and got his lawyers to sort it out. If I was a real journalist, he had just given me an even better story.

Then it hit me. Ruby was blackmailing Guisse Zeit. That made more sense. That must have been how Ruby and Rufus got the money in the first place. They hadn't conned someone; they had blackmailed him. There was one flaw: Lina was adamant that it had not been Guisse Zeit, but I still had no reason to trust her.

Even though I had never met Ruby and knew virtually nothing about her, not even what she looked like, I felt that I understood her. Blackmail was exactly the sort of thing that she would do.

Chapter 27

Be suspicious of people who act suspiciously.

from *The Private Investigator's Handbook* Jeremy Shard

I wondered what to do next. I had originally planned to go home and change, but I was loath to risk seeing Cassiopeia. Anyway, the need to change was no longer as urgent due to my shoe choice. Also, my good dress had lost all its crispness after being thrown out of the Zeit building and scrambling over the glass rocks. Trying to keep it 'good' seemed like a lost cause. I hoped no-one would notice the hole in my stockings or my grazed knee.

The waiter from La Sardine had told me to come today after the lunchtime service. He would want money for whatever he told me, and I was low on funds. I had hoped that Guisse Zeit would tell me something and I wouldn't need the waiter. Obviously, now I did.

It was too early to go directly to La Sardine when I got off the waterbus. I remembered the ice-cream shop that I had gone to before. I was suddenly hungry and realised that I hadn't had breakfast. Nor had I eaten much yesterday or the day before.

Two people pushed in front of me and the staff didn't even seem to care. All the aches and pains of the morning began to throb. When I was finally served, I took my ice cream outside and ate it under the shade of a large tree until the day had settled into the afternoon and I could visit La Sardine. Gone was the soft light and hope of the morning. And we were still a long way off from the twinkling darkness and mystery of the night. It was all harsh, bright light as I waited for one thing to change into another. I hate afternoons. There are morning people and night owls, but no-one ever talks about afternoon people.

I opened the gate to La Sardine's courtyard. The waiter was sitting on the same rock as before, smoking. This time he was watching the entrance. I had the feeling that he was waiting for me. He seemed jumpy and ill-at-ease.

I could hear the sound of people inside La Sardine. Perhaps he was scared that his boss was about to appear and tell him to get back to work.

'Well,' I said, when I got close enough to speak.

'I've got something for you.'

'What?' I asked.

He held out his hand.

'Come on, I'm not going to just hand over money, I need to have some idea of what I'm paying for.'

'A sighting of Ruby.'

'When?'

I commended myself. At the beginning of all of this I would have settled for 'a sighting of Ruby' and passed over the money, only to discover that it was last year and somewhere that had now closed down.

'Recently.'

I handed him a note.

He kept his hand out.

'Actually, the last two nights.'

I still had a lot to learn, I thought, as I handed him another note.

'At Frutti di Mer.'

Hmm. I was more inclined to believe him now. Frutti di Mer

was close to La Sardine and patrons could move easily from one to the other. It opened at around eleven and didn't shut until the sun came up or the last customers had gone home. It was built practically on the beach and in the style of a traditional fisherman's cottage. It was very exclusive.

'Was she with Guisse Zeit?' I asked.

The waiter shrugged. I was surprised that he hadn't asked for more money. Maybe he thought that he had taken enough from me, already.

'And I have something else,' he added, 'but this will cost you.'

Or maybe not.

'What is it?'

'A photograph of Ruby – and someone else.'

'Can I see it?' I asked.

He threw back his head and laughed.

'You can see it as much as you like when you buy it.'

'How much?'

He named a figure, and I shook my head.

This was less about a hard negotiation and more because he had named a price that I just didn't have. I was running out of money. I had used all the petty cash and some of the money that Lina had given me. The initial sum was supposed to cover some costs, but you still wanted to make some kind of profit.

A door opened and closed.

'Okay, how much do you have?' he said.

I told him.

'Fine, give me that.'

I kicked myself for telling the truth. How could I have been so stupid? But he had developed a sense of urgency which was catching. I handed him a fistful of notes. I did not give him the full amount, hoping that he wouldn't bother to count it. To my surprise, that worked. He stuffed the notes into his pocket and handed me an envelope. Then he jumped to his feet to terminate the meeting. I was about to take the photograph out to check it when he snapped.

'It's her all right,' he said. 'Now you've got to leave.'

I was about to argue, but I didn't particularly want to spend any more time with him.

He watched me leave. Something about his posture reminded me of a runner waiting to start a race.

I was impatient to get on the waterbus and examine the photograph of Ruby. I made my way to the back and got comfortable. As I reached into my bag, something fluttered out: the card Cassiopeia had put in with the watch she had wanted me to take for repairs. She had written the address on it. It was in the same street as the office. I had never noticed a watch-maker there before. Being observant is one of the most valuable traits for a private investigator, Uncle Timeon often said. Actually, my art teacher used to say the same thing. About being a painter, not a private investigator, obviously. Then I saw that Cassiopeia had written 'above du Trims barbers' under the address. I suppressed a shudder. I shoved the card back into my bag and the promise to take the watch in for repairs to the back of my mind.

I examined the photograph. Ruby was being helped into a long, slinky coat by someone unseen. She had turned to face the camera and was smiling. The waiter had been very cagey about how he had got it. He had adopted a take-it-or-leave-it approach. He had reassured me that it was recent. Though why I should trust him was anyone's guess.

Ruby's long hair was loose and fell down her back in waves. She had a different kind of beauty from Astrid. She was much sexier and more seductive looking. She had that quality that meant it would be difficult not to look at her. The picture was in black and white, but I imagined it in colour. I could see the red of her hair and the green of the eyes. I imagined her lit up by an invisible light from within.

She was talking to a man. He was half in the shadows, but I recognised him. It was Guisse Zeit.

Chapter 28

Anyone can become a ghost, but some people are more susceptible than others.

from *The Evolution of Ghosts, Birds and Humans*
Sister Assumpta, Abbess of the Burning Heart Convent

I spent the remainder of the afternoon in the office. I wrote down everything that had happened and everything I needed to do next. I should visit Frutti di Mer and also go and see Lina and show her the photograph. The fact that I had acquired a solid thing made me feel like I had discovered something. I needed to talk to Lina about what she wanted me to do now. And, more importantly, the burning question of money – or the lack of it. I realised that the time was growing ever closer when I would have to make a choice. I really didn't want to think about it.

As I passed du Trims, I remembered Cassiopeia's watch. I took one look at the great glass display of rotating blades and had an even more visceral reaction than usual. I was overwhelmed by queasiness. It has been a long day, I thought; a long and, at times, unpleasant day. The watch could wait.

As I was about enter the house, I remembered my dishevelled appearance. I really did not want Cassiopeia to see me like this. It would no doubt prompt lots of questions. I decided to sneak in, creep upstairs, change and come down again. I would wait for the cuckoo clock and grandfather clock to create their usual racket and go in under the cover of that.

I stood with my ear against the letterbox. I suddenly had an image of Cassiopeia opening the door. I was just trying to think of a reasonable explanation when I heard the familiar click that the grandfather clock makes just before it starts to chime.

When the clocks interrupt a conversation, they seem to go on for ever. Now that I had actually found a use for their din, it didn't seem to last nearly so long. I had just reached the top of the stairs when they fell silent and I heard Cassiopeia's voice float up from the drawing room.

'I'm worried about her. Maybe we should contact him?'

'Contact Timeon?' came the reply. 'Whatever for?'

To my horror, I realised that it was my mother.

I felt dizzy and clung onto the banisters.

'I'm worried about her,' said Cassiopeia again.

'Worry, worry,' exploded my mother. 'I know all about worry. I worry about her every single day, every single day since that first day, when I held her in my arms for the first time and she looked up at me. I worry about her all the time. That's what being a mother is all about.'

Her voice was like a cutting edge.

'And since this working-as-a-private-detective nonsense and moving-out-of-home-to-live-here nonsense, I've worried about her more and more and now – now! – you want us to try and hunt down that reprobate Timeon. What good will that do?'

'She is getting paler and paler,' said Cassiopeia.

'Not eating enough or not enough of the right sort of food and staying out too late,' was my mother's predictable response.

'No, I think that she's disappearing.'

'Of course, she's disappearing; young ladies are always disappearing these days. That's what young ladies do now, especially young ladies living in places without enough rules. They stay out late, stay out all night and get up to all sorts. And all sorts can happen when you don't come home and sleep in your own bed.'

I was quaking. I could almost imagine my mother looking straight at me, sensing that I was there.

'And I'm sure you know exactly what I mean by that; you don't need me to spell it out,' she continued.

'No,' said Cassiopeia. 'She's vanishing. I'm scared that she's turn–'

At this point my mother sneezed and I missed what she said. No doubt my mother would blame it on Cassiopeia not dusting enough or not dusting in the right way or having the wrong sort of feathers in her cushions.

'That's why we need to call Timeon; he may have experience in this sort of matter.'

'Nonsense,' interrupted my mother. 'Fanciful nonsense.'

'I just think we should get Timeon.'

'Of course you do,' replied my mother, with a humourless little laugh.

'I've seen this before in the village where I grew up,' said Cassiopeia. 'It happened to a girl there, a girl like Vulpe, who was very sensitive.'

'Highly strung,' said my mother.

'Creative.'

'Over-imaginative,' said my mother.

'She was like Vulpe and had had her heart broken.'

My mother snorted; she did not believe in broken hearts. My mother believed in getting on with things. Anything else was wallowing.

'That's what made her vulnerable,' continued Cassiopeia. 'She allowed herself to be overwhelmed by love and longing – so her substance was easily swept away or subsumed by him.'

Oh my God, Cassiopeia knew that I had let Finn stay the night whilst she was away and now she was throwing me out.

'Well, you'd know all about being overwhelmed by love and longing,' said my mother.

'The girl in my village looked the way Vulpe looks – bright-eyed and feverish – but each day there was less and less of her; she became increasingly insubstantial. And that is what is happening to Vulpe. In the end, her parents had to take her far into the woods to a wise woman. She burned sage and wild herbs and chanted over her and called her back to herself. That's why we need Timeon. He will know what to do.'

My heart was racing, and my palms were sweating. I did not like the sound of this one bit.

'Enough!' shouted my mother. 'I have had enough of all this nonsense. I can't comment on what happens in the north with all its superstitions and other foolishness. People cursing cows and witches souring the milk. But things like that do not happen in the City. We are a bright, modern place, free of all that ancient nonsense. People don't grow horns or wings; succubi don't come down chimneys and a fine silver mist no longer rolls off the sea and steals away golden-haired children.'

She was shouting. 'And Vulpe is not turning into a ghost.'

I clutched the banisters in shock. For once, I was in full agreement with my mother.

I thought that I heard one of them move towards the door. Maybe I did, maybe I imagined it. But it spooked me. I scurried up to my bedroom.

What on earth was Cassiopeia talking about? Could she really think that I was turning into a ghost? What did that even mean? Could living people turn into ghosts? Or did Cassiopeia think that I had died?

I was overwhelmed with a dizzying panic. For a moment, reality slipped and slid around me. It seemed a lot less substantial than it normally did. What if I had died and not realised it? My breath came faster. 'Stop it!' I pinched my arm hard. It hurt but that felt like a relief. I wasn't dead. I almost laughed that I was having to reassure myself of that. It was like one of those ridiculous philosophical conversations you sometimes have with friends.

I could imagine, once upon a time, live people turning into ghosts here. That wouldn't surprise me. Nothing would surprise me about the City. But that was in the past, in the magical days when it was the dark City and full of fantastical things.

But now we lived in the City of Light. A city of steel and glass. I thought of the Zeit Building. You couldn't get any more modern than that. There was no magic hovering around there. The whole thing was nonsense.

My mother might think what Cassiopeia was saying was ridiculous, but that wouldn't stop her taking me home. In fact, it would encourage her. 'Obviously I had to remove you from that madhouse as quickly as possible,' I could just hear her saying. Pointing out that I had a job wouldn't help. My mother didn't really believe in my job, and she would remind me that Timeon was away. And if I told her what I was up to, that would horrify her even more. I imagine that she would not be happy to hear that I was going around pretending to be people that I wasn't – in other words, lying – and getting thrown out of places.

But could she force me? I was an adult after all, not a little girl. I would be very firm and refuse.

The relief was short-lived. That would work if Cassiopeia was happy for me to stay here but she wasn't. She obviously wanted me to leave. That is why she had called my mother.

I needed to get out of the house and away from them. I shoved a few items of clothing and underwear into a bag. As soon as the clocks started again, I slipped down the stairs and out of the door.

I went to the office. It occurred to me that, if I didn't arrive home, my mother and Cassiopeia might come here looking for me. But I often didn't go home until late and so I felt that I had plenty of time yet before they started searching for me. I changed out of my good dress. I feared it no longer deserved that title. It looked like a limp rag when I hung it over the back of a chair. I comforted myself with the thought that I didn't really have any occasion approaching where I needed to look smart.

There was a first aid box in the office. It was just a tin with some plasters and a bottle of liquid that stung when applied to cuts or grazes. I put a plaster on my knee but avoided the liquid. I had had enough stinging experiences for one day.

I had to convince Cassiopeia that I wasn't a ghost. The whole thing was ludicrous. I had no idea what had come over her. Coming from the north, she is a bit superstitious at times, but I had never seen her behave like this before.

People from the City are superstitious too, of course, but not like that. They just take lots of precautions to avoid bad luck and acquire good luck. Somehow that seems typical of people in the City. Our superstition is a transactional kind of superstition, based on pleasing, appeasing, and not annoying in order to get what you wanted.

But we don't go around accusing people of being ghosts. The whole thing was just absurd. I had no idea even where to begin dealing with it. So, I decided that I wouldn't; well, at least not at the end of such a long and trying day. Instead, I would focus on finding Ruby. If I could find Ruby, then things would be better. If I succeeded at something, then everyone would accept that I was all right and stop all this ghost nonsense. Suddenly I was angry at the injustice of it all.

I was hurt as I had always believed that Cassiopeia was on my side. I had believed that she was my friend. Also, if they told Timeon, he would certainly stop me, if only because I wasn't getting paid. I couldn't tell them what I was doing as they wouldn't let me do it. They would rob me of my chance to succeed. And I needed to succeed to prove to them that I was okay.

Suddenly I thought of Finn. But this time I felt very angry with him. He had robbed me of a chance too. He had disappeared and robbed me of my chance of love. He hadn't even given me any explanation or any way of making things right.

I thought of art college. They hadn't given me a chance. They hadn't let me prove myself either. They had just told me that I wasn't good enough.

I was angry with them all. I was trapped.

Well, I would find Ruby and prove them all wrong. I would go to Frutti di Mer that night and look for her. Let's face it, I had nowhere else to go.

Chapter 29

Not everything you read in books is true but quite a lot of it is.

from *The Cod that Swallowed a Diamond* Freddie Fortune

Before I left, I took out the secret petty cash box. This was different from the petty cash box which was now empty. This was another petty cash box that Uncle Timeon had stashed away for emergencies. He didn't know that I knew where it was. So, it was a tiny source of triumph to me that I had discovered it. I had come into the office one day and thought that he was looking strange. He was standing near the bookcase by the window. Later, I realised that what he was looking was shifty.

The next time he was out, I found the box, hidden behind a loose brick. Uncle Timeon wasn't always quite as clever as he believed himself to be. And maybe I wasn't as bad a detective as I had thought myself to be. I felt guilty, though, as I took out a handful of notes: so guilty that I put some of them back. I had now reached the stage that I was having to steal money in order to continue looking for Ruby. I told myself that the money was only a precaution, to be used in absolute emergencies. I would return what I didn't spend and pay back what I did.

I was glad to have a reason to go to Frutti di Mer. It was for the type of people for whom the night was always young: people who didn't have to get up for work the next morning. I thought of how the night City came alive as the day City went to sleep. Finn and I had been residents of the night City. Now I felt as if I had been expelled from that place. I wondered if Finn was still there. Walking home in the darkness, hand in hand with someone else. I forced myself to stop thinking about him. The problem was that Frutti di Mer did not open until late. I had a lot of time to kill.

I watched the City go by. I wasn't going anywhere. One of the waterbus routes did a long loop round the City. Sometimes visitors just sat on it to see the view. I decided that I could stay on it for a few loops. I was worried that Cassiopeia and my mother would try and find me at the office. This was much safer.

I huddled in my seat. I didn't feel as if I was entirely there. I watched the people get on and off. Families with young children. Little girls with bows in their hair clutching stuffed rabbits or teddies. Groups of friends laughing. Young ladies who would slip off their uncomfortable shoes and flex their feet for a few minutes. Couples holding hands. Or other couples, for whom the tiniest touch – the brushing together of their arms or the back of their hands – was enough to demonstrate a flicker of intimacy that illuminated them from the inside out for a few seconds before fading, like the striking of a match. How I envied them.

The waterbus finished its second loop. I sank even further into my seat in case someone told me to get off. But no-one seemed to notice me. I felt cold and stiff, which surprised me as I thought that the evening was going to be hot and sticky. My fellow travellers thought so too as they had taken off their jackets and were wiping sweat from their faces.

The stop after the next one was close to Frutti di Mer. I would get off there and have a look around.

Frutti di Mer was all closed up and shrouded in darkness. It was hard to believe that in an hour or so it would be alive with music, dancing, and people talking. I could sense people moving around inside, preparing the magic and razzle dazzle.

Nearby was the Gaslight Café, a small place, full of the hiss from the coffee machine and the tempting smell of fried food. My stomach gave a little growl, and I realised that I felt hungry for the first time in a long time. I ordered a sausage and bread to go with my coffee.

The Gaslight was half-full or was it half-empty? Was it a day place winding down or a night place winding up? A couple sat looking intently at each other, their fingers touching across the table. He said something and she smiled and looked lit up like an angel in an old-fashioned painting. She gazed at him with absolute devotion. He smiled back, but I thought I saw him look over her shoulder at the waitress bringing my coffee.

I looked for some loose change; I really wanted to avoid using the stolen petty cash money. I had to empty my bag and, in doing so, pulled out the Dr Dorridorri book that I had taken from the library, in spite of the strict prohibition. I imagined the look of horror that Miss no-Mercy would have if she knew that I was exposing it to coffee and grease stains. She may have despised the content, but I suspected that she believed that all books, especially her library books, should be treated with reverence.

I remembered that there had been something in it about people turning into ghosts. I looked at the book fearfully. Maybe I didn't want to know. This was ridiculous, I thought; fanciful nonsense. I opened the book to find the place. But I did wipe my hands with a napkin first.

'...The City was full of ghosts at the time, as there had recently been many deaths from plague. Ghosts are spirits who struggle to let go.' That seemed obvious to me, but there was also a theory that ghosts could turn the living into ghosts too. Often, they could do this without the living person realising. In most cases, the living person was unaware that they had even met a ghost.

There was something about the atmosphere in City which meant that ghosts found it easy to appear solid. It may have been to do with the density of the darkness; the air of the City was closer to that of the density of ghosts than most places. This also meant that ghosts flocked to the City like migrating birds in winter; another reason why the City had so many of them.

This phenomenon seemed to remain, even after glass came to the City and it became the City of Light. Some said that darkness had woven itself into the fabric of the City and could never be removed. Others that the City never forgot, that it clung onto the memory of the darkness and the memories of itself, just like the ghosts clung onto the memory of their life and it was this that connected them. Each made the other more real.

The belief was that ghosts sucked the life-force out of people they believed would complete them, and this was how the living could end up as ghosts. Some theories even suggested that certain kinds of people were also drawn to ghosts. These were often people who felt incomplete themselves and were searching for completion. Apparently, they could almost manifest ghosts or make it more likely that the ghost would manifest in solid form.

The book ended with a quotation from *Ghosts – Parasites or Epiphytes?* by Sister Assumpta. She described being turned into a ghost as 'a condition that most return from, but a few do not.' She also said, 'But, perhaps, it is beneficial to have an encounter with a ghost in this life as it is a warning for what may befall you in the next one if you do not change your ways or thoughts or behaviours.' I closed the book sharply. A tiny seed of panic took hold. I thought of the line 'a condition that most return from, but a few do not.'

I would have to summon up the courage to read *Parasites or Epiphytes?*

I regarded the closed book in front of me. I was almost scared of it. This was ridiculous, I thought. 'But Cassiopeia thinks that you're a ghost,' a little voice whispered.

Another thought crept into my head: If I'm a ghost, then Finn must have been a ghost too. He's the most likely person to have turned me into a ghost.

I am not a ghost, I told myself firmly. But I will go and read Sister Assumpta just to be certain. And Finn wasn't a ghost either. I remembered how his hand had felt in mine that night as we walked home. How safe he had felt. Despite everything, I smiled at the memory. And I indulged myself in pretending that he was still around, that I was going to meet him now instead of trying to sneak into Frutti di Mer for the most tenuous of reasons. In the few moments that I imagined it, I felt happy again and then I remembered that it wasn't true and went back to feeling sad.

Chapter 30

Everything happens for a reason. It's just sometimes it's not the reason you want.

from *Ways to be Rebellious* Kathy Redditch

Frutti di Mer was still closed but I could see light from inside. The entrance had a green canopy with Frutti di Mer written in gold lettering. A doorman appeared carrying a large plant in a pot which he placed outside. Of course, there would be a doorman. I hadn't really thought this through. There was no way that I was going to get past a doorman: I was nowhere near rich or beautiful enough. No amount of Uncle Timeon swagger would suffice.

I walked round the back. Here was another door, with a small window. That would be worth a try but probably best to wait until it was busier. I carried on to the side closest to the sea. The air smelled of seaweed and I could hear the slap of the waves against the rocks. There was another door here. I was just wondering what it was for when it opened, and a girl emerged carrying a stack of empty boxes. She completely ignored me. Maybe it's because I'm a ghost, I thought. I tried to make it a jokey thought, but even so I felt a chill. Or maybe she ignored me because the boxes were obscuring her vision.

Then I had a crazy idea. If I was turning into a ghost, I should be able to walk in and no-one would notice. So that's what I did. But I added a little touch of swagger just in case.

I strode along the corridor. I didn't encounter many people and those that I did paid me no attention.

The main room of the club was long with a low ceiling. It was painted in black with splashes of dark green. It reminded me of being inside a cave. In one corner was a bar with a couple of barmen checking the bottles and glasses. Next to it was a platform where a jazz band was setting up. A row of raised booths ran round the perimeter of the room. The seats were covered in dark green velvet. There were more tables and chairs and a dance floor. Dance floors always look much smaller when you see them empty. It's like a magic trick, how many people you can squash onto one.

Frutti di Mer looked like any other nightclub. I suppose it was the people that made it exclusive, not the club itself. Outside the main room was the cloakroom. Two girls threaded paper tickets onto hangers. Beside this was the ladies' bathroom. I slipped in and locked myself in one of the cubicles. I could stay here, I thought, and then emerge when the place gets busy.

I felt trapped for what seemed like forever. I was stiff and sore. It still sounded quiet outside, but I could stand it no longer. I tiptoed out. The band was playing to an almost empty room. I crept back into the bathroom. I would wait until it got busy.

I stayed there until I could tell that the place was definitely beginning to fill up. I could hear conversations punctuated by the occasional laugh or shriek of excitement. I could sense the atmosphere building up and breaking like waves on a shore.

The door opened, and I heard the voices of two young women. Although I could not see them, I knew that they were fixing their make-up. One asked the other how she looked. The other told her that she looked lovely. The first girl disagreed and then listed all the reasons why she didn't. Then the second voice asked the first how she looked, and they repeated the process. Then they mentioned the names of certain men and wondered would they be there that evening. And if they were, how they could get them to notice them. It was the same conversation that happened in every bathroom of every nightclub that I had ever been into. The same conversation I had used to have with my friends. I would have imagined that because Frutti di Mer was filled with the very rich and the very beautiful they would not have to have these conversations.

Then again, I had had the same conversations with Astrid, and she was rich and beautiful. I suppose that I never believed that she really needed to have those conversations, that she just had them because everyone else had them. I never believed that her insecurity could be the same as mine. I thought that she said those things to make me feel better. I had never really believed that Astrid could possibly doubt herself.

I heard the door opening – the sound of outside rushing in – and then the door shutting. A few moments later I walked out myself. I glanced at myself in the mirror. I was very pale and unkempt. I searched in my bag and found my lipstick. I wondered what the reaction of the two girls from earlier would be if I asked them how I looked.

I walked out of the toilets trying to look confident in a way that I did not feel. The main room was now about three quarters full. There was a queue of people at the bar and others clustered round the tables. The band was in full swing, and the dance floor was a writhing, shimmering mass of moving bodies. I felt a pang of regret that I was here, like this. Underdressed and snooping around. I would much rather be drinking cocktails and dancing, sitting in one of the booths, holding hands. I shook Finn from my head. I had work to do.

I had decided on just walking round and trying to spot Ruby.

I couldn't pretend to be a customer. I certainly wasn't dressed correctly. I had thought about pretending to be a member of staff but the waitresses were also dressed up, in sparkly, slinky outfits.

Yet again, I had the idea that if I was turning into a ghost people wouldn't see me. Thinking about it, it might actually be advantageous to a private detective to be a ghost. It was all nonsense and yet I was beginning to incorporate the idea that I was becoming ghostly into my plans.

As I made my way around the room, it occurred to me that I might be able to acquire invisibility without actually becoming a ghost. How many other times in my life had I felt under-dressed and invisible? How many times had I been out with Astrid and felt that I almost disappeared when I was beside her? It was really just the same in here. Why would I be noticeable amongst all these fabulous, shiny creatures? I was like a sparrow amongst tropical birds.

I decided that if I did see Ruby, I would keep her under surveillance until I had a good chance to catch her on her own – say, if she went to the bathroom. If that didn't happen, then I might try to follow her when she left. Or if the worst came to the worst, I would question the staff about her. If I had to do that, I would just tell them the truth – that I was a private investigator. Well, obviously, not the whole truth. There was no need to be that truthful.

No-one paid the slightest attention to me. In many situations this would have been upsetting, but now it was a bonus. Everyone was too absorbed with their own night. I decided to risk getting a drink. Frutti di Mer was famous for its cocktails. It seemed a shame to miss the opportunity, even if I was going to have to pay with the secret petty cash money. I felt a wave of guilt.

Waitresses brought drinks to the table but there was a little bar in the corner. If I really was a ghost, I could just float to the front of the queue, I thought, and help myself; no one would notice. But can ghosts drink? Finn had drunk; I saw him. Stop this, I told myself firmly. You are not a ghost, and neither is Finn.

I got myself a sour cherry cocktail. The barman paid me no attention whilst I ordered. My drink was black until the light caught it and it glowed a dark crimson. It was very good but very expensive.

Frutti di Mer was full now. The air was thick, and condensation ran down the walls. Everyone was pressed, almost melded, together, like a myriad different coloured candles all running into one. I had to jab a few people sharply in the ribs to get past, but they hardly seemed to notice. The dance floor was a mass of writhing bodies. The music was fast and frenetic. I was amazed that anyone could find the space to move, let alone dance. But each couple did, oblivious to everyone else around them. And as the music got faster, more and more pushed their way on.

I looked across the crowd. This is crazy, I thought; I will never find Ruby in here. I should call it a night. But I was reluctant. Now that I had got here, part of me was determined to hang on to the bitter end. Also, I was disinclined to leave as I was scared to go back to Cassiopeia's house. I imagined her waiting up to tell me that she was sending me back to live with my mother.

My feet were sore. I wondered if the Gaslight Café was still open. I should have checked. It had the feel of a place that stayed open to serve a late-night snack or very early breakfast to revellers. If it was, I could wait there and then come back here at the end of the evening and talk to the staff. I longed for a quiet space and a cup of frothy coffee.

It had reached that raucous part of the evening where most people were squashed onto the dance floor or were on their feet, trying their best to mingle. I might be lucky and find a corner to tuck myself into. So, it was when I stopped scanning the crowd for Ruby but, instead, was searching for a seat, that I thought I saw her. A statuesque woman with long red hair hanging in waves and a green shimmering dress. She was laughing. Then a group of people pushed in front of me, and I lost her. But I was sure it was her. I felt it as well as knew it. It was intuition.

Uncle Timeon, naturally, has no time for intuition. 'It doesn't exist, we just tell ourselves it does. It's your subconscious. Your subconscious is constantly taking in facts, noticing things, solving things and then trying to attract your attention. When it eventually does, you attribute it to intuition. I don't believe in intuition, but I do believe in the subconscious. It's incredibly clever and not given nearly enough recognition. Many's the time I've gone to bed unable to solve a crossword clue and then woken the next morning to discover that my subconscious has done it for me. Sometimes it gives me the answer as images in a dream.'

I pushed through the crowd to try and get to where I thought I had seen Ruby. It wasn't easy; people were so tightly packed now that they were practically on top of each other. I had to use a degree of force. They hardly seemed to notice. They were too busy drinking, dancing, and having a good time. I pushed through groups of friends, couples, and across a corner of the dance floor. When I eventually got to where I thought I had seen her, I looked round desperately.

I had convinced myself that I had either imagined her or she had gone, when I saw her again, moving through the crowd, a flash of red and green. She disappeared through the door. I reached the hallway, but I didn't see her. I ran into the bathroom. A group of women were standing around the mirror. They were all taking about how bad they looked and reassuring each other that they didn't. They were too absorbed in the conversation even to notice me. Two of the three cubicles were occupied but whilst I stood there, two non-Rubies emerged.

I ran back into the hall. The outside door was open and one of the doormen stood just inside it. He was a huge man with no neck and a head that looked like a block balanced on his shoulders.

'Have you seen a woman with long red hair in a green dress?'

He looked at me with absolute amazement.

'She's just left,' said the tallest woman I have ever seen. She was wearing a silver dress and looked like a giantess. The effect was partly due to her very high shoes and her platinum-coloured hair which was piled on top of her head. But even without these she would still have been very tall. I thanked her and ran outside. There was no sign of Ruby.

Maybe she is in the Gaslight Café, I thought. This was more wishful thinking on my part than anything else. I imagined her sitting alone having a coffee. I could just sit down and join her. And what then? She would apologise for everything and give me the money she had swindled to return. I would give it to Lina, she could pay me, and we would all live happily ever after.

Ruby was not going to be in the Gaslight Café and even if she was, what was I actually going to do? At least I will have found her, I told myself. I opened the café door. Ruby was not in the Gaslight Café but plenty of other people were.

I went back outside. It suddenly occurred to me that I had not thought about how I was going to get home. The waterbus would have stopped running. A water taxi would be very expensive and I had no idea of how to get one.

As I headed back towards the nightclub, I noticed a familiar figure, standing a little to the side of the club, smoking. Then he abruptly dropped the cigarette and strode towards the beach.

Chapter 31

Look what the tide dragged in.

from *A Whiff of Malice* JJ Black

It was Blockhead, the doorman from earlier. He broke into a run, heading towards the beach. On the way, he had to pass a small, wooden shelter. He stopped and looked like he was talking to someone. The figure of a young man emerged and began to jog back in my direction.

Blockhead continued running and I had a sudden, horrible idea what this might be about. This was the stretch of beach where they found the dead mermaids. There were men right down on the shore now. They were nothing more than shadows. I could only just make them out.

I started to walk down to the beach. I couldn't bear the idea of another dead mermaid. But I had to find out. I desperately wanted to be wrong. I kept on walking, occasionally breaking into a run. As I passed the shelter, a female voice called out to me.

'Excuse me, but I wouldn't go...'

I ignored her. I saw three male figures down near the water's edge. I recognised Blockhead. I ran to where they were.

'Stop!' called out one of the other men.

There was a body. Of course there was a body. The head was turned away from me, but I saw red hair falling over a green dress.

'Ruby!' I gasped.

'You know her?' asked one of the men.

'Yes. No. Sort of.'

We were joined by three other men, two young and one older. One of the young men was panting.

'I found the police,' he said. 'They were called to a disturbance at the Gaslight.'

'The Gaslight?' I looked up. 'I was just there and didn't see a disturbance.'

'That's because there wasn't one,' said the younger policeman.

'Lucky,' I said and gave a hollow little laugh. It sounded almost hysterical.

'Yes.' He repeated the word 'lucky' in a thoughtful way.

'She says she knows the victim,' said one of the men.

'Really?' said the older of the police officers. He had a brusque manner that I did not like. 'Was she a friend of yours?'

'No,' I said. 'She was –'

'How did you know her then?'

I opened my mouth to start to try and explain but he either ignored me or didn't notice.

'Who are you and what are you doing here?'

He was one of those men who made everything sound rude.

'She's a journalist.'

I looked around in surprise. I hadn't really paid any attention to the two men with Blockhead. Now I saw that this was, in fact, Guisse Zeit. He stood in the middle of the two and Blockhead held his arm in a firm, doorman grip.

'A journalist?' said the police officer. 'And what exactly are you doing here?'

For a moment or two I could not answer. I was transfixed by Guisse Zeit's hands. They were covered in a substance which dripped off them into the sand. It was hard to say for certain what it was, but I was pretty sure it was blood.

'A journalist,' repeated the policeman, investing the word with a certain amount of hostility, which implied to me that he did not approve of it as a career.

'I'm not a journalist, I'm a private detective.'

'Really? Can I see your licence?'

'I don't have it with me,' I mumbled. I couldn't be bothered going into the actual story. Or, put another way, I couldn't face telling the truth. 'I work for my uncle, Timeon Tempest.'

'You're Timeon's niece?'

I had never really thought about who Uncle Timeon knew. But I suppose that he must have some sort of relationship with the police.

'Can you fetch him now?' he continued.

Something about the way that he said this filled me with relief. It implied that he believed me; he just wanted to deal with Uncle Timeon because he was a man, and he knew him. Under normal circumstances I would have been annoyed; now I was just pleased that he believed me.

'He's ...' I was about to say on holiday when I stopped myself. 'He's not in the City tonight.'

As far as the police were concerned it was better to create the idea that I was working with him on this. Saying he was away for the night implied that he was on other business and had entrusted this to me.

'You said that you recognised her?' said the younger of the two police officers.

He smiled at me. He was standing close now and I could see that his eyes crinkled up when he smiled.

The older one gave him a look.

'I'm not sure. She might be someone I'm looking for, someone called Ruby Alleck, but it's hard to say when I can't see her face.'

'Come round here,' Crinkly Eyes said, guiding me round the body. 'You will have a better view.'

He walked with me and laid his hand gently on my arm. It felt surprisingly comforting. I glanced down. She was still beautiful; that was the first thing I noticed. I had never seen a dead body before, so I didn't know what to expect. I imagined it would be horrible, but if I focused on her face, it was not.

It was only horrible because I knew that she was murdered.

'Well?' he asked.

I thought it was, but I had never seen Ruby in the flesh. I brought out the photograph of Ruby with Guisse Zeit and handed it to the policeman. He looked at the photo and then at Guisse standing close by and raised his eyebrows.

I looked down at Ruby, or the presumed Ruby, again. I felt very strange, and her face seemed to swim in front of me. Maybe I was going to faint. I had never fainted before, but this seemed like the kind of situation where one would faint. I clutched Crinkly Eyes' arm for support.

'What the ...?' he said, as someone else gasped.

I looked at Crinkly Eyes. He was staring at Ruby. I followed his gaze. He was not looking at her face but the lower half of her body. Her green dress seemed to shimmer and shake. It made me dizzy, and I clutched his arm even tighter. I screwed my eyes shut and when I opened them the shimmering was slowing down. When it came to a stop, the bottom half of Ruby's body had been transformed. It was now a sinuous, green tail.

'She's a mermaid,' said the man who had come with Blockhead.

Guisse Zeit didn't look surprised.

More people arrived. I assumed that they were connected with the police. I saw Crinkly Eyes talk to the older officer. He came over and said to me that I looked 'done in' and suggested that he take me for a sit down. I was too 'done in' to do anything but agree.

We went to the Gaslight Café, and he ordered me a frothy coffee and a pastry. It seemed a lifetime ago that I'd sat here and read about ghosts.

Crinkly Eyes was actually called Constable Rock. And the older policeman was Inspector Stone.

'I know,' said Crinkly Eyes. 'I don't think he is very happy about that. He thinks that Rock somehow outranks Stone, and my name is a challenge to his authority.'

'Well,' I said, 'at least he isn't called Inspector Pebble or Shingle or something like that.'

Crinkly Eyes – or should I say Constable Rock? – smiled and that made his eyes crinkle even more. I noticed that they were a very nice shade of blue.

He explained that he would need to take a statement from me. He could do it now, but he understood that I was exhausted and, no doubt, distressed about what I'd seen. In that case, I could come to the police station, when I felt better.

Uncle Timeon had always impressed upon me the need to put everything down on paper as soon after the event as possible. I had only ever helped him out in the most minor of ways but afterwards he always made me sit and write the whole thing out. I was just about to say that I would give my statement now, but the memory of Uncle Timeon made me hesitate. Should I wait to see him before I said anything?

The waitress brought our order. I had a sip of my coffee and took a bite of my pastry. They tasted heavenly. I suddenly realised how tired I felt. But the thought of going to sleep frightened me.

Constable Rock let me eat and drink in silence. When I looked up, I caught him watching me intently.

In the end, I decided to tell him. I was too tired not to. I just wanted to talk. Constable Rock was easy to open up to. Of course, I only told him about the case. None of the stuff like Finn and my fear that I was becoming a ghost.

I told him about the case from the first day when Lina came to the office and asked me to find Ruby. He was concentrating, but I saw his eyes crinkle a couple of times at certain parts of my story. I assumed that he was smiling. I didn't go into the bit about the business cards. I didn't think he needed to know about my previous friendship with Astrid. And I was concerned that, technically, I might have stolen them. This was the sort of thing that I really should check with Uncle Timeon. When I came to the part about Guisse Zeit, he stopped writing and looked up.

'What did your uncle say about that?'

'Ahh...' I replied.

I took a mouthful of my coffee. It had gone cold. Constable Rock asked me if I would like another.

'So ...?' he said, as we waited for it to arrive, and then he looked at me intently. His eyes were very piercing, and I had the sensation that I could not hide from his questions.

'Well, the thing is,' I began, 'I haven't exactly told my uncle. He is away...'

I was going to say on business, but Constable Rock was recording what I was saying. I did not want some kind of official record of me lying.

'I'm supposed to take the details of potential clients,' I continued, quickly, 'to see if they are suitable. Not so much the clients, but the cases,' I added.

'Vet them?' asked Constable Rock.

I nodded. This wasn't entirely true either, but it was close enough to the truth that I might be able to get away with it.

'I know that I probably should have checked before going to see Mr Zeit but' – I struggled to find a way to describe it – 'I didn't want to ask for permission in case I was told no,' I finished.

Constable Rock looked at me with those blue eyes and nodded as if he understood. I thought of Inspector Stone, and it occurred to me that maybe he did. Constable Rock read back to me what he had written down and got me to sign it.

'We may have to call you to the police station,' he said, 'to answer more questions, and please come by at any time if you remember something else. Often people remember after the event and sometimes they don't understand the relevance of things until later.'

He tore a page out of his notebook and wrote down his name and the address of the police station where he worked. It was the one near the office, on Martinet Street.

Chapter 32

Day was breaking by the time we stopped talking. The sky had lost its darkness. It looked colourless as if it were waiting for the day to come and fill it in. As we said our farewells, a thin line of rosy pink appeared at the horizon.

We were standing outside the Gaslight Café. I shivered, partly owing to the coolness of the early morning, but also because I had been awake all night. Constable Rock offered to arrange some transport home for me. I declined. 'The waterbus will be running soon,' I told him. I didn't want to go home. I was scared about what might await me there and I was scared to go to sleep. I wanted to delay it for as long as possible.

Constable Rock smiled and touched my arm as he said goodbye. He told me to contact him if I remembered anything else. I always find it strange saying goodbye to someone I don't know but have shared something with. When the intensity has been broken, the whole thing feels strangely anti-climactic.

As soon as he left, I went back into the Gaslight Café and ordered a third cup of coffee. I began to think about what had happened. People always talk about being frozen by shock but when you are, you don't realise it. Sitting there, I felt my brain begin to thaw out.

I saw the images clearly: Ruby lying dead and then Ruby

turning into a mermaid. But in my mind, I turned my gaze out to the edges. I saw Guisse Zeit standing there, being held by Blockhead. Guisse Zeit with blood on his hands.

Guisse Zeit had killed Ruby. Because she was blackmailing him, presumably.

Did Constable Rock suspect already? He had noticed Guisse Zeit in the photograph. He had asked me what Uncle Timeon had thought. I wished I knew. I really needed to speak to Timeon about all of this.

Then I felt irritated. Constable Rock might have seemed all kind and easy to talk to but he was just a man who was more interested in what another man had to think than in what I had to think. All these men thought that I was stupid. Maybe I wouldn't tell him, then.

When Ruby turned into a mermaid Guisse Zeit hadn't look surprised. Then it hit me: Ruby was *another* dead mermaid. All the other mermaids had been found around this stretch of the beach. Had Guisse Zeit killed them too?

I jumped as the waitress asked me if I wanted another coffee. It would have been my fourth. I was tempted but even I realised that that would be excessive. I had something to do now. And I needed to do it quickly. More importantly, I had a reason not to go home. I no longer needed to sit in the Gaslight hiding from life.

I sat in my favourite seat at the back of the waterbus and watched the morning take colour and shape. The few passengers ignored me. It might just have been the disreputable air I had of someone who had stayed out all night.

I had to go and see Lina. It was early but I reckoned that by the time I got there she would just be waking up. I needed to tell her about Ruby before she read it in the paper or heard about it another way. The news would get out quickly. That sort of news always got out quickly.

I looked around my few fellow passengers. I knew something that most of them did not. No-one had positively identified the body, but I was sure that it was Ruby. The police would, no doubt, want to speak to Lina. That was another reason that I needed to get to her quickly. I felt obliged to warn her.

In some ways, this was it: the case was closed. I had found Ruby. I thought about the money that Lina said that Ruby had taken from Rufus. I wondered where it was. Perhaps it was all spent. Ruby didn't look like a saver. I had no desire to get involved with anything to do with the money. I had the sense that it would be crossing a line into something illegal.

Also, now I had spoken to the police, I needed to contact Uncle Timeon. I was not looking forward to this and I imagined that he would tell me to drop everything immediately. I felt that there was a good chance he would tell me to cut all contact with Lina. That was yet another reason I needed to see her without delay.

In my mind's eye, I saw Ruby again lying on the beach, turning into a mermaid. That was a whole other thing I had to tell Lina. And then there was the fact that Guisse Zeit was a suspect for her murder. I needed to be careful about this. I did not know for sure if he was a suspect; I just suspected that he was. Guisse Zeit was not the type of person who would take kindly to being called a murderer. So perhaps I should wait until there was some sort of official announcement.

Had Guisse Zeit killed all the other mermaids? Ruby hadn't been mutilated. She had merely had her throat cut. So maybe he hadn't killed the others, and it was just a coincidence that Ruby was a mermaid. I could see Uncle Timeon raise his eyebrows.

Coincidences were another thing that he was suspicious of. Maybe Guisse hadn't mutilated Ruby because he didn't have the opportunity. Blockhead had arrived and caught him in the act.

I remembered the way Lina had over-reacted when I had mentioned that Ruby might know Guisse Zeit. That was another mystery and I wanted to try and get to the bottom of it. I couldn't leave it alone until I understood why. That was so typical of me. I had no real interest in where the money went but I had a burning curiosity about why Lina had behaved the way she did.

The café closest to the waterbus stop was just opening as I alighted. It was too soon for another coffee, but I was tempted. Maybe I would get one on the way back.

I was so deep in thought as I walked to Lina's that I didn't even notice the steep hill until I was more than halfway up it. I nearly stopped for a break but pushed myself on. I was at that stage where if I stopped, I would never start again.

I knocked on Lina's door with a hopeful tap, which turned into a loud banging. When that didn't work, I called her name.

Finally, I heard the sound of a lock being turned and Lina appeared at the door and practically pulled me in.

'Shhh,' she hissed.

I heard the sound of Mrs Bird's door opening behind us and then closing again. For a few seconds, Lina and I stood frozen, not saying a word.

'Sorry,' I finally said, in a whisper.

'It's very early,' said Lina, but she was so sweet-natured that it didn't really sound like a reprimand, more of an observation.

Sleep still clung to her. Her blonde hair was tousled and stuck out in all directions. It reminded me of candyfloss. She was wearing a silky robe covered in a pattern of fish and shells. I could smell the sea and the scent of the beach in the morning. I noticed a damp towel by one of the doors.

'I have something I need to tell you.'

Lina had started to make coffee in a pot by the stove. She had her back to me so I waited. I accepted a cup of coffee. Force of habit. Finally, I had her full attention.

'Lina,' I said 'I have something to tell you and it's...'

I tried to think of the best word to describe everything that had happened.

'...and it's quite shocking; actually, it's very shocking.'

I leaned across the table and gently took hold of Lina's hands.

'Lina, Ruby is dead,' I said.

She looked at me and her big, blue eyes widened. For a moment, an image of Constable Rock popped into my head. His eyes were a darker blue though.

'And she was murdered.'

'What?' said Lina. 'How? I... I...'

Lina seemed more bewildered than upset. Of course, they weren't really friends; Lina had just made that up. But it had stuck in my head, and I had to remind myself that she never knew Ruby. That made me feel better. Lina had only lost money and not a friend. That would be much easier to deal with. It wasn't even her money that had been lost. Though she had better warn Rufus quickly, as the police would definitely want to speak to him.

I told her that I had had a tip-off (I got a thrill saying the words 'tip-off') that Ruby might be at a nightclub called Frutti di Mer. Lina nodded. Whether this was to indicate that she had heard of Frutti di Mer or that she was following the story was unclear. I described catching sight of Ruby, trying to follow her, losing her, going outside, and finding the body on the beach.

'There's another thing. Her body, well, she...'

'How do you know that it's Ruby?'

'Well, she has not been officially identified yet, but I'm pretty certain. I have a photograph,' I said as I reached into my bag.

I had decided against mentioning Guisse Zeit. I really did not want to be accused of starting rumours. I imagined that he was the sort of man who would have a lawyer. Or lawyers. However, I decided that I would show Lina the photograph with Guisse Zeit in it and watch her reaction. I handed the photograph over.

'Lina, there is something else, something fantastical. Ruby was a mermaid.'

Lina looked at me.

'I saw it for myself. She changed, right in front of me, into her mermaid form.'

As I said this, I started to cry. It took me by surprise. I had tried not to think about that moment and now I had. There was something so magical, so precious, so wondrous about that moment but at the same time she was gone. Something beautiful had been destroyed and would never come back. I felt cheated that the only time I had got to see a mermaid was like this. It felt like I had just missed out on something. I realised how selfish that would sound and felt ashamed.

Lina looked at the photograph. I could see her body go rigid.

'No!' She shouted loud enough to make me jump. She was on her feet and halfway across the room.

'No,' she said again, but this time it was a mumble to herself. 'I don't understand.'

She disappeared through one of the doors and I sat at the kitchen table, not entirely sure what to do. She emerged a few minutes later in a blue dress. Her hair was still rumpled and fluffy.

'I have to go out now, Vulpe,' she said, going into what I imagined was the bathroom.

I sat at the table and looked at our undrunk coffee. I decided that it was best to leave. I slammed the door behind me to alert Lina to the fact that I had gone. I walked down the hill and when I saw a tree on the other side of the road, I crossed over and stood behind it, hoping that it concealed me. A few minutes later, Lina left the building and walked down the street past me. I let her get ahead and then started to follow, praying that she wouldn't look round. She was walking so fast that it was hard to keep up. I realised how exhausted I was. It was twenty-four hours since I had been to bed. At the bottom of the hill, I followed her to the waterbus stop. She broke into a run and jumped onto a waiting waterbus just before they closed the barrier. There was no point in trying to catch her.

To be honest, part of me was relieved. I looked at the photograph. What had caused Lina to behave in that way? Was it Guisse Zeit or was it that Ruby was a mermaid? Or was it both? And what didn't she understand? I yawned; I didn't understand either. I needed to get some sleep.

Chapter 33

'Sometimes you just need to sleep.'

from *The Secret of Longevity* CJ Nut

I couldn't go home; I couldn't face running into Cassiopeia.

I had forgotten about the ghost business for the last few hours, but now it popped back into my head. It was all too bizarre. 'If you *are* turning into a ghost,' a little voice whispered in my ear, 'you're going to have to find a way of stopping it.' This was ridiculous, I told myself; I had enough going on at present. My priority was to contact Uncle Timeon and get him back here quickly.

I went to the office. In one corner of the room there is a large cupboard where I hang my coat in the winter. At the bottom, all folded up, were several thick blankets and a quilt. Even better, there was a pillow. I made myself a nest in the corner of the office and curled up inside it. I wondered if Uncle Timeon spent the night here sometimes. That was the last thing I thought before falling into a deep but restless sleep.

I was back on the beach. There was a mermaid lying bleeding, covered in blood. The tide had gone out and the shore was littered with fish. They too were dyed red by all the blood. They were trembling. They were the 'Jelly Fish' off the sign from the place where Lina worked. I heard a loud ringing, and all the fish began to shake. The contraption from outside Du Trims was rolling across the sand towards me. A large bell was attached to the scissors. I tried to run away but the sand became quicksand, sucking me down, and I could not move.

I woke up with a start. The phone was ringing. I had a horrible feeling that it was Cassiopeia or my mother. I was tempted to ignore it but then I thought that that might make things worse. It was better to speak to them now before they started looking for me. I would pretend that I had gone to see Astrid last night. We had had such a lovely time chatting that I hadn't noticed how late it had got. Then, Astrid had asked me to stay. If they said that I should have let them know, I would sigh and say that I was an adult etc etc.

I took a mouthful of water.

'Hello,' I said, brightly.

'Is this the Tempest and Son Detective Agency?'

Perhaps because I was so thirsty, there was something very dry about the sound of it. The dry voice introduced himself as Mr Crabbe. He was a lawyer.

'Is it possible to speak to Mr Timeon Tempest?'

I explained that my uncle was unavailable, but I could take a message. There was a long pause. Then the voice asked if I was Miss Vulpe Tempest. I had an urge to pretend that I wasn't, but I couldn't quite bring myself to do so.

Mr Crabbe said that I would have to do, or words to that effect. He had a client who wished to secure the services of the agency but would need to meet now. I felt very uneasy and was about to decline, when Mr Crabbe asked if I could come to the police station on Martinet Street.

What could happen at a police station? I thought.

Anyway, this is what Uncle Timeon had instructed me to do: meet new clients and pass the message on to him. I imagined that I was going to be in enough trouble as it was, without turning down work. Though, deep down, I didn't believe that this was a new case. But I was going to have to tell Uncle Timeon about everything else anyway, so I might as well find out what this was about. I was also aware that I had lost the business money by working with Lina and so I felt that I was in no position to turn the opportunity of some down now.

The light was beginning to fade as I walked towards the police station. How strange that I had seen the very start of the day but had then missed the bulk of it. Mr Crabbe had told me to speak to the officer on the desk and ask for him. The officer looked blank. I was just about to repeat what I had said when a door behind the desk opened. A desiccated little man in a charcoal-grey suit emerged, followed by another officer.

'Miss Tempest?' He shook my hand. 'Follow me.'

We walked down a maze of corridors that smelt of furniture polish, bleach, and scattered patches of stale cigarette smoke. The walls were painted in an industrial shade of grey, occasionally broken up with a dirty yellow. The place had an air of late nights, too much coffee, and despair.

Finally, we came to the cells. The police officer took a key on a long chain which was attached to his belt and unlocked one of the doors.

Mr Crabbe indicated that I should enter. I hesitated. I had a visceral fear of the door being slammed shut and locked behind me. Mr Crabbe tutted. I took a deep breath and went in.

Chapter 34

Guisse Zeit didn't look particularly pleased to see me.

He said, 'I wanted your uncle.'

'My uncle is' – I was about to say unavailable but thought better of it – 'indisposed. I will take the details and pass them on to him. He will obviously be in charge.'

I really wanted to tell Guisse Zeit that I didn't want to deal with him either. The last time that I had seen him in a formal setting he had thrown me out of his office. The aggression of that act hung between us. For the first time, I had an inkling of how power works. Guisse Zeit assumed that people would do what he told them and give him what he wanted. Even though he was under arrest, he still assumed that Inspector Stone would do as he was told.

Guisse Zeit's presence dominated the dingy little room. I found myself shrinking back from him. Then I remembered that whatever happened, I was the one who could leave at the end of the conversation, and he couldn't. That made me smile.

'So, what do you want Uncle Tim... us to do?'

'Prove my innocence, of course.'

I could almost hear him adding, 'What do you think I want you to do? Stupid girl.'

'So, you are claiming to be innocent then? Even though I saw you with Ruby's blood on your hands?'

A vein on Guisse Zeit's head began to throb.

'And what about the others? I have to say that it doesn't look good for you.'

For a moment I almost felt guilty, but it passed. Guisse Zeit might be feeling that he was not having a good time, but I had had a bad couple of days too. As well as the mermaid business, I was about to be thrown out of my home and forced to go and live with my mother. I had yet again failed in love and I might be turning into a ghost. I had been awake for over twenty-four hours and had caught what little sleep I could on the office floor.

'Why don't you start from the beginning?' I suggested. On the rare occasions that Uncle Timeon had let me sit in with him in interviews, I had heard him say this. He would then lean back in his chair, stretch out his legs and look as relaxed as possible. Guisse Zeit looked beyond me to where the door was. But I had the sense that he was looking inwards not outwards.

'When I was a young man...'

What? I wanted him to go back to the beginning but had not anticipated that it would be this far back. I'd expected a few weeks or months, not years. But maybe that's what happens; it's hard to find the beginning of any story. Most things start much earlier that we realise. I was trying to think of a way to hurry him along or perhaps skip a bit when I could almost sense Uncle Timeon shake his head.

'Never hurry anyone in their story,' he always said. And also, 'Let them tell you everything; often, it is not obvious what is important until later.'

'...I was engaged to be married,' said Guisse Zeit. 'I loved my fiancée very much.'

She was also very rich, I remembered reading somewhere.

'The summer before we were to get married, she went away to spend time with her cousins in the country. I missed her a lot and was very lonely.'

There was something about the way in which he said this that didn't sound quite right. I glanced up but he was still looking beyond me.

'So, it was because of my loneliness that I did what I did.'

Aha, I thought.

'I met someone else and we, we began a... I'm not sure what to call it. I wouldn't exactly call it a relationship.'

No, I thought, I'm sure you wouldn't.

'It was only because I was lonely because my fiancée had gone away.'

So, it was practically her fault then? I wanted to say. It was your fiancée's fault that you had this not-quite-relationship?

People rarely tell you the whole truth the first-time round, Uncle Timeon had taught me. It takes several rounds to get close to the truth. They often start off with what they would like the truth to be. He had certainly been proven right by Lina. And now I was having to listen to Guisse Zeit's version of the truth.

'I met her at a place I used to go to. She was very attractive. She was always coming to talk to me and asking me to dance.'

Another person to blame, I thought, your new not-quite-lover. She just wouldn't leave you alone.

'I had always told her that it would not – could not – be forever. I told her right from the beginning that I was engaged. I was always honest with her.'

Suddenly he looked me directly in the eye.

'I was always straight with her.'

Even I could have told him that that is not how love works.

Love doesn't listen to logic; it comes from the heart and not the head. Love believes that it will rise up above the constraints of this world to triumph. Love believes that it will always win. But I didn't say any of this to Guisse Zeit. I didn't even need Uncle Timeon whispering one of his pieces of advice in my ear. I could see that one for myself.

'So,' continued Guisse Zeit, 'when the summer was over, I told Melusina that we had to end things.'

My ears pricked up at the name.

'She wasn't happy,' he continued.

I bet she wasn't, I thought.

'She caused a scene, and we had a fight. She refused to leave, to believe me,' he said. 'So, I told her that I had never loved her.'

I felt that familiar tight twist in my stomach.

'I had told her that this was how it would be from the start.'

Yes, Guisse, I wanted to say, and if this was a court of law that line of defence would work, but it isn't.

'I told her to go away, and she caused a dreadful scene. But it worked and I never saw her again.'

'What happened to her?' I asked.

He shrugged. 'I think that she may have gone back home to her family. Then my fiancée came back and...'

'You married,' I finished for him.

He nodded. I wanted to say, 'and lived happily ever after,' but I stopped myself.

'Anyway, I forgot all about it all until a few months ago. I got a letter from a young woman claiming to be Melusina's daughter. She wanted to meet me.'

'Why?' I asked innocently.

'She claimed that I am her father,' said Guisse Zeit. He looked uncomfortable.

Uncle Timeon had explained that in interviews there is a time when you want people to feel uncomfortable and a time when you don't. 'How do you know?' I had asked. 'You just feel it. It's like dancing. Sometimes you want people to move forward and other times you want them to pause. Occasionally, you want to shock them into revealing something they thought that they could hide.'

I hadn't understood what he meant but now I sensed that this was a time to move Guisse Zeit forward and past his discomfort. I didn't dwell on him being her father.

'What did you do?' I asked.

'I destroyed the letter.'

I waited.

'But then I got more.'

'How many?'

'One or two,' he said.

I looked him straight in the eye.

'Well, maybe four or five.'

'And you destroyed all of them?'

He nodded.

'Then about a month ago, I received a letter from someone called Ruby Alleck. She claimed to know all about this and threatened to go to the papers. It's all nonsense, of course, but that's the problem with the papers. They don't care if it's nonsense, as long as it's a good story.'

'You could sue,' I said.

'My wife,' said Guisse Zeit, 'would be upset. I love my wife and I don't want her to leave. Things are complicated at the minute. The business is...' he paused. 'My wife has money of her own, family money.'

I was curious to hear more but, again, I sensed it would be best to move him on.

I wrote 'check Guisse Zeit's finances' in my notebook. I had no idea how to do this, but I imagined that Uncle Timeon would.

'So, what did Ruby want?' I asked.

Guisse Zeit laughed a bitter little laugh.

'Money, of course. That's all everyone wants, isn't it?'

'What about your daughter? I mean, the young woman who claimed to be your daughter?' I quickly corrected myself. 'Did she want money?'

'No,' said Guisse Zeit and looked away. 'She said all that she wanted was to get to know me, but' – he looked back again – 'she would have probably just wanted money in the end.'

'Then what happened?' I asked.

'I got a letter from this Ruby person asking to meet me on the beach. So that's what I was doing but when I arrived, she was… she was dead.'

'How did you get blood on your hands?'

'I was feeling for a pulse.'

His answer was too polished. It felt unnatural. Also, from my memory, he had had a lot of blood on his hands and Ruby had had no cuts on her wrists or arms.

'That doesn't sound right,' I said.

Guise Zeit turned away.

'I was checking under her, to see if she had a bag. If she had, I wanted to make sure that it didn't contain anything incriminating.'

'Did you find anything?'

He shook his head. 'No,' he replied. 'I would have handed it over to the police if I had.' He adopted an affronted air.

'After destroying anything that might incriminate you,' I couldn't help adding.

He ignored this last comment.

'Had you ever met her before?' I asked.

'I have seen her around,' said Guisse Zeit. 'She is very striking – was very striking – but I wouldn't say I knew her. I might have spoken a few words to her, once or twice, but I didn't know her.'

I thought of the photograph that I had of the two of them.

'You have to believe me,' he said. 'You have to help me. Now they are asking about the others, the other mermaids. I am scared that they are going to say that I killed them too.'

'Do you have an alibi?' I asked.

He looked flustered.

'No,' he said. 'That's the strange thing. I am out a lot in the evening but on all those nights, I was in.'

'What about your wife?' I asked.

He shook his head. 'She has gone to spend the summer with her cousins in the country.'

'The same ones as when you were engaged?'

He nodded. There was a certain symmetry to that, I thought.

'And children?' I asked.

'My wife couldn't...' he hesitated. 'We don't have any.'

I could see how discovering that her husband had a love child, conceived just before her wedding, might upset the current Mrs Zeit.

'Servants?' I asked.

He shook his head again.

'Not to provide an alibi. The cook left my dinner for me, but I did not see her or the maid. You have got to help me.'

I noticed, with some satisfaction, that he said 'you' and not 'Timeon'.

'Did you know that Ruby was a mermaid?'

'No,' he said, but there was something about the way he said it.

I thought about when she had changed shape and how he did not look surprised.

'Mr Zeit,' I said firmly. 'From our experience, people rarely tell us the whole truth the first-time round. It frequently takes a few interviews. However, based on your circumstances' – I gestured around the room – 'this may prove difficult.'

I felt a little smug as I said 'our experience' as I was not just quoting Uncle Timeon, but had now discovered this for myself.

'So, I suggest that you save us both a lot of bother and tell me now.'

Guisse Zeit looked away again.

'Melusina was a mermaid,' he said. 'She was a descendant of the Melusina that helped the first Guisse Zeit. I don't know if you are familiar with the story?'

So not just a love child, a half-mermaid love child. No wonder he did not want Mrs Zeit or anyone else to know.

'The thing is,' he went on, 'no-one has talked about this for years and then someone appears claiming to be my daughter and then someone else appears trying to get money from me. I didn't know for certain, but I was suspicious that they might both be mermaids.'

'I will pass all of this on to my uncle,' I said. 'I presume he should contact Mr Crabbe, your lawyer?'

'Yes,' replied Guisse Zeit.

I rang a little bell to let the police office know that I was ready to leave. Then I thought of something else.

'That is why you removed the mermaid from the Zeit sign, isn't it?'

'Yes,' replied Guisse Zeit. 'The young woman claimed that I must still care about her mother as I had the mermaid on the sign. That's why I took it off.'

Chapter 35

If you are at a loose end, then visit the library. It's a gateway to many worlds.

from *Rain at the Seaside* Carole French

I thought that I should write up my interview with Guisse Zeit, but I had still not caught up from being awake for twenty-four hours and I couldn't face another night on the floor of the office. Also, I desperately needed to wash and get some clean clothes.

It was Thursday. Cassiopeia went out every Thursday evening to play cards. She always got back late. If I went home now, I could be in bed and fast asleep by the time she returned. Then I could sneak out early in the morning.

When I got back, I hesitated. I stood outside with my ear pressed to the door. It would be just my luck if Cassiopeia hadn't gone out tonight. Or worse still, if she had decided to stay in and wait for me. That thought made me very anxious.

I could hear no sound. I was going to have to go in at some point, I told myself firmly. Imagine if I waited so long that Cassiopeia came back to find me standing here. I crept in. Even the sound of my breathing seemed unnaturally loud. I paused in the hallway. No-one called out my name nor did Cassiopeia appear. I peeked inside the living room; it was empty.

I was just about to scurry upstairs when I realised how hungry I was. Could I risk a trip to the kitchen? I waited another few seconds then hurried down the hall, grabbed a piece of bread and some cheese and got myself a glass of water. I considered making myself a cup of coffee or even a cocktail but decided that that was too cocky.

I hurried up to my room, ate my food quickly and climbed into bed. At some point, I was faintly aware of the front door opening. Then Cassiopeia was outside my door, whispering my name. She opened the door a fraction, but I lay very still until she left.

Through the night, I heard the clocks: the grandfather clock, the cuckoo clock and then another that made a sound like a honking goose. Cassiopeia must have got a new clock.

I woke with a start. It was daylight outside. I could feel my dream slipping from me and tried to hold onto it, but it was futile. I had the sense that it was important, and clocks were involved. Uncle Timeon said that you should pay attention to your dreams as they were your subconscious trying to tell you something. But it was gone. Anyway, I had no time to lie around in bed. I dressed and crept out of the house. I was going to have to face Cassiopeia at some point, but not today.

It was very early. Most places were still shut as I walked towards the office. I was relieved to see the café closest to the waterbus stop was just opening and so I was able to buy coffee.

At the office, using Uncle Timeon's typewriter, I wrote up an account of my interview with Guisse Zeit. I took some time over it as I wanted a good record of it for Timeon if he decided to take on the case.

My priority was to send a telegram to Uncle Timeon to let him know that he needed to contact me immediately about a very important case. Or, even better, to come back as soon as possible. I felt a pang as I realised this. I had been so excited about being left on my own for the summer but now all I wanted was for Uncle Timeon to come back and sort things out.

I should go and speak to Lina again. Uncle Timeon would want to know the details about her connection and, more importantly, Rufus's connection with Ruby. This might be tricky though, as I could hardly tell her about my conversation with Guisse Zeit.

I imagined that Uncle Timeon was going to be irritated that I hadn't spent more time finding these things out at the beginning. But then, I imagined that he was going to be irritated about a lot of things.

I glanced at the clock; the telegram office would soon be open. I suddenly remembered I had dreamed about Cassiopeia having a goose clock. I smiled. What crazy things we dream sometimes. I struggled to believe that this was my subconscious trying to tell me anything or anything sensible at least.

I wondered what a goose clock would be like. Would it be like a cuckoo clock with a goose instead of a cuckoo. I thought of the kitchen clock where the cat chased the mouse; maybe it could chase a goose instead.

I picked up my bag and as I closed the door, I remembered the plant. I still hadn't watered it. I probably never would.

After I sent the telegram, I made my way over to Lina's. On the waterbus, I heard the people in front of me discussing another dead mermaid. I realised, with a start, that they were talking about Ruby. I couldn't bear it and, in the end, relinquished my favourite seat so that I didn't have to listen to them.

I decided that I would see if Lina was in the Jelly Fish before climbing the hill to her house. Just as I was about to go in, the gangly youth dashed out.

'Is Lina around?' I called, as he jumped on a bicycle.

He shook his head and was off.

I climbed the hill slowly, looking out for Lina coming down on the way. I knocked on her front door a couple of times and waited. Again, I knocked, but louder. The last time I did it, I was so loud that I half expected Mrs Bird to come and tell me off, but even she did not appear to be in. There was only a heavy silence punctuated by the distant sound of the sea.

Defeated, I decided to retry the Jelly Fish. There was a small queue around the counter and an atmosphere of irritation. There was only one server, and I couldn't catch her eye. When I got near the front, I asked, brightly, 'Is Lina around?'

'No,' she snapped.

I would have ordered a coffee but she had already turned to the next person.

I walked to the café nearest the waterbus stop. The thought of a long, empty day left me feeling anxious and panicky. It was like I was cast adrift on a vast ocean. I needed to something to cling to; something to anchor me.

Someone knocked into me. They looked surprised. It was probably an accident, but it reignited my fears of turning into a ghost. I hadn't forgotten about them exactly, but I had fenced them off into an area of my brain where I didn't have to think about them. Now, no matter how hard I tried not to think about it, it loomed large in my head.

I could go and speak to Cassiopeia. Maybe it was nonsense and she was just looking for an excuse to get me to move out. That was a bittersweet thought. It was reassuring that I might not really turning into a ghost but sad that Cassiopeia wanted rid of me. I could not face going back to the house.

I remembered that I had resolved to read Sister Assumpta's *Ghosts – Parasites or Epiphytes?* Maybe now was the opportunity.

It was as good a way as any of passing the time.

When I entered the library, Miss no-Mercy was at her desk, engrossed in talking to someone. I should return the book about Dr Dorridorri, which I had in my bag. But I couldn't face Miss no-Mercy. I would leave that problem for another day.

I made my way, like a ghost, to the ghost section and found Sister Assumpta's book. She began *Parasites or Epiphytes?* by announcing that she would not go into the theories about how ghosts come into being. She had covered that in her other book, along with why there were so many ghosts in the City. Over the summer I had become something of an expert on the du Temps and Zeit families and now on ghosts. I may not have solved any crimes or found love, but I had learned some things.

Like MM Mystery, Sister Assumpta argued that ghosts are perpetually looking for humans to complete them. They could sense, apparently, the sort of humans who would be more inclined to do this and were drawn to them. Such humans were generally people who felt empty or damaged. Often a very powerful force, like two magnets attracting, existed between these humans and the ghosts. It was an intense experience, easily mistaken for love, but it was not love.

The next few pages explored theories as to what ghosts felt. One theory was that they felt nothing except the desire to complete themselves. Others proposed that the ghost could retain some of their human emotions. Some suggested that they might care about the human a little, in their own way. But, according to Sister Assumpta, it made no difference. The ghost would always leave the human in the end.

The following chapter, *How Humans can be Turned into Ghosts*, explained the ways a ghost might psychically drain vitality from a person. The ghost could curl up and take up residence in the hollow inside the human. Like a worm in a rotten apple. There was an illustration of this from medieval times. I found this a particularly disturbing picture.

Another theory was that spending time with the human allowed the ghost to pretend that they had not died. In this scenario, they did not take anything from the human. However, their presence in the human's life illuminated the emptiness inside the person. After they left, as they always did, the human found it impossible to ignore this emptiness. They became hyper-aware of it. And with that awareness, the emptiness was liable to expand, like air does when it heats. It would amplify inside the person, until one day they collapsed in on themselves and then they, too, would become a ghost.

The process of becoming a ghost was described as losing a sense of self. Or of losing a hold on the world. People would feel as if they were drifting away. One of the early signs was that people would become less tangible. They would, at certain times, begin to disappear.

I felt shaky. I wanted to put the book down and go home. It was all nonsense, I told myself. People don't turn into ghosts. Ghosts don't take up residence inside people

But I was avoiding home because Cassiopeia thought that *I* was turning into a ghost. In spite of everything, I felt compelled to read more. I turned to the next chapter.

'It is unknown how many people around us are actually ghosts (dead or alive). It is also unknown whether traditional ghosts remain amongst the living forever, or what happens to the living that turn into ghosts. In large cities like this, people disappear all the time. And no-one is quite sure what has happened to them. Perhaps some of them have turned into ghosts.'

Suddenly, I felt very angry. It was irresponsible to write this kind of thing without suggesting some kind of cure.

I flicked through the book and towards the end saw a chapter entitled *Changing Back into a Human*. I read through it quickly. Of course, ghosts who have become ghosts after death cannot change back into humans. There was a long philosophical discussion around this which I didn't absorb. It seemed to suggest that those ghosts should just accept that they were ghosts.

I was becoming fed up with ghosts. Finn flashed into my head, and I felt sick. I had avoided thinking about him. If I was turning into a ghost, which I refused to believe, then he was the ghost who had done this to me. But this was too painful to accept. Deep down, I still hoped that he would return. I couldn't bear giving up that hope.

Finally, I came to the section on how humans who were turning into ghosts could reverse the process. In some rural areas, there were ceremonies to accomplish this. These were generally conducted by a wise woman or man who had knowledge of the old ways. Occasionally, they might be performed by a religious leader. The ceremony involved 'calling someone back to themselves'. It sounded like the rites Cassiopeia had described to my mother.

Some people can reverse the process themselves. I reread this line several times. It brought me a certain amount of relief. It was, however, unclear, exactly how they might do this. I sighed: of course, I couldn't help thinking, it wouldn't be anything straightforward, like going to a churchyard and turning three times under a full moon at midnight. Obviously, I didn't believe that I was turning into a ghost, but if there was something simple that I could do, then I would do it, just to be on the safe side.

The only way to save myself would be to find a way to fill the void. But what I needed to fill the void was Finn. And according to the book, if he was a ghost, he would never come back.

A wave of frustration and anger washed over me. I didn't need another person to feel complete, I thought angrily, I just wanted the person I was in love with. Isn't everyone searching for love? Why isn't everybody a ghost then?

'The human who is becoming a ghost has to find the thing in themselves that has become lost to them.' I was not sure what it meant. I was not lost to myself. I brightened. I categorically cannot be turning into a ghost for I am not lost to myself, I thought. Categorically, I repeated several times in my head.

I shall go back and talk to Cassiopeia, I told myself. I will sort this out and there will be no more ghost nonsense.

Nevertheless, I still felt a lingering discomfort.

By the time I had finished reading, it was mid-afternoon and I faced my familiar dilemma. I felt that the best time to talk to Cassiopeia would be over a cocktail, but she would not be back yet, and I did not want to sit in the house waiting for her.

I looked around. My eyes settled on an old drawing on the wall. The building looked familiar. I went closer. A card below read, 'The du Temps family owned a clock-makers' workshop on this site and produced luxury timepieces. When the family went into decline, they had to sell their properties. This was the last to be sold. It changed owners several times but is now owned by the Zeit family. They have, fittingly, opened a watch factory here and have named it the DT Watch Factory in memory of its origins.'

Oh, I thought. That's one mystery solved again, then. Not Date and Time after all. My visit to the DT Watch Factory seemed like a lifetime ago. All that time investigating and all I've managed to work out is where the name DT Watch Factory came from, I thought bitterly.

The library felt stuffy and suddenly I longed for some fresh air. Maybe I could just sit on the waterbus for a while before I went home. The other night it had been quite soothing.

Alternatively, I could go and look for Lina again. I really did need to speak to her before Uncle Timeon got back.

It was pleasant on the waterbus and a sense of calm came over me. I told myself that I would find Lina at work. Then, I would go home to Cassiopeia. We would have a cocktail and everything would go back to normal. Something relaxed inside me at the thought of things going back to normal.

I looked out at the water and took a few deep breaths of sea air and enjoyed the combination of the warm day and the cool breeze. I imagined how lovely it would be to sit and have a drink with Cassiopeia and chat about our day. Then my imagination really took hold. Maybe Finn would contact me as well. He would get in touch. He had had to leave the City on some sort of emergency. He had forgotten to take my contact details. He was desperate. He had thought of me every moment of every day. I imagined him looking into my eyes as he said this and maybe taking my hands in his. He had bought me flowers to apologise: a great bunch of pink tulips from Violetta's. I imagined him arriving at the house with them. I would introduce him to Cassiopeia, and she would rush round trying to find a vase. Maybe two vases. We would keep some of the tulips downstairs, but I would have some in my room also.

As the waterbus docked, I pushed all these thoughts from my head and focused on finding Lina. I promised myself an ice-cream on the way back if I found her. I had not eaten for some time. I checked in the window of the first café to make sure that they had cherry flavour.

I had seen the street waking up this morning and now, in the late afternoon, it was winding down. The afternoon brightness was being replaced by the softer light of evening. Long shadows danced along the paving stones.

In the Jelly Fish the counter was surrounded by a mass of sandy children in perpetual noisy chaos, pushing and pressing each other. The waitress looked just as harassed as she had this morning, except now she looked tired as well. When she caught sight of me, she seemed to get a jolt of energy. She stood up straighter and screamed down the shop, 'No, I haven't seen her, and if you see her, tell her that she had better come to work tomorrow, or she's lost her job.'

For a moment there was silence. All the adults and some of the children turned to look at me. I had a horrible feeling that something bad had happened to Lina. All thoughts of getting myself an ice-cream were forgotten. I walked briskly up the hill, not even sure why I was rushing. Maybe I just wanted to rid myself of the terrible feeling of doom. I wanted to be proved wrong.

I ran up the stairs and banged on the door. Nothing. I shouted Lina's name. Still nothing. I didn't care if Mrs Bird came out and told me off. But no one came to the door. I gave one last desperate volley of knocks. The silence was so heavy that it had a weight to it. Then it was shattered by the sound of gulls, following the fishermen home with their evening catch.

Chapter 36

If you're in the right frame of mind, drawing can be a magical experience.

from *The Beginner's Guide to Drawing* Eloise Gray

I went straight back to the office. I remembered all the times I had been desperate for a message from Finn. At this moment, even more than hearing from Finn, I was desperate to see Uncle Timeon.

Realistically, I did not expect to see him. I had only sent the telegraph this morning. If he was in the mountains, as he claimed, it would take him a couple of days to return. I had hoped that he might be a little closer, with his lady friend. But even then, he probably wouldn't get back until at least tomorrow.

I rifled through my bag. It was full of all sorts of stuff: Sweet-and-Sours, the address of the new clock-maker that Cassiopeia had written down for me, one of Astrid's father's business cards. Eventually, I found what I was looking for. The card that Constable Rock had written his name on.

It seemed a bit extreme going to the police, but I was certain that something bad had happened to Lina.

There was no-one at the front desk. But there was a hand bell, with a sign saying, 'Please Ring for Attention.' I rang. Almost immediately a young officer appeared. He looked doubtful when I asked for Constable Rock.

'I represent the Timeon Tempest and Son Detective Agency,' I said, in my most authoritative voice, drawing myself up to my full height. 'We are assisting on the dead mermaid case. I have to speak to Constable Rock as a matter of urgency and I'm very short of time.'

Perhaps something of Uncle Timeon had rubbed off on me. The young officer hurried off and, in a moment, returned with Constable Rock.

He took me into a room just behind the desk. Inspector Stone was there and a couple of other officers. Inspector Stone looked at me with irritation. Though that might have just been his face. I was always judging him unfairly.

'Yes?' he said. 'What do you want?'

'I have some important information.'

All four men in the room looked at me. I explained that Lina and her boyfriend had hired me and had described Ruby as a friend. I decided not to say anything about the disappearing money. I realised that if I mentioned it, it could make them more inclined to be interested in Lina. However, I did not want to cause her unnecessary trouble. Even as I thought this, I had a sinking feeling as I felt sure that something had happened to Lina and that money would be the least of her worries.

'When was the last time you saw her?' asked Inspector Stone.

'Yesterday morning.'

He raised his eyebrows.

'Doesn't sound that long ago. Where have you looked?'

'Her house and work.'

'What about the boyfriend?'

I did not want to have to admit that I knew very little about 'the boyfriend', including where he lived.

'Sounds more like a case of someone who couldn't be bothered showing up to work than a missing person. A common enough problem these days.'

I could almost hear Inspector Stone add 'with young people'. It sounded like a favourite refrain.

'Sir?' Constable Rock cleared his throat. 'This Lina did appear to know the latest victim and was concerned about her. It might be relevant.'

Inspector Stone glared at him. 'We have an excess of dead mermaids and a dignitary of the City locked up as our main suspect. We are under pressure from above to find the real killer.'

As he said, 'real killer', he made inverted commas in the air with his index fingers. I got the impression that Inspector Stone was not as convinced of Guisse Zeit's innocence as his superiors wanted him to be.

'Furthermore, one of our key witnesses has disappeared,' he went on, 'and yet you suggest that we should investigate a young woman's mysterious absence from work. Of course, perhaps you think that she is the mermaid killer?'

'No, sir,' said Constable Rock.

I admired the way in which he was able to say this and not make it sound in any way sarcastic.

'I just thought I could take a few details from Miss Tempest.'

Inspector Stone muttered something, which I took to be assent, and left the room, taking the other two officers with him.

Constable Rock smiled, and his eyes crinkled up at the edges. I noticed again how blue they were. He gestured that I should sit at a desk near the window.

I answered a series of questions about Lina. I was evasive about her relationship with Ruby and was careful not to let slip anything about the money. Constable Rock wrote everything down; occasionally, I had the impression that he knew that I wasn't being entirely truthful but, for reasons of his own, did not press me on it.

'So, the last time you saw Lina was yesterday morning?'

I explained that I had gone to see her immediately to tell her about Ruby's death.

'How did she take the news?'

'She was shocked, and angry, and something else.' I thought about it, trying to put my finger on what else she was exactly.

'She seemed confused,' I said at last.

'Why do you think something has happened to her? How do you know that this isn't just the way she is?'

I just looked at him and gave a tiny shrug.

'Do you have a picture of her?'

I shook my head.

'It will be much easier to look out for her if we know what she looks like,' he said.

'I could draw her,'

He looked at me.

'If you have paper and a pencil, I could draw her.'

He left the room and returned a few minutes later with some paper and three pencils, all of different sizes. He also brought me a cup of coffee. We could hear the little bell at the front desk ring. I selected one of the pencils. The bell rang again. Constable Rock excused himself.

I closed my eyes for a moment and thought of Lina. I remembered her the first day that she came into the office. And the night of the party when she looked lit up with all the lights and love. I tried to capture her delicate face and her big eyes. I tried to capture her prettiness. She was like a fresh day down by the shore, the sound of the waves and the smell of the sea.

The window was open, and an evening breeze blew into the room, bringing with it the smell of fresh flowers and candles. Somewhere someone was playing a radio. It was classical music, a string quartet. I don't really like classical music but there was something about this that was very beautiful and I found myself drawing in time to it, as if it was flowing through me and animating my hand. Constable Rock did not return. I was not sure what was going on, but it seemed as if the little bell was ringing almost continuously.

I had forgotten how much I loved drawing. How happy it made me feel. How it transported me to a different world. I felt myself relax. The tension left my muscles. I found the whole thing a most soothing experience. I was just admiring my handiwork when Constable Rock came back.

He looked at my picture and smiled. 'Very good,' he said.

'You can't possibly say that,' I replied. 'You don't know what Lina looks like.'

Constable Rock looked amused. He took the picture from me and folded it up very precisely in half and then half again and then placed it inside his notebook.

'I don't suppose that you could draw the doorman for me?' he said. 'The one from Frutti di Mer who found the body.'

'Blockhead?' I replied, without thinking.

Constable Rock looked at me sharply. 'You know him?'

'No,' I was a little embarrassed. 'I just named him Blockhead. I don't think I could draw him. I didn't really pay that much attention to him and there was a lot going on that night. All I really remember was…'

'That he had a head like a block?' suggested Constable Rock.

I nodded.

'Why do you want me to draw him?' I asked. 'Has he gone missing too?'

Constable Rock looked round. I got the impression that he felt that he should not really have told me anything.

'I'm sure he'll turn up,' he said airily. 'That sort always does in the end.'

As I went to leave, he said, 'Thank you Miss Tempest, Vulpe. If you think of anything else, please don't hesitate to let us know.'

Outside, I realised how tired I felt and all I wanted to do was to go home. Finally, I gave in. As soon as I opened the front door, Cassiopeia was in the hallway.

'Vulpe,' she said.

She was trying to make her voice sound normal. She smiled but there was something forced about it.

'Do you want a drink?' she asked, as if it were just any other night.

I followed her into the room.

'So, what have you been up to? I feel as if I haven't seen you for ages.'

'I've been busy,' I replied.

I thought about telling her about Ruby's body, but I decided that I should not give her any more to worry about. So instead, we both made polite conversation and pretended that everything was back to normal.

Chapter 37

'It was really important that I had it, so it wasn't exactly stealing,' said Alice.

from *Don't Hold Your Breath* Scarlett West

I awoke early. At least Cassiopeia had not said anything about my becoming a ghost. Nor had she told me that I needed to leave.

Suddenly, I was gripped by an overwhelming need to look for Lina. I jumped out of bed and slipped out of the house. A mist clung to the City. The normal sounds were muffled.

The waterbus floated silently through the lagoon. It felt like a ghost ship. I imagined that I had become a ghost. Maybe I would spend forever on this waterbus: always in motion, never arriving where I wanted to be. But a few minutes later, the boat pulled into the stop I needed.

I had a cup of coffee at my now usual place. The waitress smiled when she saw me. Even the tabby cat who lived there seemed to flick her tail in recognition. I tried to formulate a plan as I drank my coffee but still did not have one as I finished it. I ordered another but I could not concentrate. My mind wandered over everything that had happened. Why could I not have spent the summer falling in love?

I finished my second coffee and reluctantly decided against a third. The mist was lifting but things were still blurred and indistinct. I walked down to the Jelly Fish and looked through the window. It was the same as yesterday: only one waitress, who wasn't Lina. I watched for a while in the hope that Lina would appear. I was unsurprised but still disappointed when she didn't. That's me, always hoping that things will be different even when I know that they won't be. There was no point in even going inside to ask. I walked back towards the hill that led to Lina's house.

I climbed the stairs to Lina's flat and stood in the hallway. The silence seemed to mock me. It was as if it were laughing at me. A wild frenzy overtook me, and I banged on the door in a crazed fashion. I kicked the door, screaming Lina's name.

I hated that door. It stood between me and moving forward. Suddenly it seemed to me that for my whole life, doors had closed in front of me, preventing me getting what I wanted. In a strange way, I felt that everything I had ever wanted lay behind that door. In that moment, I believed that if only I could break down the door, somehow, I would get everything that had been lost or denied to me.

Think, Vulpe, think, I told myself. There must be a way in.

I saw the plant on the table. I had heard of people hiding spare keys under plants. Of course, we had never done that. My mother thought the idea ludicrous. But what if Lina had? The first time she let me in, she had had her key in her bag. But she looked the sort to lose keys. What if she had hidden a spare one? What if the answer was staring me in the face?

With trembling hands, I lifted the plant. As I did so I realised that it was not actually real but made of rubber. I turned the plant over. This was easier than expected as there was no soil. It would be a perfect place to put a key. But there was nothing there.

I slapped the plant back down on the table. I looked at the door. Its presence seemed to taunt me, reminding me of all the other things I had failed at in my life, all the other obstacles which had defeated me. Think, Vulpe, think. There must be a way you can get inside.

I remembered when I had just started working for Uncle Timeon. He had not yet had a chance to get me my own keys, so there was only one set for the office. One day we left together, each thinking the other had the keys. We only realised as I slammed the door shut. Timeon just laughed. He reached inside his pocket and took out a little pouch. Inside were several pieces of wire. He selected one and placed it in the lock. He jiggled it around a few times, smiled, and opened the door.

I wished that I had paid more attention to what he was doing. Or, even better, got him to show me how. But how hard could it be? The problem was, I didn't have any wire. I was just wondering whether anywhere nearby sold stuff like that when I remembered the Sweet-and-Sours. They had little twists of wire at the end.

I picked one out of my bag and opened it. I popped the sweet in my mouth. It was sour. The two pieces of wire in my hand looked short and flimsy. Then I thought maybe I could get some more pieces and twist them together. I added two more Sweet-and-Sours to the one already in my mouth. I grimaced. They were all sour. What were the chances of that? Or maybe one was sweet and was just being drowned out by the other two.

I twisted all the wires together to create a longer, sturdier piece. I poked it into the keyhole and jiggled it around. Nothing happened. It still seemed quite flimsy. Maybe I needed more wire. I stuffed two more sweets into my mouth. It was not a pleasant sensation. I think that they were sweet, but it was quite hard to tell.

I added the wire and tried again in the lock. Nothing. A kind of madness descended over me. At that point, opening the door wasn't even about Lina. It was like a test. And if I passed it would somehow prove that I was good enough or talented enough or loveable enough.

I remembered something that I had read, once, in the paper or a magazine. The City was very old and so were its buildings, including the houses. Apparently, in many cases, the locks used were very similar. One key could open many locks. I took my keys out of my bag. I had three of them. I tried the office key and the key to Cassiopeia's house. Neither of them fitted.

The third key was to my mother's house. She had let me keep it, in case I wanted to come back. It slipped into the lock. I felt a surge of excitement. I was also amused. How funny if my mother's key could unlock many doors. That would mean other keys could unlock her door. She would not be happy about that.

But it would not move. I tried harder but still it would not move. I was about to exert even more pressure when I stopped myself. The last thing I wanted to do was to break the key in the lock. I forced myself to stop and took the key out.

I took a few deep breaths and flexed my fingers. I had read that if you thought positively about something, imagined it happening, that you could make it come true.

I closed my eyes and imagined the key turning in the lock. I could feel the movement, the give as the key started to turn, the relief of it. I imagined kissing Finn. I could feel his lips on mine, the way he tasted. The surge of excitement and joy.

I pushed the image from my head. I replaced the key in the lock, took a deep breath and started to turn it.

'What do you think you are doing?' said a voice behind me.

I had completely forgotten about Mrs Bird. She was standing at the top of the stairs, carrying a basket. I could smell freshly baked bread. She looked like she had just been to market.

'Oh, it's you,' she said, sounding disappointed.

The shock of being caught made me flustered.

'Lina is away and she asked me to water her plants,' I mumbled. 'The key is very stiff in the lock.'

'Yes, that lock can be tricky.'

There was something critical in her tone, as if tricky locks were somehow due to the fecklessness of young ladies who did not care for them correctly.

'Here let me get my key.'

'You've got a key?'

'Yes. My cat, Perdita, has a fascination for Lina.' She sounded deeply disappointed by this fact. 'Perdita is always climbing in through the open window. I have asked Lina repeatedly to close the window before she goes out, but she keeps forgetting.'

Although she didn't say it, I could hear her add: silly girl.

'So, she gave me a key to let myself in if Perdita disappeared. Wait a minute.'

I glanced down and saw the wire lying on the ground and hurriedly kicked it under the table.

A moment later, Perdita rushed out and began to scratch wildly at Lina's front door. Mrs Bird followed, looking irritated, and holding a key attached to a brown label. She plucked Perdita up, and returned her to her own home. Perdita did not go without a fight, wriggling and scratching. Then Mrs Bird inserted the key in the lock and opened Lina's door for me.

The apartment looked exactly as it had done the last time I was there. There was something anti-climactic about the scene.

Mrs Bird walked in behind me. I had the feeling that she did not quite trust me. Or maybe not me specifically but young ladies in general. I quickly looked around the room for any plants but there were none. I could feel Mrs Bird's eyes on my back. I filled a large glass with water. I heard a tutting sound. Mrs Bird had noticed the window was open and went to close it.

I darted into Lina's bedroom and closed the door behind me. There were no plants in this room either. However, I was banking on the fact that Mrs Bird had never been in here to know that.

There was a vase of flowers on a small table by the bed. They were wilting and dying. They didn't look like shop-bought flowers but more like flowers that Lina had picked herself.

Lina's room was very neat. The silk robe was hanging on the back of the door. I looked round the room wildly.

I opened the wardrobe. A few items of clothing hung on metal hangers. There were a couple of pairs of shoes stacked neatly in the bottom. I checked inside them. There was nothing hidden there. I stood on tiptoe and felt on top of the wardrobe. Only dust, which stuck to my sweaty palms. I lay on the floor and checked under the wardrobe and the bed. There was an old case under the bed. I pulled it out. It was empty.

'Are you nearly finished?' called Mrs Bird.

She sounded close to the door.

'Coming,' I called back.

For a second, I considered telling her to go ahead and I would let her know when I was done. But I felt that that was risky and would arouse suspicion. I took one last desperate look around.

The table by the bed had a drawer. Inside was a green leather writing case with a large M on the front. Inside was a photograph of Lina and a man who I took to be Rufus. I could feel Mrs Bird's presence outside the door. I shoved the case into my bag. It might contain other useful information, and at least I now had a proper picture of Lina that I could take to the police. I knew I was stealing. Then I realised that part of me already believed that I would never see Lina again.

As I walked down the stairs, I heard Mrs Bird lock the door and the sound of Perdita mewing loudly and scratching.

Chapter 38

In amongst all the noise, I heard the faintest squeak of something important.

from *The Blueprint of a Discovery* Edgar Lawrence

As I walked away from Lina's apartment, the enormity of what I had done hit me. I had gained entry and *stolen* something. I glanced nervously behind me. I don't know what I expected to see. Mrs Bird and Perdita pursuing me down the hill? My heart pounded. I broke into a little run.

I went into my café and ordered a coffee and a large pastry. They even had cherry, but my mood spoiled my enjoyment. I was acutely aware of the presence of the writing case in my bag. Part of me burned to take it out and look at it but I felt too exposed.

I took my usual seat on the waterbus. Someone knocked into me and apologised. At that moment I almost felt relieved at the idea that I might be turning into a ghost. I was too anxious to care that I was thinking that turning into a ghost was a good thing.

The one item that I had seen in the writing case was the photo of Lina. I wasn't sure about giving the police stolen property. I could tell them that I had remembered that I had it in her file. That didn't sound likely. Alternatively, it implied that I was far too scatty to be a private detective as I forgot about vital evidence.

Nearing the office, I began to feel calmer. Perhaps it was being in my own street that did it. As I opened the door, it caught on something: a piece of paper, neatly folded in half. On the front was written 'Miss Tempest'. It wasn't from Finn. I had looked at the first note often enough to know his writing and, anyway, why would he address it to Miss Tempest?

This note was from Constable Rock. 'Please come to the station and ask for me.' Surely, they could not already know that I had taken something from Lina's apartment?

Then I realised that if the police thought I had stolen something they would not leave a note. They would come and find me. I re-read the note. Constable Rock had put the date and time. He had delivered the note whilst I was still in Lina's.

At the police station, there was a young lady behind the desk. Young ladies were really getting everywhere these days.

As I was telling her my name, Constable Rock appeared. He led me into the room at the back. There was only one police officer in there this time. Thankfully, it was not Inspector Stone. He was staring at a typewriter but not typing. I recognised the expression on his face and shot him a sympathetic look.

Constable Rock fussed around getting me a chair.

'Did your mother tell you that I was looking for you?'

'My mother?' I gasped. 'You have spoken to my mother? Where did you find my mother?'

Constable Rock looked slightly taken aback.

'She was at the address you gave me,' he said.

'Oh, that's Cassiopeia,' I said. 'She is my landlady.'

I said this in a condescending fashion as I wanted to imply that I was an adult who did not live at home. I wondered if Constable Rock still lived at home. Did he have a mother who fussed over him, washed his clothes, and made him sandwiches?

'She looks like you,' he said. Then Constable Rock leaned forward and very gently put his hand on mine.

I had never been to a mortuary before. It was practically part of the police station. You just had to go out through a back door, and there it was. I wondered, if anyone saw us walking, me and Constable Rock, would they think we were just a young couple?

The mortuary was like a cross between a hospital and a police station. It had that type of quietness that makes it necessary to speak in a whisper or muted tones. And a sharp, antiseptic smell. There were a couple of men waiting. Constable Rock brought me a hard little chair to sit on. He crouched down beside me.

'Remember, you only need to do this if you are ready. You can have more time if you want.'

I shook my head. Are you ever really ready for anything?

The room was large and white. There were metal cupboards along one wall. I glanced my reflection. It was distorted, like looking into a mirror at a funfair.

In the centre was a table and an object covered with a sheet. I must have recoiled, for Constable Rock put his hand on my arm.

'Do you want more time?' he asked, softly.

I shook my head. One of the men pulled the sheet down to reveal the face. Just below, I could see the start of a knife wound. I had lived most of my life having never seen a dead body. This was my second in as many days.

'Well?' said Constable Rock.

I looked hard. Strangely, I wasn't sure. It was like seeing a picture of a building in darkness when you were used to seeing it all lit up. I studied the face as I did not want to make a mistake. I was so absorbed in getting it right that I forgot what I was looking at for a few seconds. Then I nodded.

'Yes,' I said. 'That's Lina.'

I turned to look at the white wall with the reflections of the silver cupboards dancing across it. I heard a voice call someone's name, but could not make out what they said after that.

A wave of nausea swept over me. It was mixed with grief and anger and confusion. Who would have wanted to kill Lina? I felt lightheaded. I must have swayed a little for Constable Rock put out his hand to steady me and looked at me with concern.

Everything seemed to dance in front of my eyes, like the reflections on the wall. The sheet covering Lina's body shimmered and shook. I looked up and caught the eye of one of the other men in the room. He was staring, bewildered, at the body.

'What the...?' he glanced at Constable Rock.

He lifted the bottom of the sheet. He looked up, screwed up his eyes tight and then looked back again. He pulled the sheet off Lina's body with a flourish, like a magician performing a trick. I looked away as I did not want to see Lina naked. It seemed wrong. I heard Constable Rock gasp. I couldn't stop myself looking back.

Lina had a tail. It took a few seconds to make sense of what I was seeing but there it was: a mermaid's tail in shades of blue from aquamarine through to a pearly opalescence. Constable Rock looked at me. If he was searching for some kind of explanation, he was looking at the wrong person.

I sat on my hard little chair, drinking the coffee Constable Rock had brought, and waiting. Maybe I was not waiting at all. I was avoiding having to start thinking about what had happened. Lina was dead and Lina was a mermaid. None of it made any sense.

I counted the wall tiles. I would get to a certain point, lose count, and then have to go back to the beginning again. At first, they all looked the same. But I became familiar with their quirks, their stains and their cracks, which made them individuals.

People began to arrive, rushing past with an air of importance. No-one noticed me. I wondered if it was because I was a ghost or if they were just preoccupied with what had happened. I saw

Inspector Stone but he ignored me. All the newcomers squashed themselves into the room. I could hear the low hum of voices.

Constable Rock came out to inform me that I could go home if I wanted to but that he would need to take a statement at some point. I said that I would do it now. He looked unwilling but led me into a small room. He went to get me another cup of coffee. Constable Rock knew me well.

The room looked out into a little garden with a small fountain in the centre. A statue of a woman, stained blue-green with age, held an object – I'm not quite sure what – at her shoulder, from which water flowed. Her nose had chipped off.

Constable Rock returned with my coffee. The first question that he asked me was had I known that Lina was a mermaid?

'Of course not.'

The whole idea was so ludicrous that I started to laugh. And once I started, I couldn't stop. I laughed so much that I started to cry. Great big tears ran down my face and I had to sniff to stop my nose from running. I wasn't even sure why I was laughing. Or if I was laughing or crying. All I knew was that I couldn't stop.

I eventually regained control.

'I think that we should stop now,' Constable Rock said, 'and do this at another time.'

I did not disagree.

'Can I get you someone?' he continued. 'Your landlady?'

I shook my head.

'Or what about your uncle? Is he back?'

I didn't have the energy to make up another excuse as to Uncle Timeon's whereabouts, so I just shook my head again.

'Would you like a cup of coffee?' he asked.

I didn't really want another cup of coffee, but I had come to realise that coffee was a kind of currency between Constable

Rock and me. It seemed important that I should accept. Also, it was against my nature ever to refuse a cup.

I reached inside my bag for a handkerchief and took the opportunity to blow my nose noisily whilst he was out of the room. In amongst all the tears and laughing, something was nagging at me. Irritating me, like a pebble in my shoe. When he came back with my coffee, I got it.

'Did the killer know that they were mermaids?' I asked.

A little of my coffee spilled down the side of the cup.

'Ruby and Lina both turned into mermaids after they died,' I said. 'So, when he killed them, did he know that they were mermaids? And what about the others? Surely, he must have known that they were mermaids when he killed them? He could not have killed lots of women who then all turned out to be mermaids. That would be too much of a coincidence.'

Constable Rock's eyes seemed an even brighter blue.

'We are not sure,' he said.

'How long does it take to turn back into a mermaid?' I continued. I was not really asking a question, just thinking out loud. 'What about Lina? Why did she take so long to turn back into a mermaid? She must have been killed hours ago. She took much longer than Ruby.'

'There is a professor in there who is an expert on such things. He believes' – Constable Rock stared into the distance, a look of concentration on his face – 'that mermaids who die in another form generally revert quickly back to being mermaids.'

He looked down at his notebook.

'A delay in reverting to mermaid form indicates that the creature' – I winced – 'was only part mermaid. Also' – he looked at his notebook again – 'the longer they have spent as human, the longer, after death, it will take them to change back.'

'So, he thinks that Lina was only part mermaid?'

Constable Rock nodded.

I put my handkerchief back in my bag and felt the leather of the writing case. I wondered if I should hand it over to Constable Rock. But it just seemed so complicated.

Then I thought of Mrs Bird. The police would speak to her and, surely, she would tell them about my visit. Maybe it would be better just to hand it over now. I heard the sound of voices from inside the morgue. I thought of Lina lying cold and dead in that sterile place, surrounded by strangers, some of whom thought of her as a creature. I could not bear to hand over her case and photographs to them.

'Where did you find her?' I asked.

I hoped that it was somewhere beautiful or, at least, not ugly.

Constable Rock told me. It was not on the same area of beach where they found the other mermaids. It was actually quite close to the office.

'Is that relevant?' I asked and started to cry again.

'I really think that you need to go home, Vulpe,' he replied.

I was about to leave when another thought hit me.

'How did you recognise it was Lina?' I asked.

'Your drawing,' said Constable Rock. 'It is very good.'

I could feel the tears starting again. Constable Rock reached inside his notebook and took out a folded piece of paper.

'Here,' he said. 'Why don't you take it?'

I thanked him and put it in my bag. My hand brushed against the raised M on the front of the writing case. Something fell into place. I knew who Lina's father was.

Chapter 39

'What an utter mess, both inside and outside my head.'

from *The King, the Kaiser and the Tsar* Beryl Jewel

I sat in the office and tried to sort out my thoughts. There was so much swirling round inside my head, it made me feel dizzy. Lina had told me that she came to the City to find her father. Guisse Zeit told me that a young lady had sent him letters claiming to be his daughter. Not just that, she was the result of an affair with a mermaid called Melusina. Lina was part mermaid. I thought of the M on the front of the writing case: was the name Lina a corruption of Melusina? It was all too much of a coincidence for Lina not to be Guisse Zeit's daughter.

I looked inside the case. Below the photographs was a pad of writing paper and some envelopes. I opened the pad. Half the pages remained but they were all blank. I shook the pad just in case any spare letters might fall out. I was looking for an unsent one to Guisse Zeit. Unsurprisingly, no such thing appeared. Guisse Zeit told me that after ignoring the letters, eventually he sent one to the young lady telling her to stop. That was not in the case either but I could imagine that Lina would not have wanted to save it.

Then there was Lina's strange attitude to Guisse Zeit. Had Lina just not wanted to believe that her father was a bad man; a man capable of doing bad things?

The more I thought about it, the more convinced I became

that I was right. It all made perfect sense. Unfortunately, I had no evidence.

I took out a Sweet-and-Sour. It was an orange one, sweet. I searched for the card Mr Crabbe, Guisse Zeit's lawyer, had given me with his office number on it.

It was early evening, but Mr Crabbe struck me as the kind of man who was married to his job. I phoned the exchange and waited for what seemed like an eternity to be put through. Long enough for me to finish the Sweet-and-Sour. I was just about to give up, when someone answered. I recognised the dry voice of Mr Crabbe.

I reminded him who I was. 'I have something important to tell Mr Zeit.'

'Yes,' said Mr Crabbe. His voice remained incurious.

I was about to request a meeting with Guisse Zeit when I realised that this might prove difficult or even impossible.

'And to what does this pertain?' asked Mr Crabbe.

'I know that Mr Zeit has a daughter.' I was about to change the 'has' to 'had', when Mr Crabbe drew his breath in sharply.

'I am not familiar with that piece of information,' he said.

I knew that he was lying.

'I would also be careful about repeating scurrilous gossip.'

'I also know that her mother was a mermaid,' I continued, ignoring him. He made a strange sound.

'I know who she is. I've met her, the daughter,' I added quickly. 'I just want to tell Mr Zeit about her. I think that he would like to hear about her, that's all.'

'I very much doubt that,' said Mr Crabbe.

'I don't want money or anything. I just want to tell him about her. She is lovely. Was lovely.'

'Was?' said Mr Crabbe. 'What do you mean?'

He sounded interested for the first time.

'Has she left the City?'

'No, she's, she's de...' I hesitated.

'Dead?' Suddenly, Mr Crabbe really sounded interested. 'How did she die?'

'She was murdered.' I said this quickly as I did not want to dwell on it. 'But I thought Mr Zeit might like to hear about her, what she was like.'

'When did she die?' asked Mr Crabbe.

'I could bring him some photographs if he likes.'

'When did she die?' repeated Mr Crabbe, more firmly.

For all his dryness, I could imagine that he had a temper.

'I don't know, I'm not sure,' I replied.

'When did you last see her alive?'

'I went to tell her about Ruby's death,' I said.

I was trying to sort out when that was exactly. The last couple of days were like a blur.

'So, the last time you saw her was after the other mermaid's body was found?' he asked.

I heard him speak to someone in the background.

'Yes,' I said.

'And was her murder the same as the others?'

I did not want to think about that.

'The police seem to think so.'

'The police know?'

I could hear relief and something else. Triumph, maybe.

'Look, could I speak to Guisse Zeit about this?' I asked. 'Could you request a visit?'

'Absolutely out of the question,' he replied.

Belatedly, I realised what this was about for Mr Crabbe. Guisse Zeit now had an alibi for Lina's death and that would make it harder to pin the others on him. Mr Crabbe, obviously, did not care about Lina, no matter who her father was.

And probably Guisse Zeit wouldn't either.

'I will come and speak to you tomorrow,' said Mr Crabbe and hung up.

No, you won't, I thought, anger rising. I'm not speaking to any of you.

My anger turned to frustration and my frustration turned to hot, bitter tears which burned my face and made my eyes sting. I was crying at Mr Crabbe's total disinterest in and dismissal of Lina, his casual disregard for her. Worse, I knew that Guisse Zeit would be the same. He would not want to know anything about her. He wasn't interested. He would reject her in death, just as he had rejected her in life.

He would only be interested in Lina because she gave him an alibi. There was an irony about the whole thing that, in the end, she might save him. But even that would not be enough to stop him rejecting her.

I could imagine them agreeing it was a shame, that she was a deluded young lady. No, a deluded creature who had latched onto Mr Zeit.

Then, with a certain horror, I wondered was I a creature now? If I was turning into a ghost, would people stop thinking of me as human and call me a creature? Is that why Cassiopeia wanted me out of the house? She could not bear to live with something less than human?

Uncle Timeon kept a bottle of brandy in the bottom drawer for emergencies. This was definitely an emergency. I poured a small amount into a glass and drank it down in one. I don't really like brandy, but that night I found it comforting. I hesitated and refilled the glass right up to the top. What did it matter?

Uncle Timeon was going to be furious enough with me as it was. Finishing off the brandy was the least of my worries.

On an empty stomach, it made my head spin. I felt as if I was lurching on a ship lost at sea in a storm. Now I was crying about everything. About how I had made such a mess of my life. And I realised that I had no way of solving it, or if I even had much of a life left anymore. For if I really was turning into a ghost then, surely, I would just fade away until I was nothing.

On the desk were the photographs from Lina's case. There were four of them. The first was of Lina and Rufus. They were holding hands and Lina was leaning in close to him. I wondered if he knew that Lina had died. I wracked my brain trying to remember if I had mentioned him to Constable Rock.

The next photo was just of Lina. It looked like it had been taken at a funfair or somewhere similar. Lina was smiling. The third picture was of Lina and a friend at the beach. They had their arms around each other. They looked so happy and close. It reminded me of how Astrid and I had once been, and for a moment I felt that familiar knife-like pain in my stomach.

I looked more closely at the photograph. The other girl was Ruby. The more I looked, the surer I was. It was hard, as I thought now of Ruby with her red hair. I tried to remember the photograph that I had had of her. What had happened that photograph anyway? I had given it to Lina. I wondered if the police had found it on her body. Or should I give them this one?

I began to fear I was withholding evidence. I looked at the photo again. It was definitely Ruby. But why had Lina told me she didn't know Ruby? Initially, she had said that they were friends but then claimed to have lied about that. Why change her story?

I remembered her reaction when she saw the photograph of Ruby and Guisse Zeit – the man I now believed was her father.

And I had told her that Guisse Zeit was the suspect for killing Ruby, the person who now appeared to have been her friend. No wonder she had been so upset.

Had she and Ruby been blackmailing Guisse Zeit together? Had Ruby double-crossed her and not Rufus? But she had been so shocked and distressed when I saw her that morning. And more than that, she had seemed confused.

Maybe she had told Ruby that Guisse Zeit was her father. Then Ruby had blackmailed him herself. That would explain Lina's reaction. She had confided in her and trusted her, like friends do. Then Ruby had betrayed her. Then her father had killed her friend.

But who had killed Lina and why? Perhaps it was the mermaid killer. The mermaid killer who was not Guisse Zeit. Maybe the mermaid killer had killed all of the mermaids except Ruby. Maybe the fact that she was also a mermaid was just a coincidence. That seemed unlikely.

Or perhaps the mermaid killer had killed them all and Guisse Zeit was innocent, just as he had claimed. But why had Lina lied about knowing Ruby. None of it made any sense. My head was spinning out of control now. I needed to lie down and sleep. I could not face going back to the house. The blankets were still on the floor from the other night.

I turned the photo over. BEAUTIFUL CORAL BEACH was printed on the back. Why do people write in capitals? I looked again at the photograph. There was no coral in it. That didn't make any sense. The beach didn't look that beautiful, either. Then I thought of Lina with her sweet nature and realised that she probably saw beauty everywhere.

Chapter 40

Pay attention. Often you can tell a lot from the notes scribbled in the margins.

from *An Echo in the Brain* Dearbhla Danger

When I woke, it took me a few moments to realise where I was. For the briefest of times my mind was perfectly serene until all the memories rushed in like the tide. I remembered Lina's body lying there in the mortuary and pushed the image from my head.

I stood up, felt awful and promptly had to sit down again. I looked at the brandy. I hadn't finished it, but Uncle Timeon would definitely notice that I had been at it. I got myself some water. I should just go home, I thought; I should go home and go to bed and, with any luck, by the time I woke up, Uncle Timeon would be back to deal with all of this. He could sort it all out.

I gathered up the photographs and the writing paper. When I packed them away, I noticed the folded-up picture that I had drawn of Lina. I opened it up and looked at it. It made me tearful.

There were four photographs, but I had only looked at three last night. The fourth was also of Lina and Ruby. They looked like they were at the funfair that Lina was at in the other picture. I turned the photograph over. 'Coral and me,' it said on the back.

I took a sip of water. I thought of the night that I had seen Ruby. She had long, red hair. But, thinking of it, it was a deep pinky-red. Not really ruby at all. It was more the colour of coral. That would certainly explain Lina's confusion when she saw the photograph. But, in that case, what had happened to Ruby?

I could hardly believe it; I was back at the beginning again. All that running around, following clues, finding dead mermaids, and I was no closer than I had been on that first day when Lina had walked in and asked me to find her. And now Lina was dead.

So, did it really matter where Ruby was? Lina had wanted me to find her for Rufus. Would he even care, now that Lina was dead? Maybe he still wanted his money back. Grief is a terrible thing and whilst money won't take it away, it might make it more comfortable. Had Rufus realised that the dead mermaid was not Ruby? More importantly, had he told the police?

I had the feeling that I had dug myself into a really big hole and the more I said now, the worse it would be. I thought of the money I'd spent trying to find Ruby. Not to mention all the time I had wasted. What did it really matter if she was found or not now? It wouldn't change anything.

Ruby had tried to blackmail Guisse Zeit. Good for her, I couldn't help thinking. If he was released, maybe she would try again. Even better, I thought. I wanted him to pay for his behaviour.

Perhaps Ruby would just move on to another city. She was smart. Well, good luck to her.

I looked around the room and my gaze fell upon the plant. Something else that I had failed to do all summer: water it. I recalled the rubber plant outside Lina's apartment. Was Uncle Timeon's made of rubber too?

My mind was full of unanswered questions and this one, at least, I could answer relatively easily. I dragged the set of steps over to the bookshelf until I was eye level with it. I reached out and touched it. It was rubber. Well, that was one mystery solved.

In fact, it was the only mystery that had been solved. No, I told myself, I had also solved the mystery of the DT Watch Factory's name. I started to cry again. Some of my tears fell onto the leaves and cut tracks through the thick layer of dust which coated them. It may not need to be watered, but it could be dusted and polished from time to time. I felt that that was the least I could do. I blew at one of the dusty leaves.

As I did, I clocked the picture of the red fish. It was not a painting but an embroidery. Something about the style looked familiar. I unhooked it from the wall and took it down to the desk. The plant remained on the shelf, forgotten once more.

I took a handkerchief from my bag and rubbed away the dust. I was correct; I had recognised the style. The artist's name was embroidered in familiar purple thread at the bottom: 'Cassiopeia'. Along the top it said, 'To my darling Timeon'.

I wondered if one of them had broken the other's heart. If so, they must have been forgiven as they seemed to get on pleasantly enough now. I could never imagine forgiving anyone for breaking my heart, nor being friendly with them. I couldn't imagine all that raging passion diminishing into mere fondness. They must not have really been in love. But I read the words 'To my darling Timeon' again. Cassiopeia certainly sounded as if she had been.

Below that she had embroidered 'Latin Scholar and brilliant Private Detective – but remember to beware of'... Below that was the embroidered red fish. There were letters around it, in a circle. I looked at them closely; they formed two words: 'Rubeum Allec'.

I felt a mixture of excitement and agitation. I searched the bookshelf for Uncle Timeon's Latin dictionary, but I couldn't see it. Oh, for goodness' sake, surely he hadn't taken it on his trip to his lady friend? What kind of man thinks Latin will impress a woman? I wondered if Cassiopeia had been impressed.

I had a theory as to what Rubeum Allec might mean and, if I was right, the implications were huge. I could feel them all buzzing round in my head. I just needed a Latin dictionary.

Chapter 41

'Sometimes the best hiding place is in plain sight,' said Dolores.

from *Death in the Lagoon* Julianna Maiden

I burst through the door of the library as if I had been shot by a cannon. Miss no-Mercy was at her desk. I recognised the person with her; it was Mr Academic with another long list. I didn't have the time for that.

I marched right up to them and shouted, 'Dictionaries? I need a Latin dictionary.'

Miss no-Mercy's face froze. Mr Academic had no issues with my communication style.

'Reading Room, down at the back,' he said, cheerfully.

There was only one person in the Reading Room, an earnest-looking young man. He had a large book in front of him and a dictionary. It had better not be the Latin one, I thought.

No; it was still on the shelf. I thumped it down on the table making the earnest young man jump. I started to flick through the pages. My hands were sweating, and the thin paper stuck to my fingers.

I turned to A and looked up Allec.

Allec meant herring. I had a pretty good idea what rubeum meant but I checked, just to be sure. Yes; it meant red. Rubeum Allec: red herring.

Had I just spent this whole time chasing a red herring? It seemed fantastical but it made a kind of sense. Ruby had always felt so elusive, intangible at times. Well, the reason for that was that she didn't actually exist. That would make anyone elusive.

When I had drawn her, following Gus Wilde's description, she didn't really look like anyone. I had thought it was my drawing, but maybe it was because she wasn't really anyone. But who was he describing? He had seemed confident in her existence. And the others, the waiters at La Sardine. Were they confusing her with someone else? Or had they been fooled too? But why?

Had they been paid to fool me? I could hear Gus Wilde's honking laugh. Was he honking at my stupidity? They call me Goose, Goose Wilde, Wilde Goose. I slapped my hand on the desk. A wild goose chase, that's what I had been sent on.

But it was all so elaborate, so well thought-out. Who would do such a thing?

Lina? it just didn't seem like her. Then again, I had no reason to be confident in any of my assertions. I had just spent time and money looking for someone who didn't exist.

Or the other mermaid, Coral? That seemed unlikely also, though I was basing all knowledge of Coral on two photographs and her corpse. But if she had set it up, how come she was dead? Was she working with someone, or had she just been an innocent victim of the mermaid killer?

The Reading Room was at the end of the building. On one wall was the big portrait of Vulpe and Rufus du Temps.

The Art College had told me that I needed to look at lots of paintings. I had thought this nonsense. I already looked at lots of paintings. They said that I should even look at paintings that I did not like or paintings that I found boring. That I should look at them properly, study them, take in all the details. God is in the details.

Sitting there, in the library, for the first time I couldn't help thinking that they might have had a point. Except that it wasn't God in the details. No. As my grandmother used to say, it was the devil.

It was the watch that I recognised first: the big, ornate watch hanging from Rufus du Temps' pocket. There was something about it that was familiar. Then I realised that I had seen it round the wrist of Rufus Klumpe, Lina's beloved.

I thought of all the books I had read about Rufus and his love of the dark arts. Is that what he was up to? Were they figuring out how to cheat death? I retrieved Lina's writing case from my bag and extracted the photograph of her and Rufus. I searched for a pen or pencil; I was sure I had one. But in my excited state I couldn't find any.

'Excuse me,' I whispered to the earnest young man, and asked to borrow one of his. I drew a moustache on the photograph of Rufus Klumpe. I looked from one Rufus to the other. I'd joked with Cassiopeia that the police should look for men with moustaches in order to find the mermaid killer. I wasn't laughing now. Oh, Rufus, a tiny part of me thought, you are so arrogant that you didn't even bother changing your first name. You weren't even trying to hide.

'You, you!' screamed a voice.

It was Miss no-Mercy, marching into the Reading Room. She had obviously rediscovered her power of speech and wasn't afraid to use it. Even if it did mean breaking the library rules.

The earnest young man shrank slightly away from me.

She jabbed a finger in my face. 'You took an unauthorised book from the library. There is no difference between that and stealing.'

Something about having her finger thrust in my face pushed me over the edge.

'Yes,' I replied loudly, 'and it was a scurrilous book, not suitable for young ladies.'

I jumped to my feet so that my face was level with hers.

'And, what's more, I DON'T CARE.'

I shouted louder than I think I had ever shouted anything before. It felt exhilarating. I could hear my words echo through the library. It almost felt as if the fabric of the building recoiled. I picked up my bag and pushed past her. I looked straight ahead as I marched out, but I could sense every pair of eyes turn to watch me go.

I was angry, and fed up with being lied to and taken for a fool. But, more importantly I also had a good idea where Rufus was. The mention of the Dr Dorridorri book nudged more seemingly random pieces of information into place.

The book had said that Rufus, Dorridorri and the watch-maker took up residence in the upper rooms of one of the du Temps' buildings. I marched back in the direction of the office. I may have forgotten the details, but I was pretty certain that I knew where those rooms were.

Chapter 42

If you can't find the answer to something, find the answer to something else.

from *A Guide to Getting Blood from a Stone* Melanie Bathhouse

As I marched into Du Trims, the low hum of conversation stopped, and everyone turned to look at me. Though I had walked past the barbers' before, I had never actually been inside. Everyone seemed almost alarmed by my presence: a young woman invading their sacred male sanctum. I didn't care.

'I'm looking for the watch-maker.'

'Upstairs,' several people called out.

He was sitting near the window when I entered. The room was long and thin with a low ceiling. One wall was almost completely taken up by a great window that overlooked the street. Along one side ran a bench covered with an assortment of flasks and bottles, brass instruments and the insides of clocks. Several clocks hung on one wall. All ticking together in unison, like a heartbeat. A map covered the other wall. He turned as I entered.

'Vulpe, Vulpe,' he said. 'Welcome – and "at last", I could add. You certainly took your time coming. I really had to spell things out for you at times, didn't I? But then again, I suppose, it's not as if you are a real detective. Most inconvenient that your Uncle Timeon decided to go away for the summer. He would have made a more worthy adversary.'

He gave a bitter little laugh, and twisted the ring on his finger round and round.

'So, I was stuck with you, blundering around.'

'You killed Lina,' I said.

I sounded like a little girl whining.

Rufus looked surprised, then started to laugh.

'That's it?' he said. 'That's all you can say? Of course, I killed Lina, I killed them all.'

Through the big window, something caught my eye. It was the horrible glass display on the outside of Du Trims that I always crossed the street to avoid. I watched the great glass blade cross the window. Even above the ticking of the clocks, I heard it, whirring and cutting through the air.

Rufus followed my gaze.

'So, Vulpe,' he said, 'what do you think that is?'

He leaned his head to the side and put on a high-pitched, wheedling voice, like a teacher trying to coax an answer out of a particularly difficult pupil. I looked at the machine.

'Come on, Vulpe,' he continued in the same voice. 'You can do it. I've seen you on your many little trips to the library. I even followed you there one day when I was particularly bored. So, tell me, what do you think that is?'

'It's Dr Dorridorri's ghost trap,' I said.

Rufus clapped his hands. The sound rang out in the room, drowning out the clocks.

'Well done. The harvester. Gold star. Or maybe just a silver star. You've only walked past it several times a day all summer.'

I scanned the room. There was supposed to be a tank behind the machine to contain the trapped ghosts. I couldn't see any such thing. I did notice a long thin rubber tube with a brass nozzle at the end. The pipe was currently coiled up like a sleeping snake and attached to the wall by a clip.

'Where's the tank?' I asked.

'Ah,' laughed Rufus. 'That was one of Dorridorri's more fanciful ideas. Poor old Dorridorri sometimes had too flamboyant an imagination. Other times, he lacked the imagination to see some of the more obvious predictions of what could happen.' He gave a nasty little laugh. 'But he harboured this fantasy of being some kind of sultan. He dreamed of travelling round the City in a sedan chair carried by ghosts.'

I watched the glass scissors move across the window.

'But talking of flamboyant imaginations,' said Rufus, 'were you hoping to find the tank? And then find your little ghost Finn in there? Then you could set him free, rescue him, and the two of you could live happily ever after?' He gave another nasty little laugh. 'Is that what you think happened to him? That's why he didn't want to see you again? God knows, *I've* grown bored of you over the last few weeks, so I imagine any man or ghost would quickly find you tedious. Or perhaps you are thinking of your own, personal, little ghost problem?' he continued.

I must have looked amazed.

'Oh yes,' said Rufus. 'I have been watching you, Vulpe, all this time. I've seen you diminish – you're disappearing. You're becoming a ghost and I should know. I have known so many of your type.'

He walked to the window and reached for the rubber pipe and put the nozzle to his mouth inhaling deeply a couple of times. Afterwards, he gave a little sigh of pleasure.

'That's where the ghosts have gone,' he said. 'Not into some tank to become a slave army. I don't need a slave army; I just need me. I tricked Reynardo into making it for me. Reynardo was very good with his hands, but not so good with his brains. Like that stupid watch that was supposed to stop time. He never quite got it to work, thank goodness. And he never questioned why I wanted him to convert the ghost trap into a source of energy. Nor why I thought that we should keep it a secret from Dorridorri. 'Oh, Dorridorri will spoil it, interfere, he doesn't understand your genius. Not like me,' I'd say. 'You're so brilliant that I'm sure you can do it and here, have some money as well, lots of money.' That's how you appealed to Reynardo, to his vanity and his pocket. Though I suppose I should be grateful to him in a small way. He saved my life or, more accurately, my afterlife.'

Outside, one of the blades of the machine passed by the window again.

'I was stabbed in a fight over a card game. Can you believe it? I had cheated, of course, but it was too easy not to. Too clever for my own good, that's what they used to say. I never believed it but, on that instance, maybe I did. Reynardo brought my body here and he and Dorridorri managed to find my ghost. Reynardo fed me in secret until I was strong enough to have substance again. Enough substance to kill him. I let Dorridorri live a bit longer, for we had plans; we were going to take over the City. He didn't seem to notice how strong I had become, but he was the type not to notice things that did not interest him. And that is always a weakness. Then the fool got himself killed. And do you know what he got himself killed over?' asked Rufus, banging his fist down on the table. 'Arguing philosophy with some drunks in an inn. He got himself killed over philosophy. And then, then...'

He looked agitated and inhaled from the rubber pipe again.

'Are you wondering if this is where your Finn has gone?' he taunted. 'Wondering if he is inside me, somewhere?'

He ran his hand along my cheek. I inched away and turned to look at the door. It was shut. When I looked back, Rufus was waving the key in my face. I began to question my wisdom of coming here alone to confront him.

'Obviously, Dorridorri thought that I would do the same for his ghost as he and Reynardo had done for me. He didn't notice that I had not saved Reynardo. That was Dorridorri's problem: he never noticed what he wasn't interested in.'

I tried to edge towards the door. But somehow Rufus was suddenly behind me, forcing me back into the room. Instinctively, I felt that it was best to keep him talking.

'So why did you kill the mermaids?'

Rufus rolled his eyes. 'Oh, Vulpe, Vulpe, Vulpe, you are just so sentimental, that is your problem. Well, one of your problems. *Why did you have to kill the poor mermaids?*' He imitated my voice. *'With their lovely shiny tails and beautiful hair.* Why? Because I enjoyed it,' he said. 'And I enjoyed slicing them open, dissecting them even more. That bitch Melusina ruined me. Each one I killed. I pretended I was killing her. Lina was the best, for she was actually descended from Melusina. She was so stupid she couldn't understand what was happening. I had to explain it to her twice. I thought at one point I was going to have to draw her a diagram.'

Then he burst out laughing. 'Oh, Vulpe,' he said. 'You should see your face. Why did I kill the mermaids? Why do you think that I killed the mermaids? I can't deny that I enjoyed it – I was sorry to have to stop – but come on, Vulpe, think. Why did I have to kill the mermaids and why did I need you? Well, not exactly you – I can't imagine anyone needing you – but why did I need someone in your position? Come on, think, see if you can figure it out.'

He had put on the school-teachery voice again.

'Guisse Zeit,' I said. 'You were trying to frame Guisse Zeit.'

Suddenly, Rufus had me by my arm and pulled me towards the map. He swung me round to face it. It was covered in pins.

'Do you know what this is?' he asked. 'This,' he said, 'is a map of the City and each pin represents a du Temps business or property. We owned this city. This city belonged to us; this city belongs to me. It is mine, my birthright, my inheritance. And it was stolen. Stolen by a nobody and a mermaid: Zeit and that bitch Melusina. And not just the City, but our name. Once, people bowed at the mention of the du Temps name. Now it is something consigned to history.'

He was shouting. He stamped his foot and punched the wall with his fist.

'All I want is to reclaim what is rightfully mine, that which I was denied. I want things to be as they once were, for that is how they should be.'

'But even if you do manage to get rid of Guisse Zeit, that won't mean that things will go back to the way they were.'

As soon as I said it, I realised that it was a mistake. The atmosphere changed between us, as if all the air had been sucked from the room. It felt like the drag of a tide pulling far out in preparation to rush back in as a giant wave.

'No!' bellowed Rufus, forcing his face down close to mine and screaming. 'He has what is mine. With him gone, I will get back what I rightfully own. I will be the master of this City once more.'

There in the midst of it all, trapped in this upstairs room with a mad, murderous ghost growing madder by the moment, a memory crept back into my head. I was crying and Cassiopeia had her arm around me. It was when my old lover had left me for Astrid. I was saying if only Astrid had never existed, then he would never have left me. And if only she would go away, then he would come back to me. Cassiopeia had said nothing.

Eventually, she had hugged me closer and said no, she did not necessarily think so.

'Why?' I had demanded. 'Why?'

'Because,' she said, 'often the reason for things is not as straightforward as all that and even if she did go away that does not mean things would go back to being the way they were. Time has moved on and you can't turn back time.'

I looked round the room full of clocks and the insides of clocks and the ticking of clocks and I realised that Rufus couldn't turn back time either. He might have been able to cheat death, but he couldn't manipulate time. I decided against telling him this though. I myself had not taken the news well. I had pushed Cassiopeia from me and stormed from the room. I had never quite accepted it; I had a very strong sense that Rufus would take this piece of advice even more badly than I had.

I ruined this moment of cleverness by blurting out, 'But Guisse Zeit's lawyer knows he couldn't have killed Lina, because he was in prison at the time.' Then, for good measure – or, perhaps, bad measure – I added, 'I have spoken to him.'

'His lawyer? Crabbe, isn't it? Well, isn't that another loose end to be tied up?' he said in an over-dramatic voice feigning tiredness. 'Or cut off,' he added.

Rufus moved over to the black pipe by the window and inhaled slowly from it, giving a little sigh of pleasure when he had finished. He reached for a bottle of champagne.

'Beau Vie Champagne,' he said. 'The glass for the bottles is made here in the City by none other than our old friend, Guisse Zeit. Such an enterprising family, those Zeits.'

He poured the contents into a glass and for one moment I thought that he was going to offer me a drink.

'Never waste good champagne,' he said

Then he took the bottle by the neck, raised it above his head and brought it down on the bench with a crash. Splinters of glass flew round the room. I felt one graze my leg. Rufus was left holding a long, sharp shard of glass that looked like a blade. He walked towards me.

'Come, come, Vulpe,' he said. 'Surely you didn't think I was going to let you out of here alive? I am going to enjoy killing you,' he added. 'Nearly as much as killing the mermaids. Though not quite as much. Nothing will be as pleasurable as that. It was the way they writhed and flapped around in the sand. Remarkable, really; there was something so piscine about them when they were dying. They made this strange high-pitched noise, a bit like singing, but shriller.'

I backed away from him. He pursued me at a leisurely pace, reminiscing about killing the mermaids. He was going to play with me, like a cat plays with a mouse. Then I remembered reading that if someone is coming towards you, you should also go towards them. It throws them off balance.

I took a step forward. He looked surprised and then amused and took a great step towards me. I squealed and retreated.

'People know I'm here.'

'No, they don't,' said Rufus, 'and what's more, they don't care. Nobody cares about you.'

Deep down I knew he was right. Nobody knew I was here. What would happen to my ghost when I died? Would it be trapped here, or would it be free to roam the City? I would like to see Cassiopeia again and my mother too, actually. I thought of them doing normal things. My mother cooking dinner and Cassiopeia making herself a cocktail. I would even like to see Uncle Timeon again.

I thought about Miss no-Mercy at the library. She would be the last person to have seen me alive. I remembered the expression on her face. She would probably fine me or ban me from the library. Then I realised that it wouldn't matter as I would be dead.

Nothing would matter anymore. I wouldn't matter anymore. Suddenly, I felt very angry. All I had wanted was a nice summer, to fall in love and enjoy myself. And I had ended up here. About to be murdered by a malicious ghost in the upstairs room of a barber's shop. How long before anyone even found my body?

My fury overwhelmed me and, emboldened by that and the feeling that I had nothing left to lose, I bawled at Rufus.

'Why? Why did you have to come back now, this summer?'

'I saw the signs, Vulpe. I saw the signs.'

As he said this, he began to laugh. Then he seemed unable to stop laughing. He stood there, laughing uproariously until he began to cry. Tears of mirth ran down his face, and he was doubled over. I watched him partly in astonishment and partly in disgust. Obviously, Rufus was the type of person who had never doubted his own genius or wit.

Still emboldened, I screamed, 'That's not even funny.' This seemed to set him off again.

'Oh, but it is, Vulpe. Oh, but it is.'

The excessive laughter had used up his energy and he walked over to the black rubber piping by the window and inhaled from it again. Then he was right next to me, his face close to mine.

'Right, I need to finish you off now,' he said, almost matter-of-factly. 'I've places to go, other people to kill.'

With one hand, he pushed me into the wall and with the other, tried to stick the shard of glass into my stomach. We were right beside the window. I could hear the sound of the ghost machine cutting through the air. Even before the glass came near me, I was feeling strange, as if I was being sucked out of myself.

When the glass touched my flesh, it seemed to slip off to the side.

Rufus tried again but the same thing happened. He regarded the piece of glass in confusion. Then he glanced at the ghost machine and gave a little chuckle.

'There really is quite a lot of you that is already ghost,' he said.

Was I now too much ghost or not enough human? It didn't sound that good in the long term, if I had a long term, but in the short term it appeared to be saving my life or what was left of it.

Rufus tried to push me away from the window. I realised that it must be the ghost machine that was having an effect on me, and he wanted to get me away from it. I pushed myself as hard as I could into the wall and did not budge.

Rufus gave a sound that was almost a snarl, then lunged for the rubber piping and inhaled. Bellowing, he pushed me as hard as he could. As I stumbled, he picked me up and hurled me as far away from the window as possible. Immediately, I felt more solid and gave a cry of pain as my shoulder crashed against the ground. Rufus pulled me to my feet and pushed me backwards.

'I am going to pin you to the wall like a moth.'

Remarkably, my handbag was still over my shoulder, and the movement caused it to fall down. Futile as it was, I caught it and held it in front of me like some kind of shield. Rufus swatted it away as if it were an annoying fly.

He skewered the glass into my stomach. I gasped. I thought of Coral and the smell of her blood mixed with seawater. I thought of my mother and Cassiopeia for the last time.

Maybe because I wasn't entirely human, I could feel the strange sensation of the glass cutting through me. I felt it hit something hard. I felt the edge of the glass scrape against it. I suddenly had a very strong image in my head of a closed shell like that of an oyster.

I felt the glass penetrate the shell. I watched Rufus twist it. Then I had a sensation like a 'pop' inside me, similar to opening an oyster shell with a fine knife. A stiff, fresh breeze blew through the room. I heard the high cry of a gull. I closed my eyes, and I was far out at sea. I was surrounded by ocean. I could taste the saltwater in the air.

If this was death, then it was really not too bad. Much less frightening than the fear of it. Something pulsed inside me: a feeling of excitement and exhilaration. There was a wildness about it. It was both inside me and outside me.

I had the sensation of something building up behind me: power: raw, untamed power. Then it broke. It was like the cheer of a crowd, and I felt a great wave crash behind me. This must be what happens, I thought. A huge wave sweeps you off to wherever it is you go. I simply let it.

I was tired of fighting. Not just Rufus, but everything. I had been fighting so many things for so long. I stood with my eyes closed, enjoying the sensation of relinquishing the battle. Around me, I heard the sound of roaring and crashing.

It struck me how still I was. I felt the wave move around me, but I was motionless. I waited for it to lift me up and sweep me away. But nothing happened. Very cautiously, I opened my eyes.

The first thing that I noticed was how normal the room looked. Everything was just as it had been. There were no waves, no shrieking gulls. A brass container rolled across the floor and came to an abrupt stop when it hit the wall.

Rufus was still facing me but was moving further back in the direction of the open window. The expression on his face was one of sheer incredulity mixed with rage and fear. Whatever was going on was nothing to do with Rufus. Some unseen force was dragging him towards the window. As he drew near, he grasped the black rubber pipe and gasped at it. Newly empowered, he tried to break away from whatever it was. For a second, it looked like he might just be able to manage it, but then the force increased its efforts and yanked him even closer to the edge.

He grabbed hold of the window frame, his knuckles white as he hung on for dear life or, in his case, dear afterlife. Then whatever it was seemed to give one last great pull and Rufus was dragged out.

I thought I heard the sound of singing and then laughter. He screamed the word 'bitch'. It looked like he was saying it to someone behind me. But when I looked round there was no-one there. Then Rufus was gone.

I heard a strange sound, the sound a pumpkin or watermelon would make if they were dropped onto the floor. The tips of the glass scissors veered towards the window. Rufus was impaled on them. I was mesmerised by the sight. I watched his body rotate past the window.

Then I dropped my bag. The sound brought me back to life. As I bent to retrieve it, panic flooded through me. I fled the room, taking the stairs two at a time. I arrived in the street to a great creaking sound. I looked up just in time to see the display buckle and come crashing to the ground. The glass shattered and Rufus lay motionless amongst the shards. I wondered if it was possible to kill a ghost. Then Rufus melted away before my eyes, until there was nothing left but broken glass.

I felt the sun on my skin and it was a beautiful day. From somewhere I had an understanding. (It was more than a thought; it was as if a piece of knowledge had been revealed to me. But I can never quite explain this, not even to myself. So, I never try to explain it to anyone else.) I understood that loss and pain, disappointment and grief are all part of life. You can't live without losing someone or something you love. And it doesn't happen just once, it happens time and time again. Your heart will be broken and shattered many times. But holding on to what is lost is a fool's game. For you will never get it back and all it does is keep you pinned to the past. And that is not living; no, that is not living at all.

I smelled the tang of salty air and heard the gull again. A very soft voice, no louder than a whisper, called out my name. I felt a great rush as if a tide were sweeping in and filling me up. Filling me up until I felt solid again.

It was a long time since I had felt solid. It was good to feel normal again.

But, as I thought this, I realised that my stomach felt wet. All my stab wounds had started to bleed. I pushed my hands against them to try and make them stop.

The men from Du Trims came running outside. One of them swore quietly under his breath and shouted for help. More men ran out, all carrying white towels. The last thing that I remembered was someone pressing one of them over my wounds and watching it turn a deep ruby red.

Chapter 43

Sometimes you need a lot of imagination to fully understand reality.

from *Flowers in the Wasteland*   Pansy Ackroyd

I opened my eyes, and I was in a hospital bed. My head was full of strange dreams mixed up with confused memories, all floating round like clouds in a stormy sky.

When I next opened my eyes, a nurse was standing in the room. I could see sunlight, so it must have been daytime. I had no idea how long I had been there. The nurse smiled and spoke gently to me. She helped me sit up a fraction, then opened the door and let my mother and Cassiopeia rush in. They seemed almost like friends, a development I didn't entirely approve of.

They immediately started fussing round me, pulling at sheets and pillows, holding my hand and stroking my hair. My stomach felt stiff and sore and was covered in bandages. I learned that I had been stabbed several times, in what was described as a frenzied attack. One of the wounds, in particular, was very deep.

According to my mother, the doctors said that it was a miracle that nothing important had been damaged. Over time, my mother changed this to it being a miracle that I was still alive.

'Just wait until I get my hands on Timeon,' she said. 'What was he thinking going away and leaving you alone in that place to be practically murdered.'

I looked at Cassiopeia, but her expression was unreadable.

I tried to explain to my mother that she couldn't really blame

Uncle Timeon for what had happened to me. It had all been down to me and my decisions after all. But my mother was not interested. She used words like irresponsible, lazy and old fool.

At one point when I was trying to argue she looked away and her eyes were full of tears. The nurse returned and told them that it was time for them to leave, prompting another round of fussing and kissing.

I thought about everything that had happened and could not entirely come to terms with it all. I was really very lucky that I had managed to get away and was here, being fussed over, rather than dead or trapped in some shadowy afterlife. However, I could not entirely relax as I was unsure what exactly had happened to the ghost of Rufus du Temps.

This became my routine: I lay in bed feeling stiff and sore and my mother and Cassiopeia came and fussed over me. They generally arrived bearing gifts. I was lucky to be alive.

My mother came with homemade bread and a little flask of soup. I hoped that Cassiopeia might bring me a cocktail but, sadly, she didn't. However, she did bring me my toiletries and some of my own clothes, for when it was time to leave. She also collected up some of the books and magazines from my room. These included *Scandals and the City*, which I must have taken upstairs to read one night and the stolen Dr Dorridorri book. Miss no-Mercy's face flashed into my head and I wondered if I had been banned from the library.

One afternoon, the door was flung open, and three men strode in: Constable Rock, Inspector Stone and a man whom I did not recognise. I got the impression he was important. Constable Rock ran around, arranging chairs for the others before taking up a position by the door.

The important-looking man introduced himself as the Chief Commissioner of Police. He voiced the hope that I was feeling well. I detected a certain anxiety in his voice. It occurred to me that, perhaps, it might not look too good for the police that I had nearly been killed solving the case of the mermaid killings.

The Chief Commissioner asked me to tell him exactly what had happened. So, I did. Well, some of it, not everything. I didn't, for example, say anything about breaking into Lina's apartment. I just said that I had become suspicious when I realised that Rubeum Allec was Latin for red herring. I said this in a breezy kind of way, as if I was a Latin scholar and frequently translated things in my head.

I went on to say that I had realised that it was Rufus's ghost from 'my research.' I felt that they did not need to know that I had stolen a book, which I could see out of the corner of my eye, where Cassiopeia had left it. I also omitted all the stuff about my turning into a ghost.

I said that Rufus had attacked me, and I had closed my eyes as I thought that I was going to die. Then when I opened them, I found Rufus being dragged from the room by an invisible force.

'Mmmm,' said the Chief Commissioner. 'It all sounds a bit, well, fanciful to me.'

To be honest, I couldn't entirely fault him. It all sounded a bit fanciful to me and I had left out some of the more unusual events.

'And,' he continued, 'I have found, from experience, that young ladies can sometimes be a trifle...'

He gazed into the distance, concentrating.

'Hysterical,' said Inspector Stone. 'Young ladies can often be hysterical.'

I instinctively glanced down at my bandages. This was not

lost on the Chief Commissioner. He shot Inspector Stone a very dark look.

'Miss Tempest has been through a terrifying ordeal,' he said, 'at the hands of a maniac that you, so far, have failed to catch. No-one is suggesting that she is in any way hysterical. I was merely saying that young ladies can sometimes be...'

He gazed into the distance once more, searching for the right word, but failed and had to settle for fanciful again.

'Creative,' said a voice from the door.

We all turned to look at Constable Rock.

'Young ladies can be creative, Sir. Miss Tempest is a talented artist. I imagine she is very creative.'

'Yes, yes, exactly the word I was looking for,' said the Chief Commissioner.

'And sensitive, Sir,' continued Constable Rock.

The Chief Commissioner nodded.

'What I reckon happened was...'

Inspector Stone shot him a murderous look, but the Chief Commissioner beamed encouragingly.

'...Miss Tempest bravely, but rashly, went to confront this Rufus Klumpe, who was pretending to be Rufus du Temps. Who knows? Maybe he even believes that he is. When confronted, he attacked Miss Tempest. This must have been terrifying for her.'

The Chief Commissioner nodded.

'Miss Tempest tried to escape and there was a scuffle, sir,' said Constable Rock, 'and Rufus went out the window. Now, I reckon he must have stumbled. Maybe he even jumped,' suggested Constable Rock. 'In the confusion, Miss Tempest thought that she had pushed him. This idea is, of course, abhorrent to her, as it would be to any young lady. So, her imagination creates the story that he was dragged out the window by an unseen force, to protect her from the idea that she might have been responsible for hurting him.'

I looked at Constable Rock incredulously. I had no problem with the idea that I could have hurt Rufus. The Chief Commissioner, however, was still nodding enthusiastically.

'Yes, yes,' he muttered. 'I have heard of such things happening.'

'And what about Rufus?' asked Inspector Stone.

'I reckon he ran away,' said Constable Rock. 'But he might be injured, so we should check the hospitals.'

'Yes, yes, good idea,' said the Chief Commissioner. 'I assume we have already put checks at all exit points out of the City?'

He smiled at Constable Rock.

'We should search the area where we found the body of his accomplice,' he added.

'Accomplice?'

Constable Rock mouthed the word 'Blockhead' at me.

I thought back when we found Ruby's body, or, rather, Coral's body. Blockhead had been first on the scene. Rufus must have paid him to make sure that Guisse Zeit didn't manage to get away before other witnesses arrived. Rufus must have killed him, too.

'And as for you, Miss Tempest, I would put all anxieties about harming this man out of your head,' said the Chief Commissioner. 'Look at you, you're just a slip of a girl...'

He assumed the air of a man who has just sorted everything out and earned himself a large drink. Still beaming, he got up out of his chair, perhaps to go and get one as soon as possible.

'What about Zeit?' asked Inspector Stone.

The Chief Commissioner shot him a look that – I might have been being fanciful here – seemed to imply that Inspector Stone was an idiot. The two men swept out of the room, but Constable Rock lingered by the door.

'Here,' he said. 'I have something for you.'

He was carrying a brown paper bag from which he produced the bag that I had dropped whilst fleeing from Rufus.

'Oh,' I said. 'You have put my bag in a bag. Were you scared that if anyone saw you carrying it, they would mistake you for a creative young lady?'

Constable Rock smiled, and his blue eyes crinkled up round the edges.

'I found it in Rufus's hiding place,' he said, 'and I thought that you might like it back. Otherwise, it would have been searched and, perhaps, there might be something in there that you would rather the police didn't see. I had to conceal it; that's why I put it in the bag. I was being a creative young gentleman.'

I was trying to think of something sarcastic to say when I remembered that Lina's letter case and photographs were in the bag. Constable Rock was right; I did not want the police seeing those. I wondered if he had looked, and studied his face. But he was unreadable.

'Thank you,' I said, for it would have been churlish not to.

'Well,' he said. 'I'm glad you're –'

'Not dead?' I interrupted.

Constable Rock laughed. 'Not quite the words I would have used.'

'So, what words would you use? As you seem to be the one with all the good words today.'

'Alive,' he said. 'I'm glad that you're alive, Vulpe.'

Chapter 44

Every now and then you can catch a glimpse of the landscape and see the place as it once was.

from *The Lilac Forest* Maeve Fitzwilliam

After Constable Rock left, I lay back and shut my eyes. I was angry with the police. They had not believed me and, worse than that, they had made out that I was silly – or 'fanciful', to use their word. Even worse, they were searching for Rufus as if he were a normal man.

I should be grateful to Constable Rock for bringing me my bag. I would not have liked to have to explain the photographs to them. I imagined Inspector Stone, in particular, being delighted to have an excuse to charge me with something. I was also pleased to see my bag for its own sake. We had come through a lot together and I was glad that I had not lost it. I remembered the Sweet-and-Sours that were in there. I quite fancied one, a sweet cherry one. Actually, any sweet one would do. I was not up to anything sour today. But that was the risk you took.

I reached in my bag, but something felt odd. I tilted my bag to the light and looked in. The Sweet-and-Sours appeared to have melted. They had all fused together and formed one large mass. As I lifted it out, I saw that some were stuck to the front of Lina's writing case. I managed to prise them off. No harm had been done. I felt protective of the writing case. It was all that was left of the Lina that I had met.

I took out the photographs. The first two were of Lina and Coral. The third was the one I remembered of Lina and Rufus – but Rufus had vanished. The photograph was now just of Lina.

I must have made a mistake. This must be a different photograph. Maybe the one of Lina and Rufus had got caught up amongst the pages of the writing paper. As I lifted out the paper, my fingers brushed against something else. I felt that pulse, I heard the cry of a gull. Momentarily, I was out at sea, with the spray on my face and the salt in the air.

It was a folded piece of paper, charred slightly at the edges. I unfolded it. It was the drawing that I had done of Lina.

As I studied my drawing, the sense of the deep water came and went. I felt it right on the edge of my consciousness. I tried to concentrate but that seemed to make it worse. Like squeezing something delicate. A lighter touch was needed.

I tried to let my mind relax and ran my fingertips over the paper. Then I got it. I smelled a candle, and, in the background, there was the sound of a bell. Had I read something about this? I reached for *Scandals and the City* and flicked through the relevant chapters, but they didn't contain what I was looking for.

I picked up *The City – the People and Places Who Shaped It* and there I found it: the chapter on Madame Grise and how she enchanted paintings and pictures. There were several accounts of the process. People described the smell of candles and fresh flowers and the sound of a string quartet and the ringing of bells.

I recalled drawing the picture in the police station that stood on the site of Madame Grise's house. Had her power worked its way into the fabric of the building? Or had she somehow found a way of leaving something behind as a parting gift to the City? I peered at my drawing again and gently touched Lina's face. Is that what had saved me from Rufus?

I turned back to the book. There was the image of the painting of Melusina by the unknown artist. The first time I had seen it, I thought that she had looked like someone. Was it Lina?

No, I'd thought that she looked like a mermaid. Actually, I had never seen a mermaid except for the grainy pictures of the dead ones in the paper and it wasn't them that Melusina resembled.

Then it dawned on me. She looked like the mermaid on the old Zeit Glass sign. I had the sensation that this was somehow important. It was important that the mermaid on the sign was Melusina. I had a memory of Rufus laughing maniacally.

'I saw the signs, Vulpe. I saw the signs.'

I had thought that he was being cryptic. He wasn't. He was being literal. No wonder he was amused. Melusina had visited Madame Grise regularly after Rufus had left her and, suddenly, I knew what they had been up to.

Madame Grise and Melusina had been enchanting the signs to protect against Rufus. And it had worked. It had worked down the years and continued to protect against his ghost. The magic must have been powerful for, even when they reproduced the signs, it remained. And somehow it enchanted my drawing of Lina, Melusina's descendant.

The problem started when Guisse Zeit changed the signs. He took them all down and many of them had been thrown away or destroyed. I contemplated how many Zeit Glass signs there were all over the City. They were everywhere. And I thought of them all over the Zeit building. The signs hadn't just been protecting Zeit Glass from Rufus. They had been protecting the whole City from him. And now they were gone, leaving the City undefended.

Panic rushed through me. I had no idea where Rufus was now. Perhaps my enchanted drawing had been enough to destroy him.

Perhaps he was gone forever. But I didn't feel in any way confident about that. I had the horrible fear that he could reappear at any moment.

I had to tell Guisse Zeit to put the mermaid back on the signs. And to do it quickly. He needed to do it before Rufus had the chance to try something else. I lay thinking about how I was going to manage this.

If I could get to a phone, then I could call Mr Crabbe. Cassiopeia had brought me my own clothes. I could get dressed and slip out. I did not know the area round the hospital well, but I knew that it was close to a waterbus stop. More and more coffee shops were getting phones. I might be lucky and find one nearby. if I didn't, I could get on the waterbus and go to the office.

The nurse arrived with my evening meal. I would wait until she had cleared away the tray and then go. I picked at my food and pushed the plate away. A short while later, the nurse came in to collect it.

'Are you feeling all right, Vulpe?' she asked. 'You look pale.'

'I am just tired,' I said, and gave an exaggerated yawn. Actually, I *was* tired. It must have been all the excitement of the day. After she left, I reached down to the cupboard in the bottom of my bedside table for my clothes. I winced. I told myself that I would feel much better once I started to move around. The nurses were talking in the corridor. I would wait until they had gone. I closed my eyes to rest them. When I opened them again, it was morning.

Although I was irritated, in some ways it would be easier to look for a phone in the daytime. The only problem was my mother and Cassiopeia. They came in most mornings and stayed until the afternoon.

The nurse came in with my breakfast, smiling brightly.

'And how is my favourite patient this morning?'

I made a sad face, raising my hand dramatically to my brow.

'I feel very tired,' I said in a small voice. 'Like I need some rest.'

The nurse looked worried and took out a thermometer.

'You don't have a temperature,' she said, 'but you are still pale.'

'I feel like I need a nice, calm, quiet day.' I looked at her meaningfully. 'One in which I can focus on recuperating and not have to deal with anything else.'

Patting my hand, she said, 'Don't worry, I'll see what I can do.'

At the usual time, my mother and Cassiopeia came in and started their usual fussing.

'How are you today?' said Cassiopeia, setting down yet more magazines for me. There was so much stuff on the bedside table, she had to put them on one of the chairs.

'I'm feeling tired,' I said. I was going to have to play this bit very carefully.

They both looked at me in alarm.

'Apparently, it's normal at this stage in the healing process,' I added. 'The doctor warned me that it would happen. My body is working hard to heal itself and, sometimes, people need to retreat into themselves for a day or so. Like an animal hibernating,' I added, to make it sound more scientific.

At that point, the nurse bustled in.

'Good morning, ladies,' she said. 'Now, I'm afraid that I'm going to have to be strict and will only be allowing you half an hour today.'

She had an air of determination about her.

'Our patient needs her rest. It's what the doctor ordered.'

It looked like I wasn't the only one prepared to use the doctor to get what I wanted. My mother and Cassiopeia looked at each other.

'No arguing,' said the nurse drawing herself to her full height. 'It's for the best and I'm sure that you both want Vulpe back to normal and home as soon as possible.'

They nodded, grappling with long term gain versus getting what they wanted in the short term.

'Of course,' said Cassiopeia, and my mother acquiesced reluctantly.

The nurse was good to her word and returned after thirty minutes to encourage them politely to leave.

I waited until the sound of their voices and footsteps had disappeared. Then I waited a few minutes more. The last thing I wanted was to turn a corner and find my mother and Cassiopeia arguing with one of the nurses.

When I was happy that I had waited long enough, I cautiously sat up and swung my legs out of bed. I reached down for the bag of clothes. Cassiopeia had packed the wide-legged trousers that my mother didn't approve of and a purple sweater. To be honest, putting the trousers on was much harder than I had anticipated. My wounds pulled when I bent down. I kept on having to pause. Eventually, I got them on, but then I had to rest. Footsteps sounded in the corridor. Then the nurse's voice.

'She is not really supposed to have any visitors today, but I'm sure that she would love to see someone like you. Only a short visit though, she needs her rest.'

In a panic, I got myself back under the covers. The effort of doing this quickly, combined with the stress, was overwhelming. It left me breathless, so I was lying there panting when the door swung open, and Astrid entered the room.

Her blonde hair hung loose round her shoulders. So far, she had resisted the fashion to have it cut. It looked like it was made of spun gold. She was wearing a sweater made of fine, soft wool that set off the blue of her eyes. She looked like an angel or an illustration from a book of fairy tales of a princess off to minister to the poor.

In one hand, she carried flowers wrapped in Violetta's distinctive violet paper. It was a bunch of pink tulips, premium-size. In the other, she had a box of chocolates from Carmelo's. Carmelo was another one of the discarded du Temps women. Again, it was premium-size and, as she got closer, I could see from a little label, that it contained chocolate covered cherries. Astrid took one look at me and promptly burst into tears.

'Oh, Vulpe,' said Astrid, looking around for somewhere to put the flowers and chocolates. Due to the overcrowded bedside table, she, too, had to put them on the chair, balancing them precariously on top of Cassiopeia's magazines.

'Oh, Vulpe,' she repeated. 'I'm sorry, I'm so, so sorry.'

This made her cry even more. Obviously, Astrid cried very prettily. Her big blue eyes sparkled as they filled up with tears.

She took a deep breath.

'I'm so sorry for everything that happened. And he didn't love me. He was only interested in me because of how rich my father is. Anyway, he's gone, he's left the City to find his fortune. I don't think that he even liked me that much. He always said that no-one could ever make him laugh as much as you could.'

Astrid sounded a little sad as she said this, as if it had hurt her. However, it did not make me feel as pleased as I imagined she thought it would. But that's life; you always want the gifts you don't have and don't value those that you do.

She started to sniff as her nose began to run. So, I thought, there is even a limit to how long Astrid could cry prettily for.

'And, you know, I don't care that he's gone,' she said. 'I don't think that he was that nice a person.'

I felt a surge of anger. She might not care, but I did. I hoped that he might come back to me. Then I realised that, actually, I didn't. It all seemed so long ago now. And there was some truth in what Astrid was saying: he wasn't that nice a person.

'And,' continued Astrid, 'I realised that I miss you so much more than I miss him. And now you've been hurt. Look at you,' she wailed, 'and you're being so brave and I'm the one crying. I'm so selfish,' she said.

It all flooded back. The hurt, the pain, and the betrayal. How much Astrid and my former lover had hurt me and how much I had hated them. And now I had Astrid, like this, in front of me. I wanted to take the knife and twist it just that little bit more.

Suddenly I felt that hard little shell inside me again. I got an image of it and a thin blade twisting and I felt the pop as it opened. I heard the cry of the gull and tasted salt and was back out where the deep water is. The whole thing was so strong that it made me wince and catch my breath. My hand went instinctively to my wounds, and I cried out.

'I'll get the nurse,' Astrid said, alarmed, and went to the door.

'No, Astrid,' I managed to gasp. 'Wait, wait for a moment.'

She turned back again.

'Astrid, I've got a problem,' I said. 'I need help. Can you do me a favour?'

'Of course, Vulpe,' she said. 'Of course.'

'I need you to take a message from me to Guisse Zeit, the –'

'Uncle Guy?'

'What?! Guisse Zeit is your uncle? How did I not know that?'

'Not a real uncle,' said Astrid. 'His wife and Mummy are some sort of cousins, but I always call him Uncle.'

Of course they are and of course you do, I thought. I remembered how, at one point, I was going to pretend to be

Astrid to get in and see Guisse Zeit. I felt very relieved now that I hadn't. Suddenly I wondered whether it would have changed things in any way if I had. But that was one of those pointless things to think about, for I would never know the answer. Nevertheless, I felt relieved that I hadn't tried.

'This is all going to sound a bit strange,' I said.

'Wait,' said Astrid, opening her bag. 'I will write it down.'

She produced a notebook with a picture of a bird surrounded by a garland of flowers on the front, and a mother-of-pearl pen.

I explained that Guisse Zeit needed to put the old mermaid signs back up again; that despite what the police were saying, Rufus Klumpe was the ghost of Rufus du Temps and the image of the mermaid was the only thing that could keep him away. When I had finished, Astrid read it back to me.

I nodded. 'It all sounds a bit incredible,' I said.

'Don't worry,' said Astrid. 'I trust you.'

She put the notebook and pen back in her bag.

'I could be your secretary,' she said, smiling.

I laughed.

'Don't laugh,' said Astrid. 'Father thinks that I should get myself a job. He says that as I am showing no inclination to settle down and run a household, I should get myself a job like other young ladies are doing nowadays. He thinks that I am turning into a very silly person and wasting my time at parties and frippering around. I told him that he should get himself a dictionary as frippering isn't even a word, and, anyway, look at Mother, all she does is go shopping and out for lunch.'

Although her tone was light, I sensed that she was hurt by her father's words.

'Well, he should speak to my mother,' I said. 'She is determined that I give up my job.'

We both looked at each other and laughed. For a moment it was like we were back to the way we used to be with each other. Then everything that had happened rushed in between us like the incoming tide and separated us again.

Then Astrid said, brightly, 'Well, I'll go and deliver this immediately. Don't worry, I will make sure that Uncle Guy listens. I'll try his work first and if he is not there, I'll go to his house.'

'Well, if you're going to his work, be careful. He has a dragon of a secretary who guards him fiercely.'

'Oh,' said Astrid. 'I'm sure she is a pet, really.'

I was about to say that the only way that you would think that is if you were the kind of person who thought of guard dogs as pets, when it hit me that, where Astrid was concerned, she probably would be a pet. In no time, she would be asking Astrid where she bought her sweater and telling her how lovely her hair was. I felt the little hard shell inside me again and the twisting. I must have made a noise, for Astrid looked at me with concern.

'Astrid, will you come and back and visit me?' I asked.

'Of course, I will. Do you need anything? I could bring you some books and magazines. Or, I know, I could get you a gramophone and some records or a radio.'

I shook my head. 'It's fine, Astrid,' I said. 'I would just be happy with the company. Your company,' I added and I realised that I meant it.

Astrid gave a great beaming smile which seemed to fill up the room. The nurse arrived with a vase. She smiled at Astrid as she left.

'Now, isn't she just lovely?' she said to me. 'And so pretty.'

'Yes,' I said. 'Yes, she is.'

Chapter 45

If you're waiting for your prince to come, you'll spend your life waiting, not living.

from *A Heart that's Cracked and a Heart that's Broken* Emerald O'Brien

The door swung open. In strode Uncle Timeon.

He, too, carried a bunch of Violetta's flowers, mixed blooms, standard-size, and a box from Carmelo's, chocolate assortment, standard-size.

'You're not expecting your mother or Cassiopeia, are you?' he asked.

I shook my head.

'They are both very angry with me. Perhaps justifiably, but I think it is best to keep out of their way for a while.'

He set the flowers and chocolates on top of the ever-growing pile on the chair.

'And how are you feeling?'

'Much better.'

'Good, good.'

For a moment, neither of us said anything.

'I'm sorry,' said Timeon. 'I hold myself fully responsible for this. I should never have gone away and left you on your own.'

I reassured him that I did not blame him; I had got myself into the situation, after all. I considered telling him about the money or lack of it. And the fact that I had used up the petty cash. But I decided against it. For the time being.

'Don't feel you need to rush back to work,' he said. 'Take all the time you need; you are only to come back when you are fully recovered.'

I felt a twist in my stomach. I could see how this was going to play out. No-one would say that I couldn't go back to work, but every time I suggested that I did, I would be told to take more time as I wasn't quite ready yet. And I would never be quite ready, and everyone would just stop mentioning it after a while.

'When you are feeling a little better, I will pay for you to go to the place in the mountains where I have just been. You can go there to recuperate. The fresh mountain air is most invigorating.'

I smiled sadly and said that was a very kind offer.

'Right then,' he said. 'I had better leave you to get some rest.'

He reached down and touched my hand awkwardly. He seemed genuinely upset. As he stood up to go, he said, 'Don't tell your mother I was here.'

I assured him that it would be our secret. At the door, he stopped. He just stood there, totally still.

'How did you do it?' he said.

'What?'

'How did you figure it all out?'

'Well, it's quite a long story,' I said.

Uncle Timeon smiled. 'As long as you aren't expecting your mother, I've got all the time in the world.'

He pulled up the empty chair, the one recently vacated by Astrid, and hung his coat carefully over the back. He stretched his long legs out in front of him. Then he reached across for the chocolates that he had brought and opened them. He popped a chocolate-covered cherry in his mouth.

I told him everything, starting from the day that Lina walked into the office looking for a private investigator. Well, not quite everything. I didn't tell him about Finn and nearly becoming a ghost. I really didn't think that Uncle Timeon needed to know about any of that.

Uncle Timeon sat quietly whilst I spoke. That's what he had always told me to do if I was asking people to tell me anything. 'Let people tell their stories,' he would say. 'Save your questions for the end.'

He smiled when I described how I had got in to see Guisse Zeit. When I had finished, he nodded.

'Well done,' he said. 'Very well done, indeed.'

I looked at him in amazement.

'You believe me?' I asked, astonished.

'Of course, I believe you,' said Uncle Timeon. 'Why on earth would you make something like that up?'

'The police don't believe me.'

'Forget about the police.' Uncle Timeon waved his hand, dismissively. 'There are certain things that the police can't believe, even in the City of Light. At least, things they can't publicly admit to believing,' he added. 'I met Rufus Klumpe a few times myself. I did feel that there was something off about him, but I never guessed that he was a ghost.'

'Where on earth did you meet him?' I asked.

'Oh, buying coffee, on the street, at the barbers.'

I shivered.

'Oh, and we had a drink together one night at the bar, after work,' he added. Cassiopeia told him about me and then he introduced himself.'

'Cassiopeia?'

'Yes,' replied Timeon. 'He was the one that repaired that dammed cuckoo clock of hers. He said something in Latin, and she told him about me.'

'So, it's all Cassiopeia's fault then,' I said, and we both laughed.

'Well, don't tell her that,' said Timeon. 'She will be most upset. She is very fond of you, you know. She thinks of you as a...' He hesitated. 'She thinks of you as a daughter. No, you did very well. Of course, you made a few errors. The most significant was going to see Rufus alone, without a backup plan and without even letting someone else know where you were.'

I instinctively placed a hand on my stomach.

'But I reckon that a lot of those were my fault.'

'How?' I asked.

'I need to start training you properly. How about, when come back to work, I make you my official apprentice? I will get a licence from the City, and train you up properly. You're good,' he added. 'You've got real talent; it would be a shame to waste that.'

I burst into tears, taking both of us by surprise. For so long, I had believed that I was a failure at everything. I was overwhelmed to find out that someone thought that I was good at something.

'I'm sorry. I am just happy that you will have me back.'

Neither of us spoke. The silence worked its magic and I found it necessary to confess to the fact that I hadn't made any money and, worse, I'd spent the petty cash. And the extra petty cash.

'Oh, don't worry about that,' said Uncle Timeon, airily. 'I spend the petty cash all the time.'

He stood up and fixed his trouser legs and helped himself to another of my chocolates.

'Don't tell your mother about any of this,' he said, 'and don't worry. I will sort it all out.'

There was another knock at the door. I thought that it might be Uncle Timeon returning to remind me not to tell my mother about something else. But there was something about the knock that was too neat and precise to be Timeon.

The door opened and a figure entered the room. He was half hidden behind a large bunch of flowers, Violetta's deluxe-size mixed blossoms, and he was carrying a deluxe-size box of assorted chocolates from Carmelo's. It was Mr Crabbe.

He looked round for a free surface on which to place the flowers and chocolates and finding none, set the large box on the floor and laid the flowers on top of them. For a moment, I thought of Rufus raging about all that the du Temps family had lost. The same couldn't be said for their discarded women. They had gone from strength to strength. They appeared to have the monopoly on selling luxury goods within the City. I remembered Rufus's fury and felt a little jolt of pleasure.

'Miss Tempest, my employer, Mr Zeit, heard of the unfortunate incident which resulted in you being in hospital. He has sent me to wish you a speedy recovery and to give you this.'

He handed me an envelope made of stiff white paper. Inside was Guisse Zeit's business card and a cheque for more money than I had ever seen, made out to me.

'What?' I said, in confusion. 'What is this?'

'Mr Zeit employed you to prove his innocence. This is your payment.'

'But I didn't do any of it to prove his innocence. I did it to...'

I wasn't entirely sure why I had confronted Rufus. I hadn't been thinking clearly but Guisse Zeit and his innocence had been the last thing on my mind.

'I did it for me,' I said, 'and Lina. For Lina, his daughter.'

I looked pointedly at the lawyer as I said this.

'Mr Zeit is aware of the cr...'

He was about to say 'creature' but must have seen something in my face and changed it to 'young lady'.

'He is sorry that this young woman was one of the victims of the killer. But she is not connected to Mr Zeit in any way and is certainly not his daughter.'

I looked at the cheque in my hand.

'Is this a bribe to prevent me going to the papers and telling them the truth about Lina?' I asked.

'That is the money Mr Zeit owes you for services rendered,' said Mr Crabbe. 'You are entitled to go to the papers if you so wish, but if they publish lies about my client, we will challenge them – in the courts if necessary. Mr Zeit has always had an excellent relationship with the papers,' he added.

'Well, I don't want it,' I said.

I held the cheque out towards him, but he made no attempt to take it.

'My employer no longer considers that his money. It is money owed to and paid to you.'

'Well, I will rip it up then,' I said defiantly.

'It is yours now. What you do with it is your choice and your choice alone. If you choose to rip it up, then that is your prerogative.'

He stood up and smoothed down his overcoat.

'Mr Zeit extends his thanks to you for doing a good job and wishes you a speedy recovery.'

As he left, I remembered about the mermaid on the sign. But I had no energy to call after him. He wouldn't believe me anyway.

A short while later, the nurse came in. Her face fell when she saw all the flowers and chocolates. No doubt she was horrified that I had had so many visitors when I was supposed to have had none. Or maybe she just didn't want to go searching for vases.

'What pretty flowers!' she said. 'I will go and find something to put them in.'

She looked like someone who was ready to go home.

'It's fine,' I said. 'You really don't need to.'

'Of course, I do,' she replied. 'Otherwise, they will die, and we can't let that happen.'

'Why don't you take them?' I said. 'And the big box of chocolates too.'

'Oh, I couldn't do that,' she replied.

'Of course, you could, please, I insist. Take them and share them with the other nurses. You have all looked after me so well.'

My hands instinctively touched my bandages.

'Don't you worry,' she said. 'You'll soon heal and be as good as new. Of course, there will be scars but everyone has at least one scar somewhere. Someone young and healthy like you, they will fade quickly until you hardly notice them at all. At least he didn't get your face, such a pretty face,' she said, smiling, as she left the room, with her arms full of flowers and chocolates.

Chapter 46

'Maybe it wasn't a happy ending, but it was a satisfactory one and, in many ways, that is better.'

from *The Missing Morning* Babybel

I was discharged from hospital a few days later, into the care of my mother. I fretted that now I was back at home I would never be allowed to leave again. One evening, Uncle Timeon and Cassiopeia came to visit. After seeing me in my room, they went back downstairs to talk to my mother. I crept out and stood on the stairs, but they had closed the door and I couldn't hear anything. I considered eavesdropping, but it was too risky. My mother had no loud clocks.

Afterwards, my mother brought me a plate of small almond cakes and a cup of hot milk sweetened with honey, as she used to do sometimes when I was a child. She stroked my arm gently.

'I know that you think that you are all grown up now, but to me you will always be my little girl,' she said. 'All I want to do is protect you and keep you safe, but I realise that I cannot stand in the way of letting you live your life. So, when you are well enough, you may go back to work for Timeon and live with Cassiopeia, if that is what you want to do. But please try to be careful and not do anything reckless or put yourself in danger. Also, it would be nice if I could see you more often. I miss you and sometimes I' – she looked away – 'and sometimes I feel lonely. Cassiopeia has suggested that I come and join you both for dinner once a week.'

'That would be so nice!' I was surprised to find I meant it. We hugged each other.

I took Uncle Timeon up on his offer to go and recuperate in the mountains. The final surprise of the summer was that he had, in fact, been enjoying the clear mountain air and not the company of a lady friend. Nevertheless, the woman who owned the bakery in the nearby village went very pink when she found out that I was his niece and insisted that I take a cherry pie back for him.

I wasn't allowed to go on my own so, after much discussion, it was agreed that Astrid would go with me. We did not share a room, as we would have before. However, I enjoyed spending time with her. We are slowly repairing our friendship, but it isn't yet back to what it was. Maybe it never will be. We both changed in our time apart.

I have not seen Guisse Zeit again. Well, not in real life, but I do see his picture from time to time in newspapers or magazines. Ironically, a couple of months after everything had happened, he appeared in *Jolie* magazine's special 'How to be Successful' issue.

There I learned that Guisse Zeit's favourite food was his grandmother's soup. As if he had the kind of grandmother that ever made her own soup! And his favourite smell was the sea. In his opinion, the way to become a successful businessman was by paying all your debts immediately, and working very hard.

The day after Astrid had delivered the message, she came to the hospital with a fruit basket and a worried expression. She had tried to tell him about the mermaid, but he had just laughed, patted her hand, and said, 'You young ladies are all so creative nowadays.' He had offered to find her a nice young man to show her round the Zeit building as her father had told him that she needed a job. Astrid had declined. I wasn't really surprised.

But I was very worried that Rufus might return. I asked Uncle Timeon to talk to Guisse Zeit. If he wouldn't, I would. Uncle Timeon had looked very stern and told me that, on no condition, was I to go near Guisse Zeit and that I was to forget about Rufus. He assured me that everything had been taken care of and I must trust him.

But I could never quite relax. I was always fearful that Rufus would return at any moment. I made sure that I had Lina's drawing with me at all times for personal protection, but I still fretted that it might not work a second time.

One day, many months later, I was walking through the City and arrived at the bridge which turns at right angles into Fibonacci Street. I was surprised, for I had not thought I was close to it at all. But that is the thing about the City: sometimes, you end up in the most unexpected of places.

This was the bridge where Finn and I had kissed so long ago. I had been avoiding this part of the City, for the memories were too painful. I remembered that night, how happy I had been, and I thought of all my hopes and dreams that never came to be.

I looked at the bridge for a long time. I couldn't walk away. Then I took a deep breath and forced myself to step on to it. I stopped in the centre, exactly at the point where we had kissed. Standing there, the past seemed very close. For a moment, it felt like I could almost reach out and touch it. But I couldn't. The past was gone and gone for good.

I looked both ways and then crossed the bridge to the other side. And once I had turned that dark little corner, I emerged, blinking, into sunshine on Fibonacci Street. The first thing that I saw was a large poster for Zeit Glass. I felt something, like an undertow, drag me back.

Looking at the poster, I noticed something that had not been there before. Down in the bottom right-hand corner, in one of the panes of glass that made up the Zeit building, was the reflection of a mermaid. I wondered if Guisse Zeit listened to me after all. It must have been a trick of the light because, for a moment, I was certain that the mermaid smiled at me.

Going to the mountains was not the only offer I took Uncle Timeon up on. I also decided to become his apprentice. It was all very official. He had to apply for a special licence and we both had to sign a contract. But we agreed that I would only work part-time. I thought a lot about the cheque that Guisse Zeit had given me. In the end, I realised that there was no point sending it back or ripping it up. Guisse Zeit considered the matter closed and was not interested in what happened to the money. He would not even notice. So, I decided to keep it. The first thing I did was to pay back the petty cash. I wanted to give some of the money to Uncle Timeon but he refused. He told me to think of it as my first pay cheque as a proper Private Investigator, but to accept that I would never again be paid that much for a case.

I used some of it to pay for new paper and paints and also some private art classes, for I have decided to reapply to Art College next year. Since I last tried to get in, I have moved out of home, got a job, had my heart broken (twice), partly turned into a ghost, solved a crime, and been nearly killed. I reckon that I have had enough life experience to last me, if not a lifetime, at least a very long time. I have also learned the importance of looking at all paintings very carefully.

Acknowledgements

I would never have written this book if it had not been for the support, encouragement and friendship of great mentors. I would like to thank Diane Samuels whose Monday night writing group I have attended for over a decade and Claire Steele for her Magical Journeys Writing Holidays and Constellations workshops. They both created magical spaces in which my imagination and creativity was able to flourish, and guided me in the writing process. I would also like to thank all the wonderful people I have written with over the past twelve years in their workshops.